Vilna My Vilna

D1501040

Judaic Traditions in Literature, Music, and Art
Harold Bloom and Ken Frieden, *Series Editors*

Vilna
My Vilna

STORIES BY
ABRAHAM KARPINOWITZ

Translated from the Yiddish by
Helen Mintz
Foreword by Justin Cammy

Syracuse University Press

Syracuse University Press
Syracuse, New York 13244-5290

First Edition 2016
16 17 18 19 20 21   6 5 4 3 2 1

∞ The paper used in this publication meets the minimum requirements of the
American National Standard for Information Sciences—Permanence of Paper for
Printed Library Materials, ANSI Z39.48-1992.

For a listing of books published and distributed by Syracuse University Press,
visit www.SyracuseUniversityPress.syr.edu.

ISBN: 978-0-8156-3426-3 (cloth)   978-0-8156-1060-1 (paperback)
                                     978-0-8156-5352-3 (e-book)

Library of Congress Cataloging-in-Publication Data
Names: Karpinowitz, Abraham. | Mintz, Helen, translator.
   Title: Vilna my Vilna : stories / by Abraham Karpinowitz ; translated from
the Yiddish by Helen Mintz ; foreword by Justin Cammy.
   Description: First edition. | Syracuse, New York : Syracuse University
Press, 2015. | Series: Judaic traditions in literature, music, and art | Includes
bibliographical references.
   Identifiers: LCCN 2015037080| ISBN 9780815634263 (cloth : alk. paper) |
ISBN 9780815610601 (pbk. : alk. paper) | ISBN 9780815653523 (e-book)
   Classification: LCC PJ5129.K315 A2 2015 | DDC 839/.134—dc23 LC record
available at http://lccn.loc.gov/2015037080

Manufactured in the United States of America

Contents

Illustrations

Figures

Maps

Foreword

Jewish intellectuals and writers have written about Vilna since the origins of modern Yiddish literature. If the historical shtetl was appropriated by the generation of classic writers who emerged in the mid- to late nineteenth century as the mythopoetic center of a new literature in need of its own native ground, for the writers that followed, the Jewish city was the setting from which to symbolically stage the confrontation between Jewishness and Europeanness, tradition and secularization, and to engage the challenges of class stratification, urbanization, the new politics of the Jewish street, and the competing languages of contemporary Jewish experience.

This volume of stories by Abraham Karpinowitz (1913–2004; Avrom Karpinovitsh in Yiddish) situates its narratives of interwar Jewish life in the author's hometown of Vilna, with special attention to extraordinary characters from among the city's ordinary street people. They are in conversation with a long tradition of Jewish writing about Vilna that sought to construct, challenge, interpret, and redefine a specific cultural myth of Jewish urban space. Insofar as Karpinowitz found his literary voice only after Vilna's destruction, he also must be read within the broader context of Holocaust literature, specifically within the subcanon of Yiddish texts that spoke to a global readership that had suddenly lost its Yiddish-speaking heartland. One senses that Karpinowitz approached his writing as a sacred duty, in which the personalities he encountered as a young man were reanimated to resist the finality of their destruction. Their vibrant presence and life impulse is Karpinowitz's preferred mode of post-Holocaust witnessing. While Abraham Sutzkever and Chaim Grade, the most famous of Vilna's young Yiddish writers to survive the war, honed a highbrow literary aesthetic in their postwar engagement with their hometown,

Karpinowitz found his talents best suited to a popular idiom. Vilna's Yiddish-speaking alleys, brothels, taverns, and street corners would find their voice in him.

Given that Abraham Karpinowitz departed Vilna in 1937, drawn as a twenty-four-year-old to Stalin's Jewish autonomous region in Birobidzhan, and then spent the war years in the Soviet Union, his confrontation with the completeness of his community's destruction upon his brief return to Vilna in 1944 was all the more shocking. He had not lived through the final years of Polish rule, when the struggle for Jewish rights against nationalist xenophobia reached its peak, nor the city's occupation under the Soviets when Jewish political and cultural expression was severely curtailed, nor its liquidation under the Nazis. His imagination remained frozen in the heyday of Vilna's cultural dynamism. Soon after arriving in the new state of Israel from a Cypriot Displaced Persons camp in 1949, he joined the short-lived Yiddish literary group Yung-Yisroel (Young Israel). For the next three decades, in his spare time as manager of the Israeli Philharmonic Orchestra, his literary attentions would alternate between stories of Vilna and tales of life in Israel. Writing allowed him to navigate the distance between an organic Yiddish-speaking world *dortn* (over there) and the new politico-cultural landscapes of the Hebrew-speaking state in which Yiddish was permitted to exist publicly only on the margins. With this in mind, it is no coincidence that Karpinowitz's first story in *Di goldene keyt*, the flagship journal of Yiddish literature and culture in Israel, was titled "Never Forget."[1]

---

1. Avrom Karpinovitsh, "Farges nit," *Di goldene keyt* 7 (1951): 174–79. The story appeared in a section dedicated to "young Yiddish literature in Israel," a group of recently arrived writers who, under the encouragement of *Di goldene keyt*'s editor Abraham Sutzkever, formed the nucleus of the Yiddish literary group Yung-Yisroel in the 1950s. The story was reprinted as the opening selection in Karpinowitz's first book, *Der veg keyn Sdom* (The Road to Sodom, 1959), a volume focused on the years of Israel's founding. In this story, a young man who escaped the slaughters in the ghetto is now an Israeli soldier whose conscience is haunted by the final Yiddish words of his mother when he comes face-to-face with his enemy: "Never Forget!" The story perfectly situates the competing imaginative claims on Karpinowitz that would define the remainder of his career as his prose alternated between

Vilna, Real and Imagined

Vilna, known affectionately as the Jerusalem of Lithuania, cultivated a myth of place in which layer upon layer of historical experience added to the city's reputation as harbinger of the most important trends in Eastern European Jewish culture. Indeed, no other Jewish city in Eastern Europe maintained a level of attachment from its natives, expatriates, and visitors that compelled them to so lovingly advertise its achievements. To be fair, until the twentieth century, there were not many big Jewish cities in Eastern Europe that could rival Vilna's religious and cultural pedigree. For all of Warsaw's new demographic strength and Lodz's industrial power, they lacked the deep tradition of which there was a surfeit in Vilna, which was already known as a city of sages in the seventeenth century. Vilna's reputation was sealed through the towering rabbinic scholarship of its most famous resident, Elijah ben Solomon Zalmen, the Vilna Gaon (1720–1797). The Gaon's example set Vilna's standard for intellectualism, diligence, creative reinterpretation, and openness to worldly knowledge. By the nineteenth century, the city was home to many leading intellectuals, *maskilim*, proponents of the Jewish enlightenment, and also a center of Hebrew and Yiddish publishing. Both Yehuda Leib Gordon and Avraham Mapu, respectively the most important poet and novelist of the rebirth of modern Hebrew literature, were residents of the city. Later, Vilna was a staging ground for the development of Jewish political awakening. Not only was it the birthplace of the socialist Bund (the General Jewish Worker's Union) in 1897, but it hosted early circles of Hovevei Zion (the Lovers of Zion) and was the organizational base for Mizrahi, the most important early Zionist religious party. By 1902, Vilna could also boast its own radical martyr in the person of Hirsh Lekert, punished for an attempt to kill Vilna's tsarist governor. The city continued to break new ground in the realm of the competition of ideas by hosting *Literarishe monatshriftn* (Literary Monthly), the first Yiddish scholarly journal. When Vilna (now

---

Vilna and contemporary Israeli settings. As coeditor of the 1967 *Almanac of Yiddish Writers in Israel,* he remained committed to the cultural imperative of Yiddish writing in Israel and to Yiddish literature's integration of Israeli realities into its imaginative universe.

Wilno) was incorporated into the new Polish state following World War I, its standing as a center of popular and scholarly Yiddishism was confirmed by the decision to headquarter there the Yiddish Scientific Institute (Yidisher visnshaftlekher institut, or YIVO), the most advanced center for scholarship on the history and culture of Ashkenazic Jewry. Vilna's civic pride, rooted in a respect for tradition and for the city's pioneering spirit, inspired its intellectuals and writers to rally behind the concept of *nusekh Vilne*, the Vilna way. As Max Weinreich, the director of YIVO proudly proclaimed, "In Vilna there are no ruins, because aside from its traditions Vilna has a second virtue: momentum. It is a city of activism, of pioneering."[2] Or, in the words of a popular folk saying that distinguished between material and cultural security, "Go to Lodz for work, to Vilna for wisdom."

A great deal of the city's creative energy emerged from a specific cultural geography that allowed Jewish writers to map their desires into a reading of its urban space. Of course, it is important to remember that Vilna was not an imagined city but in fact several competing imagined cities, each claimed by a different national group. To the Poles it was Wilno, where Catholic pilgrims flocked to see the famous virgin in the Ostra Brama church and whose central hill was punctuated by three crosses. Its spiritual capital for Poles was magnified by the words of hometown poet Adam Mickiewicz, whose Romantic epic *Pan Tadeusz* claimed the city and its surrounding lands as native ground: "O Lithuania, my country, thou art like good health. I never knew till now how precious you were, till I lost you." For Lithuanians, the city was Vilnius, where one of their own princes built his fortress on a local hill as the city's founding act, the ruins of which remained one of its defining sites. Though the Jews could not boast ownership over its cathedral or churches, its fortress or hilltops, their geographic center was marked by the crooked lanes and distinctive archways of the traditional Jewish quarter, where streets were referred to by the city's Jews according to their Yiddish names, many in memory

2. Max Weinreich, "Der yidisher visnshaftlekher institut," in *Vilne: A zamlbukh gevidmet der shtot Vilne*, ed. Yefim Yeshurin (New York: [n.p.], 1935), 323, 325.

of local personalities. At its center was the *shulhoyf*, a courtyard complex that boasted the Great Synagogue, many smaller prayer houses (including that of the Gaon), several communal institutions, a public bathhouse and old well, and a clock marking the time for prayer. The *shulhoyf*'s more traditional spaces later competed with those that attempted to bridge the divide between observant and modern Jews, such as the Strashun Library, bequeathed by a local benefactor in the late nineteenth century, whose reading room became a neutral, shared space for Jewish scholars and writers of all religious and political stripes. By the interwar period, the area was also a hangout for local toughs, actors, and writers, many of whom congregated in bohemian spaces like Fania Lewando's vegetarian restaurant and the neighboring Velfke's café. If the traditional Jewish quarter was the symbolic heart of the community, by the twentieth century it existed as only one axis in Vilna's expanding geocultural matrix. Others included Pohulanke, a newer, well-heeled neighborhood with broad boulevards and tree-lined streets that attracted the city's intellectuals and many of its newer communal institutions. The YIVO building, the Maccabi playing fields, the Jewish Health Protection Society, the library of the Society for the Promotion of Culture, and several modern Jewish schools were among the many institutions that were built there, beyond the tangled streets of the traditional Jewish quarter, to represent the contemporaneity of Jewish life in Vilna. Across the city's iconic Viliye River was the hardscrabble neighborhood of Shnipishok, where many working-class Jews resided, including several of those who would go on to form the nucleus of the literary and artistic group Yung-Vilne (Young Vilna) in the 1930s. Karpinowitz's boyhood and early twenties was lived within this Jewish matrix where past and present, traditional and secular Jews, workers and intellectuals, a Jewish underworld and burgeoning middle class, Yiddishists and Hebraists, Zionists, socialists, Territorialists, and Jewish communists argued the world and contributed to Vilna's dynamic expression of Jewish popular and high culture. Since neither the city's Polish nor Lithuanian residents constituted a majority of Vilna's population, the linguistic and cultural assimilation that significantly affected Jews in other Eastern European cities was mitigated for Vilna's Jewish population, allowing them to rally around their own languages and culture.

By the interwar period, *nusekh Vilne*'s self-promotion as both a defender and producer of contemporary Jewish culture was continuously deployed to distinguish the city from its biggest competitors. From the perspective of Vilna's Yiddishists, the future of Eastern European Jewry rested upon several pillars of which their city was a prime example: pride in the Yiddish language and its distinct culture as evidence of the Jews' status as a nation; a commitment to *yiddishkeit* as the manifestation of Jewish secular humanism; a sense of civic pride and ownership over a traditional past in which the Gaon could be claimed as a folk hero by even secular Jews; and a firm sense of *do-ism* (here-ness) that envisioned a Jewish future in situ, in the Eastern European heartland of Jewish life, rather than elsewhere. Vilna served as the citadel of this modern conception of Jewish nationhood.

The number of modern histories and anthologies designed to assert Vilna's reputation suggest that the age of nationalism created a need among Eastern European Jews for a capital of an imagined Yiddishland as a way to press their own distinctiveness as a people. Pride of place drove Vilna's admirers to advertise and celebrate its centrality. While it was still under the control of the tsars, these included the enlightenment writer S. Y. Fuenn's *Kiryah ne-emanah* (The Loyal City, 1860) and Hebraist Hillel Steinschneider's *Ir vilnah* (The City of Vilna, 1900). The community's travails during World War I, when it was briefly occupied by Germany, inspired Tsemakh Shabad and Moyshe Shalit's *Vilner zamlbukh* (Vilna Anthology, 1916, 1918), Khaykl Lunski's *Fun Vilner geto: geshtaltn un bilder geshribn in shvere tsaytn* (From the Vilna Ghetto: Portraits from Challenging Times, 1918), Zalmen Reyzin's *Pinkes far der geshikhte fun Vilne in di yorn fun milkhome un okupatsye* (Chronicles the History of Vilna in the Years of War and Occupation, 1922), and Jacob Wygodski's *In shturem: Zikhroynes fun di okupatsye-tsaytn* (Eye of the Storm: Memoirs of Occupation, 1926). These volumes shaped a local, popular historiography during a period of dissolution to assist in reconstruction and the preservation of collective memory. Efforts to promote the city's reputation in the interwar period were taken up by Morits Grosman's *Yidishe Vilne in vort un bild* (Jewish Vilna in Word and Image, 1925), Israel Klausner's *Toldot ha-kehilah ha-'ivrit be-Vilnah* (History of the Jewish Community of Vilna, 1938), A. Y. Grodzenski's *Vilner almanakh* (Vilna Almanac,

1939), and Zalmen Szyk's *1000 yor Vilne* (One Thousand Years of Vilna, 1939), the last the most detailed Yiddish guidebook ever produced of a Polish-Jewish city. Even those who left Vilna behind claimed the city as an important *lieu de memoire*, as when Yefim Yeshurin published *Vilne: A zaml-bukh gevidmet der shtot Vilne* (Vilna: An Anthology Dedicated to the City) in New York in 1935.[3] Local patriotism manufactured the need to export an image of the city in which the richness and diversity of Jewish culture nurtured, sustained, and inspired its population. This might explain the tension between YIVO director Max Weinreich's desire during the 1930s to promote Vilna as possessing "genius of place"[4] and American Jewish historian Lucy Dawidowicz's admission many years later that her exposure to the city's contradictions "shattered my sentimental notions about the viability of the realm of Yiddish."[5] Of course, after World War II, the impulse to memorialize Jewish Vilna took on new urgency for its former residents. We see this not only in the immediate postwar effort to publish memoirs of the city's last days but most impressively in the work of Leyzer Ran, whose three-volume *Yerushalayim d'Lite* (Jerusalem of Lithuania, 1968–1974) attempted to reconstruct the full cultural milieu of interwar Jewish Vilna through the careful collection and reproduction of photographs and documents. Karpinowitz's literary engagement with Vilna after the war is indebted to this historical and anthological imagination that produced an image of Vilna as model Jewish urban space.

3. For more on the history of chronicling Vilna, see Anne Lipphardt, "'Vilne, Vilne unzer heymshtot . . . ': Imagining Jewish Vilna in New York," in *Jüdische Kultur(en) im Neuen Europa: Wilna 1918–1939*, ed. Marina Dmitrieva and Heidemarie Petersen (Wiesbaden: Harrassowitz Verlag, 2004), 85–97. The list above does not include Israel Cohen's *Vilna* (Philadelphia: Jewish Publication Society, 1943), which appeared in New York while the city was under occupation, and those works by witnesses to and refugees from the Holocaust that explore the fate of the city in its final years. See, for instance, the diaries of Herman Kruk and Yitskhok Rudashevski, and memoirs by Mark Dworzecki, Shmerke Kaczerginski, and Abraham Sutzkever.

4. Weinreich, "Der yidisher visnshaftlekher institut," 323.

5. Lucy S. Dawidowicz, *From That Place and Time: A Memoir, 1938–1947* (New Brunswick: Rutgers University Press, 2008), 144. Dawidowicz spent the academic year 1938–1939 under Weinreich's tutelage as part of YIVO's *aspirantur* (graduate fellows) program.

Vilna in Yiddish Literature[6]

Surprisingly, it was not until after the destruction of Vilna Jewry that the city became a significant theme or locale in Yiddish *prose* writing. Though Isaac Meir Dik, one of the nineteenth century's most popular Yiddish writers made his home in Vilna and drew on its environment for his maskilic narratives, the city had no novelist who did for it what Sholem Asch or I. J. Singer accomplished for Warsaw or Lodz in the first decades of the twentieth century. Instead, Vilna's literary image was constructed in poetry, which can be divided into three general stages: (1) the poetic romanticizing of Vilna as utopian space, a process that began during World War I and continued through the interwar period; (2) the period of counter-myth dominated by the Yung-Vilne generation of writers in the 1930s; and (3) the lamentation and epic poetry emerging from the Holocaust and its immediate aftermath. Each of these contributed to Abraham Karpinowitz's creative inheritance and situated him within an established tradition that, only after the war, would expand significantly into prose where he would join such fiction writers as Chaim Grade, Joseph Buloff, and Ber Halpern[7] in contributing to the fourth stage of Yiddish writing

6. For more on the representation of Vilna in modern Yiddish literature, see Avrom Novershtern, "Yung-Vilne: The Political Dimension of Literature," in *The Jews of Poland Between Two World Wars*, ed. Yisrael Gutman, Jehuda Reinharz and Chone Shmeruk (Hanover, N.H.: University Press of New England, 1989), 383–98; Novershtern, "Shir halel, shir kina: Dimuya shel Vilnah be-shirat yidish bein shtei milhamot ha'olam," in *MeVilnah LeYerushalayim: Mehkarim betoldoteihem u'betarbutam shel yehudei mizrah eirope*, ed. David Asaf, Israel Bartal, Avner Holtsman (Jerusalem: Magnes Press, 2002), 485–511; Justin Cammy, "Tsevorfene bleter: The Emergence of Yung-Vilne," in *Polin: Studies in Polish Jewry*, vol. 14, ed. Antony Polonsky (London: Littman Library of Jewish Civilization, 2001), 170–91 and Cammy, "The Politics of Home, the Culture of Place: 'Yung Vilne': A Journal of Literature and Art (1934–1936)," *Judische Kultur(en) im Neuen Europa: Wilna 1918–1939*, 117–33. Yiddish readers in search of an anthology of writing about Vilna should consult *Vilne in der yidisher literatur* (Vilna in Yiddish Literature), vol. 84 of the series Masterworks of Yiddish Literature, ed. Shmuel Rozhanski (Buenos Aires: YIVO in Argentina, 1980).

7. See, for instance, Chaim Grade, *Der mames shabosim* (translated as *My Mother's Sabbath Days*), *Der shulhoyf* (translated as *The Well*), *Di agune* (translated as *The Agunah*), *Froyen fun geto* (*Women of the Ghetto*), *Beys harov* (*The Rabbi's House*), *Di kloyz un di gas* (translated as

about Vilna: the construction of thick landscapes of memory that offered detailed prose narratives of prewar Jewish life.

The first attempts at the poetic mythologizing of Vilna begin in World War I and extend through the early 1930s. This period witnessed the publication of several dozen poems that were interested in the ways in which Vilna's urban landscape could be read and interpreted as a cultural text, and thereby contribute to the imperative of *landkentenish* (knowledge and possession of place). Yiddish writing was harnessed to perform the Jews' at-homeness in Poland by demonstrating the degree to which they were an integral part of its built and human landscapes. These early images of Vilna in Jewish poetry tended towards naïve odes to the city, often composed by expatriates or admirers. They often served as textual guides to the city for nonnatives, providing a visual panorama of its major sites. A. Y. Goldschmidt's "To Vilna" (1921) is an early example of the sentimental strain that dominated Yiddish writing about the city in this period, one that emphasized harmony between the city's natural beauty and the Jews' organic presence there. Later, emigrant nostalgia prompted the composition of what would become the city's unofficial anthem, A. L. Wolfson's saccharine folk song "Vilna" (1934, music by A. Olshanetski), originally solicited for the celebratory anthology *Vilne zamlbukh* by the Vilna branch of the Workman's Circle in New York City and premiered at the concert marking the volume's publication. The song constructs Vilna as simultaneously an object of longing and a model for a holistic Jewish universe in which past and present are integrated. It speaks to the city as a spiritual and national inheritance, passed down from one generation to the next. Its effacement of the city's multinational nature is a response to the context of its composition during a period in which Jewish rights were increasingly under attack by the authorities and local thugs. The song aggressively claimed Vilna as Jewish space (*yidishlekh fartrakht*, "Jewishly conceived"), with a refrain that roused its New World audiences for

---

Rabbis and Wives), *Der shtumer minyen* (*The Silent Prayer Quorum*), *Fun unter der erd* (*Beneath the Earth*); Joseph Buloff, *Fun altn markplats* (translated as *From the Old Marketplace*); Ber Halpern, *Mayn yikhes* (*My Lineage*).

"Vilna, Vilna, our mecca." When the song migrated back to Poland and was embraced by the city's residents, the lyrics were changed from "our mecca"—a site of spiritual pilgrimage and longing—to "our hometown," allowing it to serve as an anthem for more immediate political exigencies, including its collective articulation of local pride and resilience when it was later sung at community events in the ghetto.

If Wolfson's song proved effective in extending Vilna's populist, transnational reputation, it was Moyshe Kulbak's earlier neoromantic "Vilna" (1926) that opened it up as a legitimate theme for Yiddish high art by taking more seriously its complexities and contradictions. Even when Kulbak sought out cosmopolitan excitement elsewhere, he would confess "Ikh bin nokh alts a Vilner" (When all is said and done, I will always be of Vilna). Though the dominant color of Kulbak's ode is gray and a funereal atmosphere punctuates its lyrics, they evoke an undeniable mystique. The city is repeatedly compared to a text, ranging from a psalm to a prayer, an amulet to a hymn, parchment to book, suggesting that its very existence is the source of its own poetry that invites praise, meditation, lamentation, and interpretation. By the end, the speaker's public confession "I am your gray! I am your dark flame! I am the city!" transforms the city into a symbol for Polish Jewry's dreams and anxieties, its commitments and its ambivalences. The fate of Vilna and the fate of the Jews have become synonymous.

When the local writers of the literary and artistic group Yung-Vilne appeared on the cultural scene in the late 1920s, they capitalized on the city's reputation in new ways. Its members were united by a common generational experience (all of them, like Karpinowitz, were born in the years immediately before World War I) and shared a commitment to Yiddish as the medium through which they would serve both the needs of their community and the cause of Yiddish literature. The group's populist streak promoted a counter-myth of Vilna that was truer to lived experience and more amenable to destabilizing and subverting its inherited images. In poetry, these included biting parodies of local heroes and landmarks by Leyzer Volf (see, for instance, the manner by which his poem "The Vilna Synagogue Courtyard" deflates the city's sense of sacred space), expressionist evocations of political radicalism by Chaim Grade, meditations on the generational mood by Abraham Sutzkever ("hear the fever of a mute generation"), and attempts to provide an enlarged vision of the region's multicultural diversity through Shimshon Kahan's engagement with its Gypsy and Belorussian presence. Elsewhere, Kahan's "Vilna" (1938) challenged Kulbak's carefully constructed urban mystique with a poem that suggested that the layers of inherited tradition and divisiveness of contemporary politics contributed to a toxic atmosphere in which it was barely possible to breathe.

Yung-Vilne's fiction writers, Shmerke Kaczerginski and Moyshe Levin, established the group's credentials with the Jewish street by taking up its prosaic concerns. They shared a commitment to socially engaged writing that was an important part of the group's local popularity. Readers found their own lives and concerns expressed in the social realism and naturalist stories of these young writers.

Kaczerginski excelled in his preferred genre of reportage. It allowed him to describe life in Vilna's streets and back alleys and focus attention on the experience of workers and activists. His ear for idiomatic Yiddish interspersed with Polish curses expanded the register of literary language deemed appropriate by the city's leading Yiddishists, a technique adopted later by Karpinowitz.

Levin, the group's main fiction writer, undermined romantic readings of Vilna by offering up angry vignettes of working-class life. The condition of his subjects is frequently one of anomie, alienation, humiliation, and fallen virtue. The Vilna that emerges in Levin's stories is intimately tied to the material struggles of its inhabitants. It is a world where a Jewish droshky driver picks up a pair of police officers who need to be taken to the station, only to realize that their detainee is his estranged prostitute daughter. Levin was especially keen to explore the corrosive effects of class conflict on Vilna's sense of community. The title story of his collection of stories *Friling in kelershtub* (Springtime in the Cellar, 1937) opens with the effects of seasonal floods on an impoverished neighborhood that sits along the banks of the Vilenke, a tributary to the city's main Viliye River. The threat is particularly severe to the inhabitants of this area because so many of them live below the flood line in dank cellars or in structures already damaged by years of neglect. When the Jewish community's volunteer flood committee urges Itsik, an unemployed laborer, to evacuate, he lets loose an invective that is a flood of a different sort: "Why don't you ever come down to this neighborhood on ordinary days?! Or every day! Our life is in constant danger, not just from a surfeit of water but from a surfeit of hunger!" Levin here is not interested in the extraordinariness of Vilna but rather in the ordinary struggles of its most vulnerable. He exposed the growing fissure between residents who struggled at a time of acute economic and political vulnerability and intellectuals and expatriates who promoted the city's reputation abroad.

To the extent that Levin was unabashedly *Vilnerish* in his writings, he cleared critical ground in Yiddish prose upon which Karpinowitz could later build. One of his collections included a lexicon of terms that were part of the city's specific Yiddish vocabulary in order to maintain regional distinctions. He insisted on situating his stories with precision, contrasting the illusion of grace suggested by the city's steeples and the region's natural beauty against the bleakness of material existence. Though Karpinowitz was never an official member of Yung-Vilne, the generational impact of a homegrown literary cohort that took the city seriously as a setting and theme for art impressed itself deeply upon him.

The liquidation of Jewish Vilna between June 1941 and September 1943 initiated a new stage in the Yiddish literary engagement with the city. Yung-Vilne's prewar strategy of counter-mythology was no longer appropriate to the imperatives of resistance, then mourning and memory. Once again, the fate of the city and its residents became the subject for legendizing. While the murderous grip on their hometown tightened, poets such as Sutzkever celebrated its folk heroes ("Teacher Mira"), its cultural resilience ("Grains of Wheat," "Ghetto Theater"), and its partisan fighters ("Itsik Vittenberg," "The Lead Plates of the Romm Press," "Narotsh Forest"). When its few returning survivors recognized the extent of the community's devastation, Yiddish poetry gave voice to the pain of leave-taking:

> You are my first love and my first love you will remain.
> I bear your name throughout the world
> as my ancestors bore the holy ark on their shoulders.

And anywhere I wander

All other cities will transform into your image.

(A. Sutzkever, "Farewell," 1943–1944)

Threnodies for Vilna soon gave way to the epic, as in Sutzkever's volume *Geheymshtot* (Secret City), in which a group of ten Jews form a symbolic minyan as they hide from the Nazis in the underground dystopia of the city's sewers.

If Vilna's mythopoetic reputation was first established and then repeatedly renegotiated in Yiddish poetry as the city's survivors dispersed after its destruction, fiction's strength at thick description seemed better suited to the imperative of its imaginative reconstruction. Yiddish writing after the Holocaust was self-conscious about its responsibility as the last repository for memories of specific places, personalities, and ways of life. This was certainly true of Chaim Grade, who turned much of his creative attention from poetry to prose after his arrival in New York City. Grade's turn to fiction enabled him to capture the unique brand of Lithuanian rabbinic culture that had been part of his formative intellectual universe. His interest in the contest and moral weight of ideas recovered Vilna's position as the meeting ground of *misnagdic*, Torah-centered tradition and varieties of Jewish secular humanism. His fiction delighted in exploring the coexistence of the sacred and the profane, in alternating its attention between the richness of the city's moral and intellectual imagination and the dire material condition of most of its residents who, like his mother, struggled to eke out a living while exemplifying the modest piety of Lithuanian Jewish civilization. Grade's achievements in expansive and erudite prose that conjured entire worlds were different in scope from Karpinowitz's preference for shorter, self-contained tales focused on the persons and places associated with Vilna's vernacular existence, including his ability to disrupt standard, literary Yiddish with street dialect and words native to Vilna's Yiddish speakers.[8] Karpinowitz's tales

8. One critic complained that "I have never read a book by a Lithuanian writer in which I did not understand so many words. . . . If the words are used for local color, the

take seriously the challenge of situating themselves in a specific geocultural landscape, one that recalls the street people and back alleys that were rarely the stuff upon which Vilna's reputation was exported. In the same way that Bashevis Singer's literary imagination was nurtured by the diverse human parade that came through his father's courtroom and the artist's atelier of his older brother, Karpinowitz benefited from growing up in a family where, literally, all the world was a stage. With two sisters who were Yiddish actresses and a father who managed a leading Yiddish theater, Karpinowitz spent his entire youth hanging around impresarios and theatergoers, many of whom could not afford even the modest price of a ticket but who were afforded a place on the balcony nonetheless. The Yiddish theater provided Karpinowitz with access to the broadest cross-section of Vilna Jewry, allowing him, as he admitted later, to "take in all this color . . . and feast on the thick stew of ordinary folk. . . . They were also a part of our people. . . . Why should they be forgotten?"[9] Karpinowitz took this question as his aesthetic mantra. His stories often relied on private memories or collective folklore of a specific prostitute, underworld figure, wagon driver, street activist, or lunatic. In so doing, the writer sought to reveal that which was concealed underneath layers of Vilna's stylized mythology. His was a heroism of the ordinary.

As the title of this collection of stories suggests, for Karpinowitz Vilna was a visceral possession. Though his fiction resists the strain of postwar

---

writer owes the reader a glossary with translations." What Yiddish readers from elsewhere considered disorienting, Karpinowitz considered essential to maintaining Vilna's distinctiveness and authenticity. See Shloyme Bikl, "Avrom Karpinovitshes Vilner dertseylungen," *Shrayber fun mayn dor*, vol. 3 (Tel Aviv: Farlag Y. L. Perets, 1970), 350.

9. *Monlogn fun yidishe shraybers: Avrom Karpinovitch* (DVD), interview by Boris Sandler (Forverts, 2012). For additional biographical information on Karpinowitz, see "Avrom Karpinovitsh," *Leksikon fun der nayer yidisher literatur*, vol. 8 (New York: Congress for Jewish Culture, 1981), 147–48; Helen Beer, "Avrom Karpinovich," *Jewish Writers of the Twentieth Century*, ed. Sorrel Kerbel (Taylor and Francis, 2003), 510–13. For additional critical readings of Karpinowitz, see A. Golomb, "A. Karpinovitshes *Baym Vilner durkhoyf*," *Di goldene keyt* 60 (1967), 256–60; Yitshok Yanasovitsh, "Avrom Karpinovitsh," *Penimer un nemem*, vol. 2 (Buenos Aires: Kiem, 1977), 274–79; Sandra Studer, *Erinnerungen an das jüdische Vilne: Literarische Bilder von Chaim Grade und Abraham Karpinovitsh* (Köln: Böhlau, 2014).

nostalgia that continued to press Vilna as cultural utopia, it may contribute to the creation of a no less idealized Vilna in which every simple worker or gangster shares a sense of community. In the end, readers of Karpinowitz will deepen their experience of this volume of short stories by keeping in mind that Vilna was never a fixed symbol. Yiddish writers consistently reimagined the city to respond to the needs of their cultural moment. We are left with the challenge of enjoying these narratives for their full-blooded characters and acute conjuring of a dynamic time and place that met a most violent end, while maintaining our critical recognition that the further one is from the source the more seductive is its aura.

Justin Cammy
Programs in Jewish Studies and Comparative Literature
Smith College, Northampton, Massachusetts

Translator's Note

By translating Abraham Karpinowitz's work from Yiddish into English, I hope to bring his stories to a wide contemporary audience. Like any important writer, Karpinowitz deserves the international audience that translation into English makes possible.

I have weighed the question of how much background to provide for the contemporary English reader. I have asked myself to what extent I should be acting as a cultural historian, bringing not only the language of the stories to non-Yiddish readers, but also their world. I have struggled with establishing where the breaking point lies in the tension between cultural explanation and interpretation on the one hand and loyalty to the original literary work on the other.

I have decided to provide a section of notes at the end of the book to give interested readers some background to Karpinowitz's stories and memoirs. These notes include definitions of Yiddish words that defy translation into English and that may be unfamiliar to the reader, information about historical figures who appear in the stories, and explanations about Vilna institutions and geographic landmarks. Vilna street names are retained in the Yiddish original with translation in the glossary.

In deference to readers who would like to read the stories straight through without a nagging call to seek clarification, there are no markings on the pages drawing attention to items elaborated upon in the notes.

The maps of interwar Vilna on pages 156–57 allow the reader to follow Karpinowitz's characters as they move through a complex web of small courtyards, streets, and passageways and unto outlying towns and communities.

All translations from the Yiddish that appear in the introduction and notes are by the translator, unless otherwise indicated. Justin

Cammy provided his own translations for the foreword, unless otherwise indicated.

Transliteration Guidelines

Yiddish is written using the Hebrew alphabet. I have used YIVO (the Institute for Jewish Research) transliteration guidelines unless words are commonly known in English, at which point I have used the spelling that appears in the Miriam Webster Dictionary online (http://www.merriam -webster.com). When names of individuals have already been frequently transliterated using Roman letters, as in the cases of Jonas Turkow and Zishe Breitbart, I have maintained the most commonly used spelling. Note that the final "e" in Yiddish words like *Daytshe*, and in names like *Tevke* and *Hirshke*, is not silent but pronounced similarly to the final "a" in "sofa."

For Hebrew words, I have used the transliteration most commonly used in English language texts (based on Google searches).

Acknowledgments

It took a multilingual village of individuals spread across the globe to produce this book. I am deeply grateful to all of you.

I start by thanking Sheva Zucker, who read early drafts of my translations of each of the stories in this collection, except for "Vladek," word by word, checking for accuracy of translation, making suggestions as to appropriate English usage, and engaging in discussion about translation theory and practice. I learned important fundamentals of translation from Sheva. With the gift of her teaching, I also greatly improved my Yiddish language skills.

Translating these stories brought me great joy. While never swerving from the truth, Abraham Karpinowitz answered genocide with love: love for his characters and love for his craft as a writer.

Dr. Sarah Lapickaja granted me permission to bring the work of her late husband into English. Simon Lapitsky and Anna Karpinowitz Gelbart facilitated the permission granting process. Anna also shared information about her uncle, Abraham Karpinowitz, and family photographs.

Liba Augenfed, Fania Brancovskaja, and Shulamis Zhabinskaia shared their detailed memories of life in *di amolike* Vilna and their knowledge of Karpinowitz's idiomatic Lithuanian Yiddish. When all efforts to understand the author's idiomatic usage failed, I turned to Eliezer Niborski, who always found the key to solve the translation challenge. Meir Shapiro shared his unpublished manuscript of Vilna Yiddish expressions and his extensive knowledge in this area.

Abraham Karpinowitz's good deeds and reputation have greatly benefited the look of this English language publication of his stories. Samuel Bak and the Pucker Gallery gave permission for the use, without charge, of Bak's painting *Soutine Street* for the cover. Yosl Bergner allowed us to use, without charge, his three drawings as they appeared in the original Yiddish publication of Karpinowitz's book *Baym Vilner durkhhoyf* (I. L. Peretz, 1967). Bak's painting and Bergner's drawings are the perfect accompaniment to Karpinowitz's stories. Thank you also to Reina Kambayashi for her evocative photograph of Abraham Karpinowitz, also given without charge.

Thank you to Solon Beinfeld and Harry Bochner for your wonderful and appropriately named *Comprehensive Yiddish-English Dictionary*.

I began this translation project in a class taught by Rivke Margolis at the YIVO Summer Program in New York. Katherine Silver, as part of the 2014 Yiddish Book Center translation fellowship program, helped me to find my own voice as a translator.

Benjamin Mintz created the perfect work space for me.

I would like to thank Dara Culhane, Michael Kaufman-Lacusta, Rachel Mines, Kian Mintz-Woo, David Mivasair, Rachel Mines, Elliot Palevsky, Ruth Portner, Nancy Richler, Leah Robinson, and Marna Sapsowitz, who read the translations of various stories and memoirs, providing valuable feedback. Thank you Meyer Grinshpan and Irvin Rivkin for your skilled and open-hearted teaching. Shimon Joffre and I shared some of our translations with each other. For the introduction: Dara Culhane encouraged me to express my own voice and Rachel Mines made valuable editorial suggestions.

The notes at the end of this book were made possible by the hard work and bibliographic talents of the librarians and archivists at the Jewish Public Library, in particular Eddie Paul and Eiran Harris. I would also like to thank Leo Greenbaum (YIVO), Amriel Kissner (independent archivist), and Eddie Stone (Jewish Public Library) for their research help. Also Ilisia Kissner, who donned an archivist's hat for a day.

Michael More synthesized information from many sources to create the map, repeatedly working under great time pressures. Laimonas Briedis shared his extensive knowledge of Vilna, particularly its urban geography.

Kian Mintz-Woo, Rachel Mines, and Faith Jones helped me to troubleshoot challenges as they arose. Kian offered much needed technical support.

Dara Culhane and Nancy Richler offered emotional and intellectual comradeship throughout. Justin Cammy was a great support in the crunch at the end.

Many people generously shared their knowledge of specific subjects including Sheila Barkusky, Rahel Halabe and David Mivasair (the Hebrew language and traditional Jewish religious practice), Ri Turner (the transliteration of Hebrew words), Dan Gillis and Leonard Freedman (fishing), Harold Perloff (the Yiddish bird kingdom), Carl Wong (construction of musical instruments), and Konstantin Beznosov (the Russian language). Seymour Levitan helped me compose letters in Yiddish.

Many people at Syracuse University Press helped to bring the initial manuscript to book form. Ken Frieden, Jennika Baines, and Deborah Manion offered the encouragement and wisdom I needed to refine the manuscript. Deb was determined enough to get me to finally release these wonderful stories for publication. Thank you to Brendan Missett, Victoria Lane, and Kay Steinmetz, who shepherded this book through the production process. Thank you, Lynn P. Wilcox, for the cover design.

Lastly and most importantly, I want to thank my parents, Esther Freedman Mintz and Benjamin Mintz, who instilled in me a love of learning, intellectual curiosity and independence, and a joyful pride in the Yiddish language and Yiddish culture.

If I have failed to mention anyone, please accept my apologies and gratitude.

Helen Mintz

Vilna My Vilna

Introduction

HELEN MINTZ

To earn the right to his pen, the writer must love his protagonists. He must understand them and sympathize with them.

—Abraham Karpinowitz[1]

Themcentral character of Abraham Karpinowitz's (Avrom Karpino-vitsh in Yiddish) stories,[2] lovingly rendered, is the city of his child-hood and early adulthood, the Jewish city of Vilna (present-day Vilnius, Lithuania) in the period between the two world wars. As David Volpe writes, "Vilna is the flaming center of Karpinowitz's love. He uses all the colors of the storyteller's palette to describe just one countenance—the city of Vilna."[3]

The reader is introduced to Vilna by Jack Grossman, the narrator of the introductory story, "Vilna without Vilna." An orphaned pickpocket in

---

1. The epigraph, and a number of subsequent quotations from Abraham Karpinow-itz, are from a 1995 interview conducted by Boris Sandler. This interview forms the basis for the film *A serie fun Boris Sandler: monologn fun yiddishe shraybers: Avrom Karpinovitch* (A Series by Boris Sandler: Yiddish Writers Monologues: Avrom Karpinovitch), Boris Sandler (New York: Forward Association, 2012), one of a series of DVDs about Israeli Yiddish writ-ers. Sandler was kind enough to give me access to the entire interview, which provides an invaluable window into Karpinowitz's life and work. Translations from Yiddish into Eng-lish in this introduction are by Helen Mintz.

2. "Avrom Karpinovitch" is an alternate spelling of the author's name, preferred by many Yiddishists.

3. David Volpe, "Di sheynkayt fun Vilne," *Di goldene keyt* 109 (1982): 209.

pre-Holocaust Vilna known then as Itzik the Hare, Grossman has become "a big shot" (p. 16), the owner of two hotels in Canada. Decades after leaving Vilna, he feels compelled to return to "see the city that raised me one more time. Her streets were my home; her people, my family" (p. 21). But Grossman's return to Vilna is a journey into absence, a detailed and nuanced description of a world that no longer exists:

> And on my street? On my street there was always a commotion, like in an anthill. Every building had at least ten shops selling all kinds of goods: Tsalke the Nose and Khanovitsh with their ready-made clothing, Sarah Klok with her dressmaking notions, Taleykinski's salami, Frumkin's pharmacy, Bendel's barbershop, Probe's bakery. Is there anything you couldn't find on that street? You could leave dressed, well fed, shaved, and with a remedy for a cough.
>
> Now mothers sit there with their children and old Lithuanian women knit little jackets. All on my street. Both sides of the street are now empty. You can't even get a glass of water to quench your thirst. (pp. 18–19)

Grossman mourns the city of his youth: "I stand on the corner that was once Gitke-Toybe's Lane and I wait. Maybe someone will run up to me and shout, 'Itsik! Itsik the Hare! Look at him.' But there isn't a single person left in Vilna who'd remember me" (p. 18), because the Vilna that the fictional Grossman is searching for no longer exists. The buildings and landmarks of Jewish Vilna, and more tragically, its inhabitants, have disappeared. Between 1941 and 1944, more than 90 percent of Vilna Jews were murdered, the majority of them shot and buried in open pits in the fields of Ponar, an area close to Vilna.

For the twenty-first-century reader, the Holocaust shadows the lives of all Karpinowitz's characters. But Karpinowitz steers us back to a more innocent time, when the brutality at Ponar is not only unknown to his characters but unimaginable. He guides his readers to maintain an awareness of the impending cataclysmic tragedy while at the same time cherishing the small but firmly held hopes of each character. Along with the writer, we love the characters and cheer for them, believing fully in the possibility of the fulfillment of their dreams.

From as early as the nineteenth century and possibly even before that, Vilna was known as Yerushalayim d'Lite, the Jerusalem of Lithuania.[4] The city boasted the majestic Great Synagogue as well as an extensive network of small prayer and study houses. The teachings of the Vilna Gaon, Eliyahu ben Shlomo Zalman Kremer (1720–1797), a Torah scholar and community leader, provide spiritual leadership to the present day. From the nineteenth century until the Holocaust, Vilna was famous for its publishing houses. These included both the Romm Publishing House, which in 1886 produced the revered Vilna Talmud among many other religious and secular texts, and the print shop of Rozenkrantz and Shriftzetser, where Abraham Karpinowitz's father worked for a short time. The city also boasted a number of important religious and secular Jewish libraries, including the Strashun and Mefistei Haskalah Libraries.

During the interwar period, when Karpinowitz's stories are set, the city of Vilna was under Polish rule. This was a time of rising anti-Semitism and increasing impoverishment and economic marginalization of the Jewish population. Despite these pressures, interwar Vilna witnessed a flowering of Jewish cultural and intellectual life. Under the leadership of Max Weinreich, the headquarters of YIVO (the Yiddish Scientific Institute) were established in 1925. The organization's mandate was to collect, preserve, study, and disseminate information on Jewish language and culture in Eastern Europe. The Vilna literary group, Yung-Vilne (Young Vilna), included among its members the important Yiddish writers Chaim Grade, Abraham Sutzkever, and Shmerke Kaczerginski. Vilna boasted numerous Jewish newspapers, Yiddish and Hebrew language theatrical groups, several Jewish choirs and orchestras, a Jewish opera company, and a Jewish sports club.

4. According to Dr. Izraelis Lempertas, a scholar and Vilna resident, there are various legends about the origin of the designation *Yerushalayim d'Lite* (Jerusalem of Lithuania): "It is said that when Napoleon saw [the city's] numerous synagogues and witnessed the devotion of the Jews, he exclaimed, 'It's Jerusalem of Lithuania.'" Lempertas cites another legend that places the designation in the seventeenth century in recognition of the 333 Vilna Jews who knew the Talmud by heart (Izraelis Lempertas, *Musu Vilne* [Vilnius: Leidini Reme, 2003], 12).

In his imaginative recreation of the vanished city of Vilna, Karpinowitz often blurs the line between fact and fiction. He intertwines the lived with the imagined and the realistic with the whimsical to create "literary authenticity, a storyteller's truth, which he maintains even in the sometimes implausible and fanciful situations he creates."[5] Through a lens that sometimes reflects the realistic, sometimes the fanciful, and sometimes a skillful blending of both, Karpinowitz shows us how the shifting social, cultural, and political trends that rocked Jewish life played out in the lives of individual members of the *amcha*, the poor and disenfranchised Jews of Vilna. For example, in the two linked stories "The Folklorist" and "Chana-Merka the Fishwife," Karpinowitz humanizes the activities of YIVO, the Yiddish Scientific Institute, through two fictionalized *zamlers*, or collectors of ethnographic material. In "The Folklorist," Rubinshteyn, the main character, is thrilled with the folk material he has collected from Chana-Merka the Fishwife. But Chana-Merka has other ideas, and by the end of the story that bears her name, she has moved on to collecting and sharing material herself. Max Weinreich, the driving force behind YIVO, appears in both stories as a secondary character.

Like Chana-Merka and Rubinshteyn, the characters at the center of Karpinowitz's stories are not the individuals traditionally associated with Jewish Vilna's esteemed religious, intellectual, and cultural legacy. For Karpinowitz, these people had already been adequately memorialized. In his 1995 interview with Boris Sandler, the writer explained that the Vilna of his stories is "not the Vilna of the Vilna Gaon, nor the Vilna of Grodzenski, the shammes of the Great Synagogue. It is not the Vilna of the . . . intelligentsia, exemplified by Dr. Max Weinreich, the director of the Yiddish Scientific Institute. . . . There is no end to what people have written about the Vilna Gaon. And Dr. Max Weinreich has been immortalized in Yiddish linguistics and in the history of the Yiddish language."[6]

Karpinowitz felt that it was the *amcha* who called out for his pen. He reminds us, "These individuals are also part of the Jewish people. We

5. Volpe, "Di sheynkayt fun Vilne," 207.

6. Abraham Karpinowitz, unpublished interview with Boris Sandler, 1995, Tel Aviv.

cannot separate ourselves from them. We must not allow them to be for-gotten" (Karpinovitsh 1995). The main characters of Karpinowitz's stories are fishwives like Chana-Merka, barbers, shoemakers, and people like Jack Grossman, the pickpocket, who lived outside the law.

The individuals traditionally associated with Vilna's cultural and reli-gious achievement are not entirely absent from Karpinowitz's stories. But they do not take center stage. Instead, they play secondary roles, forming the backdrop for Karpinowitz's heroes and heroines, the sets on the stage on which the *amcha*, the common people, live their lives. This is a delight-ful switch of emphasis from the relationship we have come to expect in fiction between well-known and esteemed individuals on the one hand and the "common" woman or man on the other.

Karpinowitz maintained a particular respect and affection for Jews who lived outside the law, as exemplified in "The Lineage of the Vilna Underworld." In this story, members of the Jewish underworld play pivotal roles in the lives of two important historical figures, Napoleon Bonaparte and Josef Pilsudski. The reader learns that the fictional Leybe the Fence offered Napoleon a place to stay when the Emperor retreated to Vilna after his defeat in Russia: "The emperor was sick: his bladder was weak, his hemorrhoids were torturing him, and he had stomach cramps from the terrible food. When he showed up at Leybe the Fence's inn, he was frozen stiff" (p. 96). Fortunately for Napoleon, "Leybe's wife saved the emperor. She cooked him chicken soup and gave him an herbal drink for his bladder. She also brought him a salve for his hemorrhoids" (p. 97). In this passage, we see not only a comic reversal of roles—Leybe and his wife are the saviors of the suffering Napoleon—but also an affectionate portrait of the petty criminal and his family. In a later historical period in the same story, Josef Pilsudski, who was to become the first head of state of Poland, enlists the help of the fic-tional Zelik the Benefactor, a well-respected member of the Vilna Jewish underworld, to help rob a train "carrying sacks of money." Pilsudski needs these funds to finance "military units to take up arms against the tsar and win back Poland's independence" (p. 98). During the rob-bery, "simply put, Zelik had saved Pilsudski's life" (p. 99). Again, Karpi-nowitz's skillful blending of fact and fiction allows him to affectionately exaggerate the importance of his main characters, in this case, members of the Vilna underworld.

The underworld characters in Karpinowitz's stories uphold a strong moral code. When the painstakingly assembled contents of Ortshik the Barber's shop are stolen in the story "Lost and Found," members of the Jewish underworld are outraged. They immediately set out to find the culprit and retrieve the loot. A meeting called to redress the wrong is attended by "everyone with the slightest involvement in illegal activity" (p. 77), as well as by Rabbi Kivele, the criminals' rabbi. Referring to the *Shulchan aruch*, *The Code of Jewish Law*, Rabbi Kivele informs the assembled group that unless the stolen goods are returned, the offending individual will be excommunicated. The thief will not only be banished from the community, he will also cease to enjoy the protection of "the all-powerful" in his thieving operations. The assembled crowd does not take this threat lightly. Even God, it appears, looks out for the members of the Vilna underworld.

Karpinowitz's characters, like their real-world counterparts, struggle with the harsh economic and political realities of the time. During the 1930s, large numbers of Vilna Jews were forced to resort to begging. The struggle for survival in difficult times is a theme that runs through many of Karpinowitz's stories. In the story "Shibele's Lottery Ticket," Karpinowitz sympathetically humanizes two Vilna beggars, Shibele the Conductor and his partner, Zerdel, who plays a violin without a back. In the story, "Vladek," Berke and Vladek try to earn an honest living by "working on the freight cars . . . going into Kinkulkin's mill, but it didn't pan out. One day there was work and ten days, nothing" (p. 83). To survive, the two get involved in petty illegal activity, like "wrench[ing] copper doorknobs off the more expensive doors and [selling] them for scrap" (p. 83). Karpinowitz's portraits of his struggling characters suggest that people turn to begging or crime when they have no other options; and, moreover, these "trades" can be honorable occupations if practiced honorably.

Another harsh reality faced by both historical Vilna Jews and Karpinowitz's characters is anti-Semitism. The story "Vladek," about the relationship between a petty Jewish criminal named Berke and his Polish friend Vladek, reveals the anti-Semitic atmosphere in Vilna during the 1930s. Berke explains, "Jewish students were being beaten up at Vilna University. And the anti-Semites hired guards to stand outside Jewish shops and stop Christian customers from entering. The threat of violence hung over the city" (p. 85). This story reveals the troubled and often contradictory relations between Jews and gentiles during the years leading up to the Holocaust, with real friendships and mutual respect existing between members of the two groups against a background of antagonism, hatred, and violence. As the story progresses, Berke is forced into the Vilna ghetto, established by the Nazis in 1941. In desperation, he turns to Vladek, his Polish friend from childhood, for help. The behavior of the fictional Vladek shows the reader the complex challenges faced by Poles in Vilna during the period of the Nazi occupation.

Various left-wing ideologies, promising a better life for the disenfranchised, exercised considerable influence on Jews in interwar Vilna. Socialism, Bundism (Jewish socialist trade unionism), communism, and Bolshevism all had their fervent followers, as reflected in Karpinowitz's stories. In the story "The Amazing Theory of Prentsik the Shoemaker," we see the influence of Soviet propaganda on the main character, Prentsik. Rather than looking to the God of the Torah and Talmud for salvation, Prentsik turns to the theories of the Soviet agronomist, Ivan Mitchurin, whose experiments in the genetic engineering of plants won him the Order of Lenin. Prentsik, a poor, uneducated man, "clear[s] out the nettles from the little courtyard behind his room on Kleyn Stephan Street, next to Tserile's inn, and set[s] up a zoo" (p. 23), determined to "transform nature" (p. 25) and "beautify the world" (p. 24) in a doomed attempt to apply Mitchurin's theories of the social engineering of plants to the animal kingdom.

In this story, like many others, the placement of important historic figures is complex, innovative, and effective. Yoysef Giligitsh appears as a secondary character. Giligitsh was, in fact, a beloved teacher to countless students at the Re'al Gymnasium (a Yiddish-language secondary school that Abraham Karpinowitz himself attended) and the author of scholarly works about zoology and botany. In Karpinowitz's story, Giligitsh acts as a foil to Prentsik, showing both him and the reader the fallacy of the theories of the Soviet scientist Ivan Mitchurin. Giligitsh patiently explains to

Prentsik that not only is "botany . . . not zoology" (p. 24), but "Mitchurin is bluffing. . . . His experiments are going nowhere" (p. 25).

Abke the Nail Biter, the antihero of the story "The Red Flag," is an unlikely hero in the fight for communism in Poland. A petty criminal, Abke is arrested on his way to a game of poker and falsely accused of "helping the Bolsheviks seize Poland" (p. 34). In this story, Karpinowitz paints an affectionately mocking picture of the world of Jewish communists as seen through Abke's eyes. Abke's tribulations during his arrest and subsequent imprisonment also reveal the repressive anti-Communist stance of the Polish government in Vilna. In this story, Karpinowitz introduces the lawyer, Joseph Tshernikhov, a significant historical figure in interwar Vilna, as a secondary character. As well as defending Jewish communists, Joseph Tshernikhov was a leader of the Freeland League, the Jewish territorialist organization that sought a Jewish homeland outside of Palestine. Tshernikhov's presence in the story provides Karpinowitz with the opportunity to explain Jewish territorialism and its fraught relationship with Zionism.

Karpinowitz's story "Jewish Money" reveals the influence of the Zionist dream on early twentieth-century Vilna Jews. But rather than placing a Zionist ideologue or movement leader in the role of main character, the action of the story is propelled by a nameless "every Jew" with neither friends nor institutional allegiances. Alone in his attic apartment, the man hatches a plan to manufacture Jewish money. "That way I'll get Vilna Jews used to their own money as a first step towards having their own state" (p. 103). The consequences of his efforts are both poignant and humorous.

Karpinowitz's commitment to honor the world of his characters permeates every aspect of his writing, starting with the very building blocks of his stories: the Yiddish language spoken by the real-life counterparts of his characters.[7] The writer frequently employs words, expressions, and

---

7. I hope those who can read Yiddish will afford themselves the pleasure of reading Karpinowitz in the original. A number of his books have been digitized by the Yiddish Book Center and can be downloaded from their website, http://www.yiddishbookcenter .org/books/search.

grammatical structures specific to the Litvak or northern European dialect of Yiddish spoken by Vilna Jews. He also foregrounds Vilna street slang.[8]

Karpinowitz makes a special point of preserving the language of particular Vilna trades by putting pertinent words and expressions into the mouths of his characters, sometimes even providing the reader with lists of sayings, aphorisms, and curses. In the story "Chana-Merka the Fishwife," for example, Chana-Merka provides the researchers at YIVO with a number of Yiddish expressions used in the market and the fishing trade. Karpinowitz reproduces her lists in his story, so that the fictional character becomes a real-life transmitter of lost linguistic knowledge and the reader a real-life recipient. "Lost and Found" incorporates extensive vocabulary used in the barbering trade, and "The Amazing Theory of Prentsik the Shoemaker" employs the vocabulary of the shoemaking trade.

Like many people in Vilna, many of Karpinowitz's characters were known by their colorful nicknames. In the story "Lost and Found," for example, Karpinowitz lists the underworld members in attendance at the meeting called to deal with the theft of Ortshik's barbering supplies: "Zelik the Benefactor sat at the head of the table with Prentsik and Zorukh the Double Boiler at his side to assist him. Further down the table, according to their rank, sat Avromke the Anarchist, Wise Melekh, Dodke the Ace, Elinke, Motke the Little Kaiser, both Squirrel brothers, and so on, all the way down to the little minnows at the end of the table" (p. 77).

Karpinowitz also took advantage of the versatility and porousness of the Yiddish language to animate his stories. For example, the story "Vladek," with its central Polish character, contains a large number of Polish words that were familiar to Vilna Jews. Thus, Karpinowitz uses his

---

8. Karpinowitz's stories include extensive vocabulary and grammatical syntax that are not to be found in Yiddish dictionaries or texts on Yiddish grammar. Fortunately there are many native Yiddish speakers who generously aided me in establishing the meanings of these words, expressions, and sentences. I cannot thank them enough. Their names are listed in the acknowledgments.

stories not only to memorialize but also to preserve and transmit certain aspects of the Yiddish language to post-Holocaust generations of readers.

Abraham Karpinowitz credits his success as a writer to the fact that he was raised in a theater home and had access to people from all classes of society. His father, Moyshe Karpinowitz, was an important theater impresario. As well as organizing performing tours for various Yiddish actors and writers including Sholem Aleichem, Moyshe Karpinowitz ran two Yiddish theaters in Vilna, first the Palace Theater and then the Folk Theater. Abraham Karpinowitz recalls, "The theater was an open door. Who didn't come to the theater?"[9] He said that when he walked down Sophianikes Street, "the Jewish prostitutes would yell through the windows, 'Ah, the writer is here.'" Karpinowitz elaborates, "I feasted on a bowl of thick folk soup . . . I absorbed all the color and variety, all the sadness and joy of the stage."[10] Karpinowitz's theater background uniquely positioned him to write knowledgably and sympathetically about members of all social classes.

This book includes two memoirs ("Memories of a Decimated Theater Home" and "The Tree beside the Theater") and a story ("The Great Love of Mr. Gershteyn") about the Yiddish theater in Vilna. Through the skillful interweaving of memory and imagination, Karpinowitz provides an intimate picture of the Yiddish theater world with its many personalities, challenges, and triumphs.

Abraham Karpinowitz survived the Holocaust in the Soviet Union. In 1944, he briefly returned to his native Vilna, now emptied of Jewish life. He left for Palestine in 1947. After two years in a British internment camp in Cyprus, he arrived in the newly formed state of Israel, where, following in his father's footsteps, he became a cultural impresario. He managed the Israeli Philharmonic Orchestra for over thirty years, from 1952 until his retirement. According to Karpinowitz, this work provided him with "the opportunity to travel and meet interesting people," as well as "to do the

9. Karpinovitch, interview with Boris Sandler, 1995.
10. Ibid.

ongoing research necessary to continue writing."[11] Karpinowitz died in March 2004, just two months short of his ninety-first birthday.

Yiddish writers like Abraham Karpinowitz, whose literary oeuvres postdate the Holocaust, faced many obstacles. As the Yiddish writer Chava Rosenfarb said, most of the Yiddish-reading public had "gone up in the smoke of the crematoria."[12] Furthermore, Karpinowitz's adopted country of Israel embraced Hebrew as the sole national language, providing no official support for, and even numerous sanctions against, the Yiddish language.[13] As Allison Schachter writes, "The new Israeli state . . . creat[ed] laws against printing a daily Yiddish newspaper and plac[ed] severe restrictions on Yiddish theater."[14] David Ben-Gurion, Israel's first prime minister, was not alone in his view that although "Yiddish was one of the important spiritual assets of the Jewish people, nevertheless, with respect to the State of Israel, . . . [It] belongs to the Jewish past, not the present and certainly not the future."[15]

11. Ibid.

12. As explained on page 2 of this introduction, the subjects of Karpinowitz's stories, the Jews of Vilna, were, with some exceptions, not murdered in the infamous Nazi death camps with their crematoria, but mostly shot and then buried by the Nazis and their Lithuanian collaborators in open pits at Ponar, an area close to Vilna. A number of Vilna Jews were sent to Nazi camps in Latvia and Estonia. These camps did not have crematoria.

13. Despite numerous reports to the contrary, the Yiddish language is neither dead nor dying. A large percentage of Hasidic Jews speak Yiddish as a daily language. Although it is difficult, if not impossible, to accurately assess the exact numbers of Hasidic Jews, in his book *The Rebirth of Hasidism: From 1945 to the Present*, published in 2005, Jacques Gutwirth estimated that there were between 350,000 and 400,000 Hasidim in the world at the time of publication. With the highest Jewish birth rate, this population is steadily increasing. However, the various contemporary Hasidic groups eschew "secular" Yiddish writers like Karpinowitz. The Yiddish "revival," on the other hand, celebrates the Yiddish literary tradition. Although the Yiddish revival supports the learning of the Yiddish language, its focus is on making Yiddish literature and culture available in translation.

14. Allison Schachter, *Diasporic Modernism: Hebrew and Yiddish Literature in the Twentieth Century* (Oxford: Oxford University Press, 2012), 156.

15. Rachel Rojanski, "The Final Chapter in the Struggle for Cultural Autonomy," *Journal of Modern Jewish Studies* 6, no. 2 (2007): 198.

But Karpinowitz found a community of Yiddish writers. This community was centered in Israel, but had connections with Yiddish writers throughout the world and access to Yiddish readers internationally. Abraham Sutzkever, the acclaimed Yiddish poet and editor and a childhood friend of Karpinowitz's from Vilna, also settled in Israel and had an enormous influence on Karpinowitz's life and work. In a 1995 interview published in *Di pen* (The Yiddish Pen), Karpinowitz explained, "Abraham Sutzkever offered me a way forward in literature and even in life. . . . When I arrived in Israel . . . Sutzkever organized us into a group known as Yung-Yisroel. He encouraged us to do nothing less than to write in Yiddish."[16] Karpinowitz was an active member of Yung-Yisroel, which formed in 1951 and remained active until 1959.[17] As well as Abraham Sutzkever and Abraham Karpinowitz, Yung-Yisroel members included poets Moshe Yungman, Rivka Basman, and Rukhl Fishman, and fiction writers Zvi Eizenman and Yossl Birshtein.[18] Karpinowitz's first book, *Der veg keyn Sdom* was published as part of a series of seven books written by various members of Yung-Yisroel and issued under the name of the group.[19] Karpinowitz was a regular contributor both to the Israeli Yiddish newspaper, *Letste nayes*, which published from 1949 to 2006 and to the Yiddish literary journal, *Di goldene keyt*, edited by Abraham Sutzkever, and published from 1949 to 1995.[20] *Di goldene keyt* showcased the work of Yiddish writers throughout the world and accessed an international reading public. Karpinowitz also coedited the second volume of *Der almanakh fun di yidishe*

16. Avrom Karpinovitsh, "Intervyu: Avrom Karpinovich." Fun Gennady Estaikh, *Di pen*/The Yiddish Pen 7 (February 1995): 35, 36. Oxford, U.K.: Oxford Institute for Yiddish Studies.

17. David Hirsh Roskies, "Di Shrayber-Grupe 'Yung Yisroel,'" *Yugentruf* (September 1973): 7–12.

18. Shachar Pinsker. "Choosing Yiddish in Israel: Yung Yisroel between Home and Exile, the Center and the Margin," 277–94. In *Choosing Yiddish, New Frontiers of Language and Culture*, ed. L. Rabinovitch, S. Goren, and Hannah S. Pressman. Detroit: Wayne State University Press, 2013.

19. Roskies, "Di shrayber-grupe 'Yung Yisroel.'"

20. Rachel Rojanski, "The Beginnings of the Yiddish Press in Israel: Ilustrirter vokhnblat," *Zutot: Perspectives on Jewish Culture* 5, no. 1 (2008): 141.

shrayber in Yisroel (The Almanac of Yiddish Writers in Israel).[21] He regularly lectured on Yiddish literature in Vilna, Lithuania; Poland; Russia; Canada; and Israel. He gave his last talk, entitled "My Vilna," to the Israeli group Yung Yiddish just four days before his death (Cahan 2011).

Abraham Karpinowitz wrote seven works of fiction, two biographies, and a play,[22] including five collections of short stories about Jewish life in Vilna before the Holocaust, the major theme of his literary output.[23] He was awarded numerous prizes, including the prestigious Manger Prize (1981). His work has been translated into German, Hebrew, Lithuanian, Polish, Russian, and Spanish.

★

"Vilna, Vilna, Our Native City," the epilogue story in this collection, is an eloquent ode to the "decimated beauty of Vilna" (p. 149). The unnamed narrator tells the reader: "I must confess in the name of the survivors, in the name of the small group of Vilna Jews who managed to travel to the other side and escape their native city when it was converted by the murderers into one bloody Daytshe Street; in the name of all those who escaped from the hellfire through ghettoes, through forests, through camps, combat zones, and battlefronts; in the name of them all, I must

---

21. M. Gros-Tsimerman, A. Karpinovitsh, and A. Shpiglblat, eds. *Almanakh fun di yidishe shrayber in Yisroel*, 2nd oysgabe (Tel Aviv: Fareyn fun yidishe shrayber un zhurnalistn in Yisroel, 1967).

22. Karpinowitz's publications are *Der veg keyn Sdom* (Tel Aviv: I. L. Peretz, 1959) with Alexander Bogen; *Baym Vilner durkhhoyf* (Tel Aviv: I. L. Peretz, 1967); *A tog fun milkhome* (Tel Aviv: I. L. Peretz, 1973); *Oyf Vilner gasn* (Tel Aviv: Di goldene keyt, 1981); *Tsu fus keyn Erets-Yisroel* (Tel Aviv: I. L. Peretz, 1985). *Oyf Vilner vegn* (Tel Aviv: I. L. Peretz, 1987); *Di geshikhte fun Vilner Ger-tsedek Graf Valentin Pototsky* (Tel Aviv: Vilner Pinkhes, 1990); *Vilne mayn Vilne* (Tel Aviv: I. L. Peretz, 1993); and *Geven, geven, amol Vilne* (Tel Aviv: I. L. Peretz, 1997). According to Goldberg, Karpinowitz also wrote the play "Itsik Vitenberg," which was produced in Argentina in 1958. Karpinowitz wrote a biography of the violinist Bronislaw Huberman in Hebrew, which was also published in Spanish.

23. Karpinowitz's collections of stories about Jewish life in Vilna are *Baym Vilner durkhhoyf, Oyf Vilner gasn, Oyf Vilner vegn, Vilne mayn Vilne*, and *Geven, geven, amol Vilne*. *Di geshikhte fun Vilner Ger-tsedek Graf Valentin Pototsky* is about an individual from Vilna.

confess that we were in love with Vilna. To this very day that love pierces our hearts like a broken arrow that cannot be removed without taking part of us with it" (p. 149).

Karpinowitz and his narrator do not rest in their grief and longing. Karpinowitz wants future generations to understand and perhaps vicariously experience the beauty and joy of life in Vilna. The narrator of this epilogue story urges "the last Jews of Vilna, [to] throw a green bridge over everything that has disappeared, so that our children will one day be able to set foot there and understand our past lives, our past joys. About our suffering they know enough. May they taste the water from the spring in Pospieshk. May they cool their spirits in the hidden shadows of the trees in the Bernardine Garden" (p. 153).

Without ever turning away from the painful aspects of Jewish life in Vilna and the brutal annihilation of that world, Karpinowitz offers us, his readers, his literary children, a nuanced and vivid experience of Vilna's past life with its hope and joys.

1

Vilna without Vilna

There are people who remember a man with blue spectacles who stood on the corner of Gitke-Toybe's Lane, begging, "Take me across to the other side." We never knew if he was really blind and needed help crossing the street or if he just longed for the touch of a warm hand. He wanted someone to take him to the opposite side, to the corner of Yiddishe Street, where the small pump supplied water to all the poor courtyards nearby. If no one came to help him, after a little while the man crossed the street on his own, tapping the cobblestones with his cane as he went.

Why did I think about that particular man when I stood on that same corner after so many years? Absolutely nothing remained, but when I stopped there, the man's pleas rang in my ears.

Gitke-Toybe's Lane bordered on Daytshe Street, the liveliest street in all of Vilna. It was called Daytshe Street even before the German murderers came to our city to slaughter the Jews. That street was my kingdom. I was friends with all the hucksters who eked out a living dragging customers into the ready-made clothing stores. I wasn't in their line of work—I didn't pull in customers. What I got, I took from people's pockets. The entire street knew how I, Itsik the Hare, earned my bread. When the street was in an uproar from one end to the other, the hucksters would growl, "Itsik, scram. Quick as a hare."

They didn't have to ask me twice. Quick as lightning, I ran to my regular hiding place, behind the poultry dealers on Yatkever Street. That's how I earned my nickname, the Hare.

I was still a boy then, just out of prison for the first time. I had yet to learn my trade—I was shoving both hands into my victim's pocket. Zuske the Professor, who had a bar on Konske Street, taught me what I needed to know. He had a school for pickpockets. He got some of the young guys who hung around the streets together and taught us the trade. During the lessons he'd shout, "Not with your hands, idiots! With your fingers. You have to work with your fingers."

Hokhman the Tailor gave Zuske a gift of an old mannequin with one leg. Zuske would dress the mannequin in a jacket or coat and we'd practice on it. If the mannequin jiggled when we touched its clothing, we failed the exam. That was my school.

No one dared cheat our professor. Every time we managed to extract something from a stranger's pocket, Zuske got his cut, as we'd agreed. We were orphans without a home and he was like a father to us. Even if one of the professor's students failed to bring in anything, he didn't go hungry.

It's good to remember all this. I'm a big shot in Canada now. I'm in the hotel business and Mr. Jack Grossman is a name to remember. I even have a say in the Jewish community. My lineage serves me well—someone from Vilna! After my years in the wide world, I've become a gentleman.

When I told people in Canada where I was from, a Jewish family with status cozied up to me. They matched me up with a girl in their family. No great beauty. She has a small defect: one of her shoulders is a little higher than the other. But she's very well educated, always with a book in hand, even in bed. Her family set me up. They brought me into the business. Being around her, I became respectable and left Zuske the Professor behind.

Here I stand in 1989, on the corner of Gitke-Toybe's Lane, and I think back to life in the thirties. That was a bitter time. People escaped to Russia to save their lives. They wanted to get out of harm's way, to work and learn a trade. We know how that turned out.

I also wanted to escape to Russia. What with the police and the prisons, I was fed up with how I was earning my living. I was an orphan, so what kept me in Vilna? The city itself. I swam through Vilna like a fish in the Viliye. I was at home from Sophianikes Street, with the whorehouses crammed with shiksas and a few Jewish girls, all the way up to Novogorod Street. Novogorod was right next to the slaughterhouses where they killed the animals for the butcher shops.

My pals lived on Novogorod. Those guys were always ready to pick someone's lock to help a friend in need and bring him a tasty morsel in prison. One of those guys saved my life, though not intentionally. Thanks to him, I wasn't in Vilna when the Germans drove the Jews to Ponar to murder them.

What a story. Gorgeous Grishke, as he was called, was quite the guy. He used to put train passengers to sleep with smoke from a special cigarette. He was very smart and knew many languages. Grishke was looking for a business partner to grab valises from the sleeping victims. He'd traveled with one of Motke the Little Kaiser's nephews, but they fought over the division of the loot, so he was looking around for someone else.

Grishke wanted to work with Black Leyke's bastard, but Leyke screamed and hollered that he was going to lead her kid astray. Even though she was a former streetwalker, her Elinke was not going to get involved in shady work. People in Vilna still remembered when Spokoyni the *moyel* didn't wanted to perform Elinke's bris because no one knew the father. Leyke insisted the father was Elijah the Prophet, because he'd left and never returned. Later, when Elinke studied at the Ramayles Yeshiva, his mother didn't dare come near the school.

Gorgeous Grishke was keen to work with Elinke because he was so honest. But Black Leyke kept fussing over her kid, insisting he only do honest work until important people like Zelik the Benefactor and Wise Melekh advised Grishke to look for someone else.

Grishke kept looking until eventually he got to me. "If I put a new suit on you, people'll think you're really somebody." So he said. He took me to Tsalke the Nose's ready-made clothing shop and bought me a double-breasted suit. I started to travel with him on the trains.

I traveled with Gorgeous Grishke until one of the passengers, a little aristocrat with whiskers, refused to fall asleep. He just dozed with one eye open. When I made a grab for his valise, planning to jump off the train at the next stop, just past Kraków, he started hollering. I dropped the valise, opened the train door and climbed onto the roof. I made it all the way to the Czech border, to Koshitsa. It was an international train.

You could write a novel about all the prisons and holes where I spent time before I got to Canada. Thanks to Gorgeous Grishke, I avoided the slaughter. Later someone told me they'd seen Grishke in Klooga, a camp in Estonia where they murdered Vilna Jews and burned their bodies.

I stand on the corner that was once Gitke-Toybe's Lane and I wait. Maybe someone will run up to me and shout, "Itsik! Itsik the Hare! Look at him." But there isn't a single person left in Vilna who'd remember me. If a passerby bothers to throw me a glance, it's because of my camera. I promised to bring photographs back from Vilna. I've already been to Sophianikes Street in search of the last house, right next to the old fish market. That's where Tall Tamara wanted to hang a sign, "Public School for Love."

Tamara got the idea from Siomke Kagan, the reporter from the *Vilner Tog* newspaper. He'd already tried organizing a professional streetwalkers union in Vilna with a separate Jewish section, but the whorehouse bosses on Sophianikes Street wouldn't allow it. They were afraid the girls would get it into their heads to demand overtime pay. So Siomke hatched another plan: Tamara and Black Leyke would teach young Jewish men the art of love. The teachers would earn a living and future grooms would learn what was what. "It would also be a great honor for Jewish Vilna, the first school of its kind in the world." That's what Siomke wrote in the newspaper. Tall Tamara took the scheme seriously. She even ordered a sign from Karpel the sign painter, but it was never hung. The entire business came to nothing.

I searched for that house but didn't find even a brick. All of Sophianikes Street had been mowed down like grass in a meadow. No trace left. Only the Vilenke, the stream that splashed against the back walls of the brothels still gurgles by, but sadder than before, on its way to the Viliye.

On the street where Shimon the Coachman once drove his horse and buggy so quickly the cobblestones trembled, mothers now sit on benches lined up on the dead earth and their little children play in the sand. Once mothers sat in the Bernardine Garden with their children and threw scraps of bread to a pair of swans.

And on my street? On my street there was always a commotion, like in an anthill. Every building had at least ten shops selling all kinds of goods: Tsalke the Nose and Khanovitsh with their ready-made clothing, Sarah Klok with her dressmaking notions, Taleykinski's salami, Frumkin's pharmacy, Bendel's barbershop, Probe's bakery. Is there anything you couldn't find on that street? You could leave there dressed, well fed, shaved, and with a remedy for a cough.

Now mothers sit with their children and old Lithuanian women knit little jackets. All on my street. Both sides of the street are now empty. You can't even get a glass of water to quench your thirst.

And what's left on Yiddishe Street, just opposite my street? Nothing, as though the street had never existed. Gone is Velfke Usian's restaurant where all the actors from the Yiddish theater used to come and eat. I knew them all. Moyshe Karpinowitz with his little beard ran the theater on Ludvizarske Street. He used to let me in to watch the performances, but he'd warn me, "Itsik, go up to the balcony. And keep your hands to yourself."

Gone is Yoshe with his kvass stand. Gone is Osherke the Herring's bar. They were all on Yiddishe Street. At Osherke's, people ate all the different kind of herring, starting early in the morning. They also played billiards there.

Before my eyes, I see the entrance to Velfke's restaurant. One sunny day, Avromke the Anarchist was sitting on the steps with something to say to everyone. He certainly never let a young lady, whether married or single, pass by without comment. I'd just left Osherke's bar and I saw everything. I saw Dovidke the Cheat appear out of nowhere and stab Avromke in the heart with a knife. Avromke managed to stand up, grab Dovidke by the arm, and cry out, "You too, Dovidke?" Then he hit the ground, a dead man.

My wife once took me to the theater. They were playing *Julius Caesar* by Shakespeare. A grim play with no singing or dancing. The theater on Ludvizarske was a much livelier place. With my limited English, I understood that when the senators attacked Caesar from all sides like real underworld types, he called out the very same words to his friend Senator Brutus, who shoved a knife into him just like the others.

Did Avromke the Anarchist know what Shakespeare had written or did he have the soul of a Julius Caesar that prompted him in his final moments with those same words?

Avromke sold secondhand things in the passageway. He certainly had enemies. He ruled over the entire miserable trade without allowing any competition. But he gave Dovidke a piece of the action from time to time, slipping him a little merchandise at bargain prices.

In prison, Dovidke went off the rails with remorse and stopped making sense. He tormented himself over Avromke's murder. When he went to pieces, they let him out of prison, but he was never seen on Yiddishe Street again.

Glezer Street is gone too. No, a few things remain: a wall here, a wall there, but it's no longer Glezer Street, where Zelik the Benefactor had his tavern. That's where guys like Mishke Napoleon and Kalman the Squirrel got together. I wasn't in their league, so I'd sit at a little side table and order a quarter meter of kishke. Zelik the Benefactor's wife was the queen of kishke. Her kishke melted in your mouth. It always came out brown and shiny, like chestnuts fresh from the tree. She sold her merchandise by the meter, like Sarah Klok sold elastic for underwear.

Zelik's daughter Taybke was obsessed with playing the piano. How did someone like Taybke get interested in piano? You shouldn't ask questions like that about people in Vilna. Everyone in Vilna wanted to be better and more beautiful.

In Zelik's home, they knew plenty about smuggling tobacco from Lithuania, but nothing about the piano. So Taybke went to Svirsky the Furrier's to talk with his daughter, the piano teacher. She explained that she was dying to learn to play a little but had no money for lessons. She offered to pay with kishke. When Svirsky's daughter heard the word kishke, her mouth watered and she immediately agreed. "Good, bring us kishke!"

A winter and a summer came and went and Taybke worked on her piano playing. Toothy Khatze and Iserke, auction wholesalers, sold Zelik an old piano. When you walked through Glezer Street in the evening, you could hear Taybke playing.

Taybke wasn't the only one. Boys and girls sang in choirs, played mandolins, and performed in plays. Every Friday, there was a social evening at the Re'al Gymnasium. People danced and read poetry. Outsiders often showed up and caused a commotion, trying to force their way into the hall. The teachers stationed Khayme the Dandy at the entrance to keep order. In exchange, he was allowed to dance with any girl he chose. Each girl at the Re'al Gymnasium was more beautiful than the next. I knew them all, from a distance. You could enter the gymnasium courtyard through Konske Street, just opposite Zuske the Professor's bar, my trade school. I loved watching the guys and girls strolling across the courtyard during their long break. I would have liked to join them.

Here I stand, after so many years, on the corner of Gitke-Toybe's Lane. I don't recognize my own city. It has run away from me, across the Viliye, all the way to the forest, to Volokumpie. Sometimes on Shabbes we used to row to Volokumpie in a little boat we rented in Antokl from Yane the Boatman.

And on my street, where day and night there were deals being made and a constant commotion? I am the last survivor of that street. To this day, memories of the street pierce my heart like a broken arrow that can't be removed.

The street has become part of the silent old city. The area from Shnip-ishok all the way up to the Shishkin hills that used to doze all week long is now the new city. Even the hotel where I'm staying is on the other side of the Viliye, where the rafts used to come in and the boom men took the logs out of the water for the nearby sawmills.

The shiksa at the tourist bureau offered to show me the city. Me, of all people. I could have walked the city from one end to the other with my eyes closed. I didn't know whether to laugh or cry.

At dawn, I left the hotel by myself and walked over the Viliye Bridge to my Vilna: to Yiddishe Street, to Glezer Street, to Yatkever and Rudnitz-ker Street, to what's now known as the old city.

I didn't recognize the place. There were new buildings that didn't match their surroundings, like someone wearing a tuxedo with canvas shoes. The lanes and passageways have disappeared. There are no corners to sneak into and hide. The city has grown big, puffed up like a rich upstart. There's no little nook to nestle into, no little corner to call your own.

My wife warned me, "Don't go. You'll find nothing there but grief." But I had to see the city that raised me one more time. Her streets were my home; her people, my family. Even Mr. Khayim Gordon, the stern shammes from the Great Synagogue, always had a good word for me: "Itsik," he'd say, "one day you'll become respectable."

Now I've become respectable. But who will listen to me brag? If only there had never been Germans on this earth, then Vilna would still be Vilna and I wouldn't have become respectable, with two hotels in Canada.

They've set up a kindergarten on the spot in the synagogue courtyard where the shammes, Mr. Khayim Gordon once lived. He went to Ponar with all our fellow Vilna Jews.

People will probably be offended. "Look whose Vilna he's searching for: the Vilna of Zelik the Benefactor and Tovshe the Angel." Let them be offended. This is my Vilna. Let everyone from Vilna search for their own corner, their own special spot. None of us will find anything. Nothing remains.

Here I stand where Gitke-Toybe's Lane once was and I cry. A little girl with a red bow in her blonde braids watches as I let the tears stream down my face. She stretches out her hand to me. She's holding a bright red candy. I'd like to smile but I can't. I murmur, "It's Vilna without Vilna."

2

The Amazing Theory
of Prentsik the Shoemaker

Prentsik the Shoemaker slept in his clothes. After finishing his day's work, he went straight from his workshop to bed without taking the hat off his head. He even brought his hammer with him and shoved it under his pillow. Prentsik insisted it made no sense to undress. "You barely have time to turn around before you have to get up again." It was easier to sleep in his clothes, especially since there was no one to watch him undress.

Prentsik was a lonely man.

But no one can be entirely alone. Everyone has to be involved with something, even if it's only a fly. Prentsik was involved with animals. This wasn't so much to drive away his loneliness as to prove a scientific theory and stun the world. He cleared out the nettles from the little courtyard behind his room on Kleyn Stephan Street, next to Tserile's inn, and set up a zoo. He got some cages and raised all sorts of monstrosities.

No one could figure out where Prentsik got the strange creatures. To people in Vilna, an ordinary sparrow sounded like a canary and every cat preened herself, delighting in her own beauty. People said that Prentsik's wild animals weren't local but hailed from distant lands.

One day Giligitsh, a teacher from the Re'al Gymnasium, visited Prentsik's private menagerie. He shrugged his shoulders, marveling at the exotic herd the shoemaker had assembled. Giligitsh sat in his socks for a good few hours. While he waited, Prentsik tacked new heels and sole tips onto the teacher's boots and the two men discussed zoological problems, Prentsik's obsession. Prentsik didn't spit only nails from his mouth but also random bits of theory from a certain Professor Mitchurin.

In the Soviet Union, Mitchurin had paired potatoes with summer beets and apples with cherries, hoping these matches would sire legitimate offspring. That's what Prentsik had read in the *Ovnt kurier* newspaper.

No matter how often Giligitsh explained that botany is not zoology, it made no difference to the shoemaker. Prentsik insisted that he would turn his animals into respectable beings. "It will take time, a lot of time. I will rear them and turn black into white."

Meanwhile, Prentsik's little courtyard swarmed with various creatures, dazed animals with pointy snouts and tails as hard as corncobs. A pair of brightly colored birds ran around, plucking at each other with their shiny beaks and tearing out clumps of feathers until they drew blood. All day long, there was a noisy ruckus and angry hissing in the courtyard. The animals gnashed their teeth, searching for victims.

Prentsik paid for the animals with the soles of shoes. The warden of the zoo at the corner of Zavalne Street brought Prentsik all kinds of creatures. In return, he and his family wore shoes in good repair all year long.

The Vilna zoo was a truly wretched place. There was absolutely nothing of interest to see there. The high points were a decrepit wolf with a miserable expression on its face, a pair of otters, and a limping pelican. The city was planning to build a proper zoo in Antokl, in a forest right next to the Viliye. In the meantime, the zoo was a ship without a rudder. The warden, a goy, was in complete charge and did whatever he pleased. When one of the landowners from around Vilna brought a gift to the zoo, it went straight to Prentsik. The warden always had a ready excuse: the animal had died. That's how Prentsik raised his congregation of strange creatures. It was a sight to behold. A pregnant woman dared not even take a peek.

Why did Prentsik need the whole business? What did he hope to achieve? He wanted to show Vilna that he could beautify the world with his experiments. God himself would take notice. Prentsik argued that if the Creator wanted to, He could create animals as adorable as dolls. He even had the ability to reshape Prentsik himself so that one of his eyes would no longer be closer to his ear than to his nose. Because of that defect, among others, Fanke, Prentsik's fiancée, had left for Africa in the middle of the night with a military tailor.

Vilna remembered how Prentsik changed after that. He stopped going to the meetings of the shoemaker's guild. He stopped enjoying his shot of whisky at Itsik the Redhead's bar. He also started sleeping in his clothes.

Prentsik poured his bitterness into his menagerie. He made the rounds of the butchers in the slaughterhouses and collected all sorts of bones, guts, and entrails in a sack. He didn't avoid Probe's bakery either. The animals had grown so scrawny, they started gnawing on old bread and even dried-out biscuits.

Every Sunday morning, Prentsik found a pile of uneaten cholent lying next to his courtyard. It was a present from the people on Kleyn Stephan Street. They felt sorry for the animals. Every so often, one of the neighbors would approach Prentsik and gently suggest he disband his treasure trove, but Prentsik wouldn't hear of it. He would launch into a long explanation about the meaning of his zoological experiments. His creatures would become more beautiful. With patience, he would transform nature. He had read in the newspaper about a certain professor who had done just that. Prentsik talked on and on. His visitors walked away quietly, shaking their heads as if they'd just visited someone who was very sick.

Meanwhile, Prentsik did achieve one success from his many experiments. He had a dog, a mutt without a pedigree. Prentsik insisted he would teach the dog to behave like a respectable being. He tormented and bullied the poor dog until eventually it stopped sniffing at poles and started lifting its leg. When the dog had to go, it supported its front paws on the wall of Tserile's inn and peed like a man. Everyone on Kleyn Stephan Street was amazed when they saw the dog go. After that, they left Prentsik alone.

Giligitsh brought his daughter's only pair of dress shoes to Prentsik and spoke to him again. "Prentsik, a living creature is not a piece of fruit. You can't apply Mitchurin's methods to zoology. Aside from that, Mitchurin is bluffing. I'm telling you, his experiments are going nowhere."

Prentsik banged wooden tacks into Giligitsh's daughter's high-heeled shoes and held forth: "You'll see what I'm going to do with these animals. I've already gotten them used to eating human food. The next generation's fur will be a different color. It'll also be softer."

Giligitsh couldn't stand it any longer and shouted, "There are laws!"

Prentsik wasn't at all perturbed by the teacher's shouts. "What laws?" "The laws of nature."

The shoemaker looked at Giligitsh out of the corner of the eye that was closer to his ear and stunned the teacher with his question. "And who says that nature can't be altered?"

An amputee sold birds and goldfish in a shop on Hekdesh Street. Every Friday, on his way back from Tishkevitsh's steam bath, Prentsik stopped at the shop. The amputee tried to get Prentsik to see that humans can't alter nature.

The amputee moved around his shop in a little wagon with two nickel wheels. His legs had been amputated all the way up to his stomach, and he was ashamed to be seen in public. That is, until Prentsik sat him down on a piece of heavy leather, traced a line around his body with a piece of chalk, and cut the leather to size. Then he took a linen sack, sewed it to the leather, and placed it on the wagon. The amputee had a garment both to wear and to transport himself. After Prentsik packed him into a linen bag with a piece of leather sewn underneath it, people were no longer so put off by his appearance. And the two men became friends.

The amputee's shop was filled with birds in cages and fish in jars. There was a large aquarium in the window. There, life was better for the fish. They could stretch out a fin. All day long, children stood in the street with their noses glued to the windowpane, watching the colorful fish performing their tricks, chasing each other up and down the aquarium and lounging in the water.

It was Friday afternoon. There were no customers in the amputee's shop. Even the birds in the cages were preparing for Shabbes: dusting themselves off and cleaning their feathers. The two friends sat together, one in his wheelchair, the other on a kitchen stool. The amputee tried to get through to Prentsik. "The teacher, Mr. Giligitsh, is right. I wish him good health. Not too long ago, he explained to me that there are two kinds of canaries. He opened my eyes. And you're arguing with him. What he says is God's truth. There are no tricks in zoology. Every bird has its hop.

"If you need convincing, I'll tell you a story that will explain zoology to you. One evening a cow and a goat go to a meadow. They chew the same grass. On the way home, the cow leaves a large pile of goods. Believe me, you wouldn't want to step in it. And the goat, here a pellet, there a pellet, little pieces of nothing. Mr. Giligitsh is absolutely right. 'Every creature has its ways.'"

Prentsik wasn't willing to be convinced, "And my dog?"

"If they tortured you with old cholent, you'd also climb the walls."

It was already Shabbes when Prentsik left the amputee's shop. All the shops on Hekdesh Street were closed. The gate to the Jewish hospital was also closed. A light rain accompanied Prentsik home. It was already dark. Here and there, Shabbes candles shimmered through the cracks in the shutters. Hunched over, with his collar raised, Prentsik walked through Hekdesh Street, carrying his little bundle of dirty laundry under his arm. Every drop of rain that fell on his face diluted his certainty about the zoological theory he'd been so determined to prove. He'd tried for a number of years, but no great scientific discoveries had emerged from his little courtyard. When he placed two different creatures in one cage, instead of falling in love, in no time at all one tore the other's head off.

Prentsik regretted his stubbornness. He thought about his visit with the amputee. While the man had talked, Prentsik looked around at the brightly colored birds, so unlike his own ugly creatures. Here a robin redbreast, there a finch with a colorful little cap. In one corner a bluebird, with two spots on its wings like epaulets, hopped around its cage. The canaries were as yellow as poppies and the parakeets and wagtails were so lively and proud, they were a pleasure to behold. The amputee had confided to Prentsik that if it weren't for the birds, he would do himself in. Even though he couldn't move, at least the merchandise in his shop made him happy. He'd told Prentsik that this was his only pleasure.

Prentsik came home, ate his solitary meal, and began to read the *Ovnt kurier*. The Friday edition always contained an article written by the preeminent editor A. I. Grodzenski about the latest scientific achievements. The articles were always clearly explained and spiced up with

Grodzenski's personal commentary. This week the editor had written about the sex lives of leeches.

But that evening, the contents of the article wouldn't stick in Prentsik's brain. All he could think about was his own failure in zoology. He'd hoped to prove that you could raise creatures and make those that are ugly, beautiful. It wasn't so much the creatures he wanted to transform as himself. He'd come into the world with one eye planted in the wrong spot on his face, a harelip, and ears as large as Chanukah latkes. He'd hoped to show that after much effort, he'd eventually sport a perfect face and a black moustache. He would stroll down Daytshe Street with a bowler hat on his head. Girls wouldn't run from him, the way Fanke had when she'd been only a hair's breadth away from standing with him under the wedding canopy.

Prentsik saw that nature did indeed have its laws, just like Mr. Giligitsh had said, and his own life was controlled by a cruel law.

He bemoaned his fate until deep into the night. He couldn't sleep. He knew that to honor Shabbes, he should wake in the morning with a clear head, without any thoughts about zoology. Unfortunately, he couldn't stop his thinking.

Prentsik threw down his newspaper and went into the courtyard. A large moon was shining in a perfectly clear sky. A cool breeze ushered in an early autumn. Prentsik's animal treasures were bathed in dazzling light. The creatures lay hidden in their cages, sleeping the gloomy sleep of prisoners who have long ago given up on their freedom. Only the mole, the warden's latest gift, huddled close to the grates of its cage, trying to dig under its prison.

Prentsik opened the cages, one after the other. At first, the drowsy animals didn't understand what was happening. But once they were fully awake, they fled as though from a fire. They didn't have far to run. After bounding through a few streets, they found themselves in the Zakrete forest. A few lost their way and ran in a different direction, but that was no great calamity. They made it to a forest in Antokl. Vilna had enough forests for an entire regiment of minks, martens, and other creatures.

A moment later, there wasn't a single soul left in Prentsik's zoo. Even the mole, who had no idea where in the world it was, had burrowed under a little hill close to the prison on Stephan Street. The only creature left in Prentsik's little courtyard was a hen with a goiter hanging down to the ground.

Prentsik went back to his room, turned off the light, took off his trousers, and stretched out on his bed in nothing more than his underwear. It had been a long time since he'd slept without his clothes. Before he fell asleep, Prentsik remembered the amputee telling him that if it weren't for the birds, he would do himself in. Prentsik hoped to find a creature that could make him just as happy.

In the morning, Prentsik put on his Shabbes suit, packed half a challah in the *Ovnt kurier* and walked down Daytshe Street to Cathedral Square. From there he headed to the Bernardine Garden. The path leading to the bench beside the pond was strewn with fallen leaves from the chestnut trees. As Prentsik approached the pond, his feet were buried in a soft golden carpet that lifted his mood. He felt as though he was on his way to a joyful rendezvous.

The only swan in Vilna was swimming in the pond that shone like a mirror. Its head, as white as a bridal veil, turned gracefully and ever so slightly to one side, the better to see who was throwing the little pieces of challah. The bird skimmed gracefully across the cold water towards the shore.

Prentsik sat beside the pond for a long time, feeding this creature fashioned with so much divine patience. It needed no alteration; its tiniest feather was absolutely necessary. Prentsik watched the swan's movements as it swallowed the pieces of challah. Every so often, the swan raced across the pond like a radiant ship carrying Prentsik's dream, a dream of beauty.

Prentsik stopped sleeping in his clothes. He returned to Itsik's bar for his shot of whiskey. He stopped reading scientific articles.

3

The Red Flag

Abke the Nail Biter's troubles began when he tried to do a good deed. He was thrown into prison. And not for just a summer, a winter, and then out. No, he got a good, solid sentence.

Here's what happened.

One summer evening, Abke the Nail Biter was walking down Daytshe Street when he happened on a guy hanging around the German church. The church gate was a regular meeting place for late night rendezvous. At first, Abke paid no attention to the skinny suitor standing under the electric lanterns in a wrinkled jacket and worn-out shoes. He figured the guy was probably waiting for a waitress from one of the nearby restaurants to take her to the little park on Troker Street.

Abke was on his way to Itske the Redhead's tavern. His pals had lured a gambler who wasn't from Vilna into an illegal game of poker, and they needed a fourth to sink their teeth into the sucker. The fourth had to be Abke. Abke had expert hands. Not for working, of course, but for shuffling cards. He was famous for his shuffling; he always held onto two aces.

But Abke had bad luck. The kid who'd been hanging around the church tried throwing a piece of cloth over the electric wires under Abke's very nose. Abke knew, without a doubt, that this had to be a red flag. What else would someone throw onto the wires late at night? Obviously not a shirt that had been washed and needed drying.

The thrower was clearly still an apprentice in the trade. The piece of cloth flew into the air a few times and fell back down like a bird that had been shot. The guy was incapable of throwing the flag over the wires.

Abke fumed, "Look at the kind of guy they send for the job." He ran over to the young man and yelled, "Get out of here, you bearded numbskull. If you can't do a job, keep your nose out of it."

The revolutionary acted like a big hero. "But I'm following party orders."

"You want to rot away in silence?" Abke asked.

"In silence?"

"In prison, you moron."

The young man wasn't the slightest bit worried. "We have to rally the masses."

Luckily, the street was quiet. There was only one carriage filled with drunks clip-clopping over the cobblestones. Abke cursed his fate. He couldn't stay there with the kid; he couldn't leave him. After all, this was a Jewish child. What could Abke do? Hit him on the head; that would be God's mercy. Abke had a good look around to make sure no one was looking, grabbed the flag from the kid's hand, and with one toss easily threw it over the wires. The flag, spread out like the wings of a bat, hung without a wrinkle.

The young man stood there with his mouth open, craning his neck up at the flag. He was about to deliver a speech and thank Abke in the name of the Vilna party and the world revolution when Abke hissed, "Get lost. Scram."

He didn't have to ask the kid twice. The kid had spotted someone watching them from Gitke-Toybe's Lane even before Abke did. He disappeared between two houses and from there, through a fence and onto another street. Abke didn't even try to disappear. He couldn't run like the kid because of his flat feet, so he just stood there, ready to take whatever God doled out. Panting, Susilo the Snoop pinned Abke to the wall of the church and handcuffed him.

Susilo was in the secret police. He knew the entire city and the entire city knew him. He spoke perfect Yiddish and ate cholent on Shabbes at Velfke's restaurant on Yiddishe Street. He was hand-in-glove with the underworld and knew everyone by their nicknames.

Susilo couldn't believe his eyes. He remembered Abke from a series of pathetic deals like selling a glittering ring to a poor peasant as real gold or taking someone's fur coat after a billiard game at Sztral's Cafe. But hanging anti-government flags? Susilo had clearly seen Abke do it. He'd purposely lain in wait at the corner of the lane to catch him in the act.

Abke's excuses didn't help. "Mr. Susilo, I swear to you, I was on my way to a poker game. You know me. Am I the type to . . . ?" Abke carried on all the way to the Central Police Station on Ignatover Street, the headquarters of the secret police. As soon as they arrived, Susilo telephoned the firemen to immediately take the illegal flag down from the wires.

The next morning, the masses gathered on Daytshe Street. Women bought buttons at Sarah Klok's sewing notions shop and the hucksters dragged customers into the ready-made clothing stores, praising the pants and jackets to the skies. And the flag, the red flag that was supposed to rally the masses, was nowhere to be seen. Instead they were rallied by the mild sun, the blue sky, and a feathery cloud that was as white as snow.

★

At the Central Police Station, they treated Abke like a regular. The agents barely paid him any attention. But when Susilo explained why he'd arrested Abke, there was a ruckus in every room. The agent on duty pinched Abke to make sure it was really him.

Susilo sat at the table, amusing himself by playing with the keys to Abke's handcuffs. If it had been anyone besides Abke, they would have slugged him on the spot. But they just emptied Abke's pockets, pulled out his shoelaces, and shoved him into an out-of-the-way cell until morning, when Pendzik the Cripple, the magistrate for political affairs, would arrive.

Abke didn't shut his eyes all night. Usually he slept during his arrests. He knew just about all the legal clauses and what was coming to him. They never investigated him but simply wrote out a report and sent him to the prison on Stephan Street. Abke felt at home there. He never acted like a big shot, so they always took into account the time he'd served before trial. The sentence never seemed that long: a month, more or less. But it wasn't such a simple matter this time. Abke turned himself inside out trying to figure out what he would say the next day. At dawn he still hadn't thought of anything, so he decided to remain silent to buy time.

Abke was just dozing off on the bare planks when an excuse hit him in his thick skull. He would claim that the kid had offered him money to hang the flag. He'd needed the money for a big game of poker, so he'd allowed himself to be convinced. Susilo had scared the kid off and he'd escaped. Abke hoped Pendzik would swallow the story and book him on a criminal charge. If so, once he got himself out from behind bars, he would never mess with politics again.

But Pendzik didn't swallow Abke's story. Susilo reported the details to Pendzik but the magistrate drew his own conclusion about Abke. Pendzik was never in a good mood first thing in the morning. By the time he sat down at his desk, he was in a rage with the entire world. Because of his lame leg, his nights with his wife weren't the best. She was from the village: young and good-looking, with plenty of flesh on her bones. Pendzik wasn't man enough for one of her teeth.

Luckily, Susilo was a regular visitor in their home. Every so often he spent a few hours of his working day in Pendzik's bed while the magistrate for political affairs was absorbed with defending Poland from the red scourge. As a result, Pendzik and his wife had a peaceful marriage. Every Sunday, Pendzik proudly limped to the Church of the Holy Anna next to the Vilenke River with his beautiful wife on his arm, hoping the other men would drop dead from envy.

Sitting opposite Pendzik, Abke buried his head between his narrow shoulders. He tried reading Pendzik's thin, determined lips to gauge the magistrate's response to the story Abke had hatched that morning. Pendzik's office was bathed in summer sunlight. The windows were open, and a green branch jutted into the room. Chestnut trees were growing in the closed courtyard of the Central Police Station. A sparrow jumped defiantly onto the window ledge as if to remind Pendzik that the entire world wasn't sitting in the palm of his hand. But aside from the bars on the windows, everything seemed so peaceful.

As well as communists, Pendzik also hated Jews. Why, even he didn't know. Now that a Jew, who was no doubt also a communist, sat opposite him, Penzik's hatred transformed the room into a closed jar containing a spider and a fly. Abke explained what had happened the day before. But Polish was not Abke's language. Pendzik summoned Susilo so Abke could speak Yiddish and the investigation could proceed more quickly and efficiently. It didn't help. Abke stuck to his story. Susilo translated everything and Pendzik didn't believe a single word. Finally, the magistrate gave Susilo a wink and the pair left the room. When they returned, Abke had nothing new to offer.

Susilo took charge of the situation. Before trying to break Abke, Susilo stroked his sparse, carefully groomed whiskers, adjusted his thick forelock, and buttoned his jacket. Susilo was very elegant, with a sharp crease in his well-pressed trousers. He wanted Abke to trust him. To win the confidence of the arrested man, Susilo pulled down the lower lid of his left eye with his index finger, an international sign that a person is in the criminal underworld and understands things with no more than a wink.

"Abke, stop wasting our time and stringing us along. You're trying to create a smokescreen with this story of the money, but you're just making a fool of yourself. You didn't ask for the money in advance, eh? Are you so trusting in poker?"

Abke groaned. "You're right. That was really stupid! I should have made him lay out the money in advance."

"The same lie again. I'll knock out your last pair of molars."

Trying to avoid a smack in the face, Abke buried his head deeper between his shoulders and sighed, "He cheated me."

Susilo straightened the knot of his tie and continued, "Abke, come on. Be reasonable. Tell us the guy's name. Give us addresses. Who recruited you into the party? Tell us everything and we'll return the favor. If not, things will go very badly for you. You're a young man now, but you'll leave prison with a white beard."

"I know nothing. I swear on my freedom."

"Stop telling stories. A criminal would never be this stubborn. You've obviously been well trained in the party. For many years. Your card playing and the petty theft—I see now that it was all a front to hide your political work: helping the Bolsheviks seize Poland."

Abke couldn't stand it any longer. He leapt from his chair and proclaimed, with a dignity that neither Pendzik nor Susilo expected, "Aside from what I do for a living, I'm an honest citizen. I have nothing against Poland."

Susilo almost split his sides laughing. He was barely able to translate the few words for Pendzik. Pendzik was furious. "You have nothing against Poland, eh? Well Poland has something against you, Bolshevik!"

Abke had something else to say, but he couldn't get it out. Grabbing his cane, Pendzik rained down blows on Abke's shoulders. Abke was already lying on the floor, but Pendzik continued to hit him. Susilo grabbed his boss and tore the cane from his hand. Susilo was certainly a secret agent, but he wasn't vicious like Pendzik the Cripple. By beating communists, Pendzik was searching for an antidote to his own weakness. Susilo was as strong as a horse and enjoyed Yiddish, cholent, and Pendzik's wife. So he saved Abke.

Abke's head was split open, his shoulders cut to ribbons, and his face swollen. They didn't take him to Stephan Street but instead, to Lukishke prison where they held political prisoners.

In Lukishke prison, an arrested man lived in luxury with a straw mattress and a bed sheet. Abke stretched out like a count. The prison doctor had bandaged his head and smeared iodine on his wounds. The court record documented the fact that he'd resisted arrest. The doctor had suggested Abke be placed in a hospital ward, but the prison director wouldn't allow it. "A communist is better off in a cell. He talks to the walls there."

Abke ended up in a cell with two political prisoners: Rulek Raffes and Mendel Kvartatz. They'd been caught with illegal literature and were awaiting trial. By the time the swelling on Abke's face had gone down and the wound on his head had healed, both Rulek and Mendel knew, by way of a note smuggled into the prison, that class consciousness had been awakened in Abke the Nail Biter. He'd contributed to the general struggle by putting his particular talents to work one dark night and hanging the flag of a bright tomorrow. The note included instructions to officially acknowledge Abke as an important member of the revolutionary avant-garde.

Abke wasn't used to this kind of prison. At Stephan Street, there were usually about thirty men to a cell. Peasants who'd been arrested for stealing wood from a landowner's forest told stories about she-devils, mossy creatures with three breasts. City pickpockets taught each other new tricks for taking a wallet from someone's breast pocket using only two fingers, so the victim didn't feel even a tickle. On these subjects, Abke had plenty to offer.

But here in Lukishke, he had nothing to say. Politics just wasn't Abke's area. All day long, Rulek and Mendel tore each other to pieces over politics,

but Abke couldn't slip in a single word. The only time the two revolution-
aries stopped was during the half-hour break, when they walked in single file in the prison courtyard. Otherwise, from early morning onward,
strange names, slogans, and nasty expressions flew around the cell. Rulek
and Mendel's tongues were on fire with the word "revolution." They never
cracked a smile. Abke felt very gloomy.

Abke was certainly gloomy, but he still lent an ear to their talk. He
marveled at their knowledge: young scamps and they knew so much.
How easily they threw those big words at each other.

Abke could see that the arrested men wanted to improve things, but
the capitalist world just wouldn't take their advice. As far as they were
concerned, the only country in the world worth mentioning was the
Soviet Union, truly a Garden of Eden for the downtrodden

Not long before, Gorgeous Grishke, who "worked" on the trains, had
told Abke that he'd followed an aristocrat with two suitcases all the way to
Switzerland but never got the suitcases. The guy had refused to doze off.
Grishke got to see Switzerland. "Shleymke Peyske's restaurant in Vilna is
a barn compared to the Swiss restaurants. And if they want poor people,
they have to send for them from Vilna."

"Switzerland sounds like a real paradise. Could the Soviet Union be
even half as good?" Abke wondered. But if Mendel and Rulek thought the
Soviet Union was so marvelous, maybe there was something to it. Abke
tried asking them about conditions there for thieves, but they just shot
him a dirty look.

At night Abke lay on his straw mattress, but he didn't sleep, he
thought. His cellmates had him totally confused. Both Rulek and Mendel were boys from fine, upstanding homes. Homes with real status. So
what drove them to stick up for the entire world and rot away in prison?
Maybe too much luxury. You could see from the packages they got that
they lacked for nothing at home. Salami, challah, apples, plums. Life was
obviously good, but not to them. They wanted a revolution.

The more he thought about it, the more Abke liked the situation. The
well-fed sons of the wealthy, who never had to eat bread earned from billiards or a game of cards played with a rigged deck, wanted everyone to

have a good life. For that, they sat behind bars and it didn't bother them as long as it brought what they called "the bright tomorrow."

★

One day Abke was taken to the prison office. Tshernikhov the lawyer had come to see him. Abke had been thinking that everyone had completely forgotten about him, and then, out of nowhere, who should show up to see him, but the lawyer who defended the most important political trials in Vilna. Abke had never had a defense lawyer. He usually just stood in front of the justice of the peace with a hangdog look, listened to the litany of charges, and sat out the few weeks of his sentence. The judge always grumbled and threatened him with years in prison for coming before the court so often. No one ever threw in a good word about him. And here was Tshernikhov himself. Abke was impressed.

Tshernikhov was always busy. Aside from the local court with its scandals and appeals, he was busy with other matters from which he derived only headaches, heartache, and grief. Tshernikhov was president of the Freeland League. The organization was looking for a corner of the world where Jews could be their own bosses and put an end to all their troubles. The Zionists wanted to eat him alive. "How is it possible," they hollered, "that a Jew like Tshernikhov, with his talents, doesn't understand that we don't have to go looking? The place already exists. It's called Palestine." But Tshernikhov was sure that before the British finally let Jews into Palestine, everyone would breathe their last. He dreamt about a territory where everyone would speak Yiddish, even the Supreme Court judges.

The prison director took Tshernikhov to a room with iron bars where he could spend a few minutes with his client while the authorities kept on eye on them. Abke didn't dare sit down. Such an honor.

Tshernikhov asked Abke to take a seat. He took a piece of paper from his briefcase and got straight to the point: "You should be aware that Pendzik has submitted an entire novel about you to the public prosecutor. They're going to try you with your cellmates, Mendel and Rulek, to draw attention to the case. You're going to be charged with undermining the regime and trying to tear western White Russia away from the Polish Republic."

Abke grabbed the top of his head with both hands. "What are you talking about, Mr. Tshernikhov? I know nothing about things like that."

"You don't have to convince me that you know nothing. I take you at your word. But court is a different matter. I thought I'd claim that you're insane, but that won't work." Tshernikhov rifled through his documents, pulled out a piece of paper, and read, "The accused, legally registered as Abbe Srogin and nicknamed Abke the Nail Biter, is a danger to society because of his quick reflexes and his intelligence. He demonstrated this when he used his weak Polish to convince the peasants at the Casimir fair to participate in an allegedly innocent betting game with three ladles and a pea. He skillfully moved the pea back and forth from one ladle to the next. The peasants had to guess where the pea ended up. The honest tillers of the soil didn't stand a chance. The accused cheated them out of tens of zlotys."

Tshernikhov looked at Abke with smiling eyes. "After feats like that, I can't argue that you're insane. I'll have to find another way to set you free. I know—I'll talk about your past deeds. That will convince the judge that you're not the right person to accuse of liberating White Russia from Poland."

Abke began to wriggle on his chair. "Mr. Tshernikhov, I beg you, don't talk about that in court. Because of Mendel and Rulek. They're going to try us together."

"I won't have any choice."

"But they treat me like an equal. Thanks to Rulek, I've even stopped biting my fingernails. You know, that's how I got my nickname, Abke the Nail Biter."

"Why thanks to Rulek?"

"He said it's a decadent habit."

Tshernikhov forgot that he was in a rush. It had been a long time since he'd enjoyed himself so much. Stroking his goatee, he choked back his laughter. "So did Rulek explain to you just what decadence is?"

"He explained, but I didn't understand much. I know it's not a good thing because of the faces he made."

"Okay, Abke, I'll do what I can to save you from embarrassment. We'll talk again."

"Mr. Tshernikhov, I'm totally broke right now. They squeezed me dry in a poker game that looked like a sure bet. I have no rich relatives. No poor ones either, for that matter. But I'll pay you back."

"We don't talk about money in cases like this."

"But this is obviously your bread. Why else would you do it?"

The lawyer was imagining telling his wife and son about this conversation while the three of them ate their midday meal. As though Abke read his lawyer's thoughts, instead of money, he offered merchandise guaranteed to produce peals of laughter in Tshernikhov's dining room. Abke stammered, "No matter which way the cards fall, you owe me a little favor."

Tshernikhov put on a serious face. "Really. Let's hear."

"Do you remember, two years ago, when someone took a garret full of wash from you?"

"Yes."

"And they said they'd return everything for three hundred zlotys."

"Right, I remember."

"And your wife insisted on only two hundred."

"True."

"I told the fence to make a deal. Because I was the . . . It was my merchandise."

Tshernikhov decided to play along with the arrested man to make him feel better. There were harsh times awaiting him. The lawyer got up from his chair, gathered his documents, closed his briefcase, and solemnly declared, "Abke, that good turn will serve you well. I'll do everything I can to save you from serious charges. But you won't get off scot free."

"Who's talking about scot free? All I want is a fair sentence."

The lawyer was about to wink at the guard to open the door with its iron bars, but Abke stopped him. "Mr. Tshernikhov, do you have another minute? I want to ask you something."

"Go ahead, ask."

"Tell me, who is this Trotsky, who Mendel and Rulek are so mad at, as if he'd spit in their food? If they could, they'd tear him to pieces like a herring."

"Trotsky? Forget it, Abke. It would take forever to explain." Tshernikhov thought for a moment before he spoke again. "Since we're asking, I have a question for you. Tell me, why did you do it? Why did you throw the flag over the wires?"

Abke took a deep breath, as though he was letting a heavy load fall from his shoulders. "The guy was so determined, I felt for him. He looked like he'd been through the ringer, like he'd gone an entire year without a solid meal. But instead of breaking someone's lock to set himself up or going off to have a good time, he risked his freedom for some crazy idea. That's why I helped him."

At the trial, Tshernikhov had to say something about Abke's background and how he earned his living. If he hadn't, Abke would have been sentenced unfairly. The judgment was longer than Abke's previous sentences, but it could definitely have been worse. He got two years. Mendel and Rulek each got five.

The public prosecutor was a different breed than Pendzik the Cripple. Although he was no less loyal to the state than the magistrate from the Central Police Station, he had a sense of humor. He was also an ardent poker player. The public prosecutor was duly impressed when, during one of the breaks, Tshernikhov told him about Abke's talent at shuffling cards.

A few days after the trial, the prison director informed the men that they would be transported deep into Poland, to Ravitsh prison, to serve their sentences. Following prison regulations, all three men stood at attention opposite the director and listened silently to the edict. Like all political prisoners, they were asked whether they had any special requests. Rulek, who knew Polish well, proclaimed, "I want to be taken to Ravitsh shackled to Abbe Srogin." Mendel smiled and nodded, pleased with his friend's gesture.

That is exactly what happened. Rulek and Abke marched in front, shackled to each other. Mendel walked behind with cuffs on his hands.

4

Shibele's Lottery Ticket

After Zerdel departed from the world, his partner, Shibele the Conductor, couldn't support himself. Their orchestra bit the dust. Before Zerdel's death, the pair had walked through the courtyards and scrounged whatever they could to get them through the day. Zerdel played a violin without a back. Shibele accompanied him on a comb wrapped in silk paper and, with his left hand, conducted. That's why he was known in Vilna as "Shibele the Conductor."

People would throw them coins from their windows. This wasn't because they liked the music, but to get rid of the two of them. Zerdel's violin made drawn-out mournful sounds, like the buzzing of telephone wires. Shibele wasn't particularly talented either. He sang whatever sounds he couldn't blow with lips that were as thick as swollen leeches. He was also very lazy. He didn't want to work too hard, so he swallowed half of every tune.

But now Zerdel's instrument hung in a corner of Sheyndel's teahouse in the synagogue courtyard. She wouldn't let anyone touch it. "I want a little something to remind me of Zerdel," she said and wiped away a tear. The courtyard folk said this was an old romance. Zerdel became a regular at the teahouse after Sheyndel's husband went to fill his bucket of water at the little pump on the corner of Yiddishe Street and never returned. Sheyndel missed her husband, the shiksa chaser, less than the bucket. But Zerdel didn't push things with Sheyndel. He loved his freedom too much. Still, of all the vagabonds who hung around the courtyards and gathered in the evenings at Sheyndel's teahouse, Zerdel always got the best glass of tea.

When he was still partners with Zerdel, Shibele also got tasty morsels from Sheyndel. But now that he was on his own, Sheyndel just resented him. She hissed that he took up space at the table but gave nothing in return. "How long should I keep feeding him on credit?" she asked.

Shibele had a talent for eating. If only he'd had half as much talent for music. Whatever Shibele laid eyes on, he wanted: a jug of buttermilk, new potatoes with baby beets, buckwheat pudding. Everything. This annoyed Sheyndel.

Shibele wasn't the only one who annoyed Sheyndel. She'd had her fill of all the trapeze artists, organ grinders, acrobats, and courtyard singers. But she'd approved of Zerdel because he'd kept himself as clean as a cat and knew how to eat a fish head.

Shibele, on the other hand, liked the ragtag gang. He was lonely and they were his family. But one Thursday, when he tried to line up at Probe's bakery with the other beggars to get the weekly groschen, they cursed him and sent him packing. With his rosy cheeks, he was too healthy for charity.

Besides being lazy, Shibele was also a dreamer. He could easily while away a summer evening on the steps of the little Gravedigger's Synagogue, daydreaming about wealth and fortune. He dreamt of owning a house in Pospieshk, at the edge of the city, right next to the forest. He'd eat sour cream with baby radishes every day and invite all his friends to visit. And he wouldn't need any favors from Sheyndel.

Shibele had already seen the house of his dreams, an abandoned dacha in Oginski's Park in Pospieshk. One day he and Zerdel went to Pospieshk to try their luck. It was summer, and the area was teaming with families staying in the dachas. But the pain had no luck, so they went off to cool their feet in the waters of the Viliye. Trudging up a hill and past a spring on his way to the river, Shibele came upon his dream. In among the tall wild grass and a few sickly trees covered with lichen instead of bark, he spotted a wooden building with open doors and broken windows. It was as if time, instead of moving past the house, had trampled it with heavy feet. The entire building was in ruins: the steps, the windowpanes, and even the chimney on the leaking roof. Old Count Oginski had long ago given up on his estate. He'd had neither the strength nor the money to look after his property, so he'd abandoned it to fate and the few families who rented the better dachas during the summer months.

Shibele and Zerdel never reached the river. They sat down on the only intact step of the ruined house. They took off their military boots and their socks filled with holes to let the breeze cool their tired feet. Shibele, who wasn't usually a big talker, found his voice. The green of the surroundings, the quiet, and the cold water from the well awakened his philosophical bent. "You know Zerdel, if you deal in honey, you get yourself a lick. And in tobacco, a sweet-smelling stick. But what do we ever get?"

Zerdel was also moved by the surroundings, by the twittering of the birds, and wanted to answer in rhyme. He didn't want to sound crude, so he said nothing. He'd been feeling very poorly lately. His lungs were whistling.

"Zerdel, how long are we going to keep drifting? We're not kids anymore, you know. When you get right down to it, we have no place to lay our heads. Pretty soon, Sheyndel's going to throw us out of her teahouse. We owe her money."

Zerdel tried to calm him. "We'll arrange something with Sheyndel. I wish I could fix my breathing as easily."

"Oh, Zerdel. If only something worked out for us. You know, if we had a little money, I would buy this place and fix it up. There's no end of fresh air here. I'd put a table out in front for everyone. On Shabbes, all the people from the street could come to breathe freely."

"Where will you get the money? From our orchestra?"

"Maybe the money will just show up."

"Right now we don't even have enough for a glass of tea. Soon we'll have to drag ourselves back to the city. I shuffle when I walk. I feel pressure in my belly, a buzzing in my ears, and my lower back is breaking. I just don't feel well."

Shibele took a good look at his partner. Zerdel looked like his strength had dwindled away. Shibele wanted to get back to the city and the synagogue courtyard as quickly as possible. If anything happened, there would be someone there to listen to his cries for help. Shibele put Zerdel's shoes on for him. They left the abandoned estate determined not to rest until they made it half way back to Vilna, to the Antokl Church.

Shibele and Zerdel gave their last concert just before midnight next to the large city concert hall. There was a foreign pianist performing that evening. The pair stood in a darkened corner next to the exit, hoping someone from the audience would stop and throw them a few groschen. Someone did stop, but not someone from the audience. It was the pianist himself. He and his accompanist were the last to leave the hall.

When the pianist first heard the strange sounds, he was completely dumbfounded. Then, in the dim light from the hall, he noticed the two musicians with their instruments, and in particular, Shibele's instrument. The pianist was overcome with laughter, as though ten demons were tickling his armpits with feather dusters. His accompanist also started to laugh. They held their trembling bellies. Shibele and Zerdel played highbrow music, doing their best to offer quality merchandise. This time Shibele didn't hold back. He hummed the entire "March of the Regiment of the Sixth Legion" without swallowing a single note. The piece of silk paper around his comb swelled as though about to burst.

After a good laugh, the pianist took a coin from his trouser pocket and gave it to Shibele. His accompanist didn't stand idle either—he handed Zerdel a coin. Shibele and Zerdel waited until they got to Sheyndel's teahouse to examine their earnings. Their eyes immediately lit up. Shibele had a ten-zloty coin and Zerdel, a fiver. Zerdel paid off their debt to Sheyndel. They had enough left for two glasses of tea and kaiser buns with salami.

Shibele placed the ten-zloty coin on the table and gazed at his own reflection in the dull silver. He had a good look at the stern Marshal Pilsudski, the founder of Poland, with his thick whiskers hanging over his mouth. Then Shibele examined the other side of the coin with the number 10 under the claws of an eagle's splayed legs. He and Zerdel were alone in the teahouse, so Shibele could sit quietly and feast his eyes on the pianist's gift. The most they ever got in Vilna was ten groschen, and for that, they had to wait for a traveling businessman. And suddenly, such a fortune. Neither of them could believe it.

Zerdel had stopped caring about things. He'd stopped grooming himself and no longer polished his shoes. Sheyndel had mentioned it. But even he was reluctant to leave the table, where the coin lay deep and wide, like a ring of fat in a bowl of chicken soup. Eventually, Sheyndel had to ask them to leave the teahouse. After all, she was also a human being and needed her sleep.

Shibele lay in the dark in the garret over the public bath with his eyes wide open. Even though there were more important people in the synagogue courtyard, he and Zerdel had permission to sleep there at night. The straw mat creaked under Shibele. He tossed and turned, unable to fall asleep. Zerdel called from his corner, "Shibele, what's bothering you? Can't you lie still?"

Shibele had been just waiting for Zerdel to say something so he could share what lay in his heart and on his mind. "You know, Zerdel, a chance like this comes once in a lifetime. He gave us ten zlotys. That's really something."

"Absolutely. If only we got that every week."

"Yes, really, and from someone in Vilna. Oh Zerdel, Zerdel. But I have something else on my mind. You're a partner, so I have to ask you. You know what I'm thinking?"

"Tell me."

"I'm thinking the ten zlotys will just disappear. We won't even see it go. You'll get a plate of cholent. Me, two or three servings of kishke. Then we'll have a hankering for some stuffed spleen, a few goose livers, and that'll be that. The few zlotys will be gone."

"So what do you want to do? Buy a house?"

"Maybe a house, maybe not. What I really want to buy is a lottery ticket."

Zerdel sat up. "A lottery ticket? With our luck?"

Shibele launched into a speech like the one he'd given on the steps of the ruined house in Oginski's Park. "Why not? We went straight from the ruined house to the city concert hall and look what happened. Maybe luck is watching us. She's probably standing behind us and snickering, waiting to see if we have the sense to grab her or if we'll just watch her disappear."

Zerdel tried to joke. "If our luck's in this attic, she won't escape. It's so dark, she'll break her arms and legs on the beams. But my guess is that she's found someplace better to sleep."

"Oh, Zerdel, you're just not yourself. You used to have more guts."

Zerdel was indeed not himself. His illness had exhausted him. Snuggling into his threadbare American coat with the deep pockets, he said his piece, "You want to buy a lottery ticket. Buy the ticket."

Shibele heard no more from Zerdel. Those were his final words for one very simple reason: he'd breathed his last.

In the morning, Shibele nudged Zerdel, trying to get him to leave the attic. Zerdel lay curled up under his donated American coat. He didn't move. His violin lay at his feet like a faithful dog.

★

When Sheskin saw Shibele the Conductor in his office, his first thought was to tell the errand boy to send Shibele on his way. Sheskin recognized Shibele from his morning performances with Zerdel in the office courtyard. But Sheskin changed money and sold lottery tickets in his office. This was no place for comb concerts. However, when Shibele explained the reason for his visit, Sheskin didn't know what to do. Shibele buying a lottery ticket! He stood opposite Sheskin in a tattered jacket, a torn shirt, pants with holes in them, and shoes without heels. Sheskin, who was taller and thinner than Shibele, bent over, looked Shibele up and down and asked him, "Are you sure you want to buy a lottery ticket?"

Shibele blushed like a virgin when her beloved proposes marriage. He twisted his swollen lips into a sort of smile and assured Sheskin, "Yes, yes. Exactly. A lottery ticket."

Sheskin felt obliged to discourage him. "What do you need a lottery ticket for? You'd be better off buying yourself a pair of trousers and a new shirt. You'd look more like a musician then."

Shibele wouldn't give up. "Mr. Sheskin, before Zerdel died, he said, 'Buy the ticket.' Zerdel never spoke without good reason."

Sheskin cut in. "He probably figured it would make no difference to him anyway, so he told you to buy the ticket."

"No, Mister Sheskin," Shibele replied, "We'd already talked about it."

When Sheskin realized how determined Shibele was, he began to joke. "Let's say you win. What'll you do? Open a business? Start lending money?"

Shibele didn't know what to say. He blushed even deeper. Finally he stammered, "I saw a house in Oginski's Park in Pospieshk. I was hoping

. . . Well, why shouldn't an ordinary guy like me have a dacha? And I want a gravestone for Zerdel. Oh, and also pants, like you said. And maybe something else."

"What else?"

"Something for a marriage proposal."

Sheskin said no more. He sold Shibele a lottery ticket. With trembling fingers, Shibele took the ten-zloty coin out of the well-used piece of silk paper and laid it on the table. When Shibele got to the door, Sheskin called after him, "Let me write down the number. If you win, I'll do you a good turn and be the first to let you know. If we need you, where'll you be?"

"On the steps of the Gravedigger's Synagogue. Or at Sheyndel's teahouse. In the synagogue courtyard."

Sheskin recorded the number. Shibele shoved the lottery ticket deep into the breast pocket of his jacket and left the office, filled with excitement. On the steps, he stroked the lottery ticket through the lining of his jacket that had known better days, when it had been strong, dark grey alpaca and the weave hadn't been about to turn to dust. Shibele placed all his faith in the square piece of paper with a number at both top and bottom and a colored crest. He fastened his breast pocket with a large safety pin and went to give a solo concert beside Velfke's restaurant on Yiddishe Street. The hucksters, the nasty jokers who dragged customers into the ready-made clothing shops, pestered Shibele all along his route, starting at Sheskin's office at the corner of Rudnitzker and Daytshe Street. Shibele didn't stop. He was afraid one of those guys would get the better of him. He would say too much and they'd cheat him out of his ticket. They could convince a peasant to buy a necktie to match his wooden shoes. Shibele quickly left the street where the gullible were so easily tempted.

Summer raged in the synagogue courtyard. With its hot breath, it blew on the heavy green branches of the only tree in the entire courtyard. The leaves crackled and then wilted, longing for rain. An orphaned page from one of the holy books lay in the corner of the courtyard, curled up from the heat and waiting to be tossed into one of the cool chests filled with damaged holiday prayer books and volumes of the Mishnah that were falling to pieces. The sun was as hot as the Friday cholent in the oven at Probe's bakery. Because of the heat, everybody had shuffled to the walls to grab a little shade. Shibele was the only one enjoying the sweltering heat. He lay down on the steps of the Gravedigger's Synagogue to warm his limbs after a night's sleep in the damp, dark garret. Putting his jacket down next to himself, he rolled what was left of the cuffs of his shirt over his elbows, and with his cap over his eyes, stretched himself out on the lowest step of the synagogue like it was the top bench of the community bath.

Half asleep, Shibele dreamt of winning. He was sure he had a winning ticket. Maybe not the big prize, but enough for the house in Pospieshk, a gravestone for Zerdel, a new pair of pants, and something for a marriage proposal.

Zerdel never spoke without good reason. During his final days, he kept saying that he was dying. No one had believed him, not even the new young doctor in the charity hospital. He'd insisted that Zerdel would be fine and prescribed Epsom salts. Zerdel had showed everyone who was right and went off and died. It would be the same with the lottery ticket. Zerdel would be right again.

As to the marriage proposal, Sheyndel was now free. After she shed a few tears over Zerdel and his broken fiddle, that romance would be over. Shibele would be able to approach her with money. She would come with him to Pospieshk and leave the teahouse with its cockroaches behind. It wouldn't even bother him if she set up a bar in the front room for the poor people who come on Shabbes with their own provisions to bathe in the Viliye.

Shibele fell asleep and dreamt one good dream after the next. Had it not been for the errand boy from Sheskin's office, he would have slept until after *Minkhe*, the afternoon prayers. But the young man kept jabbing him until he had to open his eyes. Sheskin had sent the errand boy to tell Shibele to come to the office as quickly as possible. Luckily he didn't have to search for Shibele for long. He was lying exactly where he'd said he would be. Between one yawn and the next, Shibele asked what the boss needed from him. The young man, who should have lowered his voice, squealed, "They said in the office that you won money."

Sleep took flight from Shibele's eyes like a bird with ruffled feathers. He was immediately up on his feet. He wanted to pick up his jacket and run like the devil to his luck, but the jacket wasn't lying next to him. He leapt from one step to the next. Then he raced into the vestibule of the little synagogue and from there, into the synagogue itself. He scurried to the Torah platform, searched under the ritual washstand, peered behind the curtains of the ark for the Torah scrolls, and opened the cold oven. He overturned every bookstand and shoved his hand to the back of the ark. His jacket was nowhere to be seen. Shibele figured one of the Psalm reciters must have played a trick on him and hidden the piece of clothing somewhere in the little synagogue. He ran into the synagogue courtyard and searched every nook and cranny, including the chests of old prayer books. The jacket had disappeared like the last little cloud in the sky, leaving only a cheerful patch of blue, which just looked sad and black to Shibele. Returning to the vestibule of the synagogue, with both hands he grabbed the pillory that was forged into the wall and sobbed loudly. Everyone in the courtyard came running. Shibele was sniveling like a little child. And like a little child crying for his mother, through his tears he sputtered out the story of his loss.

The story of Shibele's loss spread from Gitke-Toybe's Lane all the way to the lumber market. Sheyndel's teahouse was in an uproar. They couldn't believe the injustice Shibele had suffered. In the past, no one had ever had a good word to say about him. "With your health," they'd tell him, "you should be pushing a cart instead of playing a comb like a depressive." When Zerdel had been Shibele's orchestra partner, people had put up with their concerts. Now that Shibele was on his own, everyone just ignored him. But when bad luck struck and someone took Shibele's jacket with the lottery ticket, everyone felt sorry for him. Even Sheyndel. She said she had nothing against the thief. "May he thrive and be happy, as long as his hands dry out like splinters."

The story of the lost ticket reached Avromke the Anarchist, the chief merchant in the passageway. Wasting no time, Avromke went straight to Sheskin to see what could be done for Shibele. Sheskin shrugged his shoulders. There was nothing to be done. Shibele's ticket had won a large sum of money, but without the piece of paper he couldn't claim a single groschen. Sheskin had already informed all the agents in Vilna not to pay out any money on that number. He'd also informed the central office in

Warsaw about the lost lottery ticket, but none of that would help Shibele. The only thing that would help was if someone found the ticket. And the sooner the better. Sheskin finished with a proclamation that freeloaders, tramps, and barefoot bums should stay away from money. "They have no idea what it's worth."

Sheskin was furious with Shibele. He'd planned to write an article for the *Vilner tog* newspaper about the winner and his big prize. He'd even arranged for Zalkind the photographer to immortalize the moment when he presented Shibele with his jackpot in front of all the city big shots. The entire city would have seen the advertisement for his office. But Shibele had ruined everything. He'd lain down in the middle of the courtyard like a piece of dead meat, with his jacket beside him, instead of clutching it between his legs so no one could steal it. Avromke the Anarchist defended Shibele—how could he have known that anyone would want his old rag? And it really was a rag. The material was badly torn and the lining was in shreds. Only one of the buttons remained, hanging from a thread. The elbows were worn to nothing. Everyone had warned Shibele that the jacket would soon crumble to dust.

The jacket was never found. Avromke the Anarchist ordered all the merchants in the passageway to inspect their merchandise, hoping someone had bought the jacket without realizing it. Avromke focused his efforts on Itshe, who provided rags to the Olkeniker paper factory. Avromke got Itshe to spread all his bundles out in the passageway. No one was allowed to walk through the courtyard. The neighbors ran around in circles. Some helped by inspecting each rag separately. Shibele stood there, looking like he had a toothache. He shook his head as people shoved jackets of every size and color under his nose.

★

Years passed. Shibele had long ago lost his front teeth and could no longer play music. Besides, his mind was filled with the lost lottery ticket. He never recovered from his bad luck. He'd had all the luck he needed in his breast pocket, and it had disappeared from under his very nose. Shibele sat on the steps of the little synagogue and waited for the shammes's wife to bring him a plate of warm food. From time to time, he dragged himself to the Zaretshe cemetery to spend a little time at Zerdel's grave with its tin plaque instead of a gravestone. Standing beside the grave, Shibele let himself have a good cry about the injustice that bitter fate had dealt him. "You said yourself, 'Buy the ticket.' I was planning to put up a stone for you engraved with birds, with an iron chain around it. But my jacket and the ticket went into the ground."

Shibele never knew how true this was. His jacket with the lottery ticket really did go into the ground, as though Zerdel had begrudged his orchestra partner wealth and dragged the winnings along paths and byways, closer to him, closer to the underground realm.

One day, when Grush the Bawler was hanging around City Hall with his cronies, he drunkenly told them about the wrong he'd inflicted on his father years before. Grush's father had bequeathed his son a barrel and a horse along with the right to clean the Jewish community outhouse in the synagogue courtyard.

When the old man lay in his casket with his whiskers groomed, about to be buried, the priest realized he had no jacket. All his life, both summer and winter, Grush's father had walked around in a pair of trousers and a fur-lined cloak. But the priest said it wasn't proper to bury someone in a cloak. Besides, the cloak gave off an unbearable smell.

Grush set off from upper Nove-Stroyke, where he lived, to buy a jacket in the passageway. The casket maker had given Grush a pair of filthy cardboard shoes, so he just needed the jacket. Instead of walking down Yiddishe Street, to shorten his route Grush went through the synagogue courtyard. He noticed a jacket lying on the steps of a Jewish church. He had a good look around, but the courtyard was empty because of the heat. There was only one beggar sleeping in the sun. Grush grabbed the jacket, threw it into a bag, and with the money he saved, got good and drunk at Itske the Buckwheat Pudding's bar.

It was already nighttime when Grush dragged himself back to their hut. He was good and drunk, but he managed to lift his father up and put the jacket on him. When all of Gush's father's cronies showed up in the morning, they said the man looked like a real count and that no one had ever gone into the ground looking better. But now that Grush was older, his father visited him in his dreams and criticized his son for burying him in a stolen garment instead of buying a jacket, as it should have been done.

★

Shibele never learned the fate of his jacket with the lottery ticket in its breast pocket. Grush went blind from drinking spirits mixed with shellac for polishing furniture. In his later years, he could no longer afford straight whisky. He sold the barrel and the horse and was no longer seen in the synagogue courtyard.

Shibele still showed up in the synagogue courtyard. He sat on the steps of the Gravedigger's Synagogue humming the "March of the Regiment of the Sixth Legion" through the hole between his remaining teeth and waited for the children from Yiddishe Street to march by, laughing and shouting. One fine day Shibele also disappeared. A comb missing most of its teeth and wrapped in silk paper was found in the vestibule of the synagogue. One of the Psalm reciters placed it next to the water basin in case Shibele remembered his musical instrument and came to get it. It lay there until someone threw it in the garbage.

No trace remained of Shibele. New musicians appeared in the synagogue courtyard. On cold nights, gathered next to the oven in the little synagogue, they sometimes spoke of Shibele. The old gravediggers said he would still be making music had it not been for the lost lottery ticket, which had completely shattered him and destroyed his musical ability. "Shibele tried to become a wealthy man in a time when paupers and the sick dared not wish for such a thing. People like that should accept their lot," they said. Others disagreed. Shibele is gone, but from time to time his dream of wealth springs up in one of the other little courtyard synagogues.

5

The Folklorist

The Vilna fish market was packed. Housewives from the entire region were running through the narrow aisles between the rows of tubs. When the women from the neighborhoods of Poploves and Zaretshe heard there were cheap smelts from the Broslav Lakes, they came running to grab what they could. The market was jumping. The fishwives moved as quick as lightning. They didn't have to lift the gills of each fish to prove the flesh was red and therefore fresh. They just threw a bunch of little fish into each basket and told the customer to move on.

On that day, Rubinshteyn the Folklorist set off for the fish market to collect material. He'd come from a town that was further away than Bialystok to gather folklore in the Jerusalem of Lithuania. People in the Yiddish Scientific Institute had told him if he wanted to hear the genuine language of the people, he should hang around the fish market. Even though Rubinshteyn limped, he was willing to walk to the edge of the city for the sake of a witty saying. He got up very early that morning. It wasn't easy for him to drag his crippled leg all the way from Savitsher Street, where he had his little room, to the fish market. But was there anything he wouldn't do for folklore?

Rubinshteyn thought the Vilna sayings had to be documented as quickly as possible. If, God forbid, they were forgotten, it would be a great loss for the culture. Because of his love of folklore, Rubinshteyn was still a bachelor. No matter how many matches were proposed to him (and good matches at that), he always declined. In the Institute, they wanted to pair him up with Zelda the researcher, an old maid who specialized in Jewish cuisine all the way back to the twelfth century. But in his imagination, Rubinshteyn saw Zelda the researcher striding to the Institute on

Figure 1. "On that day, Rubinshteyn the Folklorist set off for the fish market to collect material." By Yosl Bergner from Avrom Karpinovitsh, *Baym Vilner durkhhoyf* (Tel Aviv: I. L. Peretz, 1967). Courtesy of the artist.

legs that were as long and thin as a stork's, while he limped behind her. This picture certainly didn't appeal to him. Vilna would make a mockery of them.

Rubinshteyn stood in the fish market, waiting for folklore. He didn't have the courage to walk closer to the tubs. He was afraid the fishwives might humiliate him, especially because it was slippery near the tubs and he could easily fall. So he stood at the edge of the row of tables. But he could barely contain himself. Ruzshke the Fishwife let fly with a real string of curses. From the distance, Rubinshteyn could only hear one out of every ten words, but even that made him salivate. Ruzshke was giving a housewife what for and was about to hit her with the tail of a carp.

The crowd around the tubs thinned out, and the fishwives started taking off their aprons that were caked with fish scales. The market would soon be empty.

Chana-Merka was the first to notice Rubinshteyn. Her tub stood at the very edge of the market. "Why is that man standing around without a basket? What's he doing here?" she wondered. It was as clear as day that he hadn't come to buy fish. He'd obviously been sent by City Hall to spy. Why would he have a pencil in his hand if not to check the weights? Of all the fishwives, Chana-Merka was the most likely to weigh high. Every Yom Kippur at the Yizkor service, she would wail loudly, pouring out her bitter heart. Yoel the shammes always reprimanded her. "Chana-Merka, wail less and give the correct weight."

Chana-Merka didn't just stand there. She smiled flirtatiously at Rubinshteyn, revealing the gold crown on her front tooth. "My dear man, I'll give you a kilo of tench that are so frisky, you'll have trouble carrying them home."

Rubinshteyn was befuddled and didn't know what to say. He looked foolishly at Chana-Merka. Her face was partly covered by the fringes of her woolen kerchief. Her cheeks were burning from her recent sales and her merry eyes left Rubinshteyn feeling uneasy. He stayed silent.

Chana-Merka didn't stop. "My dear man, what if I add a few barbels? Your wife won't know what to do with you."

Finally the folklorist showed some life and stammered, "I . . . I'm not looking for fish."

"That's all I have to offer. What are you looking for?"

Rubinshteyn blurted out, "Some good curses."

"What?"

"I'll explain. I collect curses. Sayings also. I was just listening to all of you talk."

A stone fell from Chana-Merka's heart. "So that means you're not from City Hall? Because I thought . . . if that's where you're from, I hope you find yourself lying face down in hell."

Chana-Merka was happy she'd escaped unscathed. Pointing to Rubinshteyn, she shouted across the entire market, "Hey, this man is collecting

curses. Who wants to give him some merchandise?" A crowd immediately formed around the folklorist. The fishwives wanted to have a closer
look at the amazing sight. Rubinshteyn tried to explain folklore to them,
but they didn't let him get a word in edgewise. The fishwives, especially
Ruzshke and Pale Tsirl, made fun of him and drowned out his words.

After that rebuff, Rubinshteyn quickly left the market. Chana-Merka
felt her heart tighten. She hadn't noticed that he dragged one leg. Was she
responsible for what had happened in the market? She reproached herself,
"Maybe this is how he earns his living."

Rubinshteyn swallowed his pride and returned to try his luck with the
fishwives. Not so much with all the fishwives as with one in particular,
Chana-Merka. He really should have been angrier with her than any of
the others, but he couldn't stay angry, no matter how hard he tried. His
temperature rose when he thought of her rosy cheeks and her eyes that
glittered like gold. During the previous few nights, while lying on his
narrow bed, Rubinstein had remembered that he wasn't only a folklorist,
but also a man.

For years, Rubinshteyn had been absorbed in collecting folk wisdom.
He was literally soaked in aphorisms, curses, invectives, and fables. From
early in the morning until late at night, he was up to his eyeballs in his
collections. He'd felt secure in his defense against all temptation. But then
along came Chana-Merka. A single smile from her had pushed him off
his path.

The folklorist tried as hard as he could to bury his feelings and to
arrive at the market with dry, scientific objectives, but it didn't work.
Thoughts of Chana-Merka whirled around in his head and stopped him
from thinking about anything else. Chana-Merka greeted him. "Oh, the
gentleman with the curses is here. I'll chop up the little door for firewood
and fry you some flea giblets. What a guest."

Rubinshteyn felt warm all over. He'd caught a whiff of folklore. He
unbuttoned his raincoat, unobtrusively took out his notebook, and immediately started writing. "Say something else," Rubinshteyn asked Chana-
Merka. "Talk and I'll write."

"Write what you want. Aren't there enough crazy people in Vilna already? I just want to know if this is how you earn your living or if you do it for fun."

Wasting no time, Rubinshteyn began to explain the lofty aims of folklore to Chana-Merka. She nodded her head while he talked. She didn't grasp everything he said, but some things made sense to her. The other fishwives edged up to Chana-Merka's tub to listen. Pale Tsirl was about to start her routine again, but this time Chana-Merka wouldn't stand for it and shouted, "If you want to give the man merchandise, that's good. If not, you can go and. . . ." She was tempted to really lay into them, but she held her tongue. She was embarrassed in front of Rubinshteyn.

The folklorist didn't collect many treasures that day, but he was as happy as could be. Chana-Merka had asked him to meet her on Shabbes morning at the little park on Troker Street for a chat.

Zelda the researcher was sitting in one of the small rooms in the Institute. She was writing about a Jewish dish called *shleyskes* and chewing on the end of a loaf of bread thinly spread with cottage cheese. Both the chewing and the writing were difficult. One of her molars was raging, and she couldn't figure out exactly what *shleyskes* were. One book she'd found implied that they were dough pellets kneaded with honey and poppy seeds. A pamphlet said they were a kind of cookie sprinkled with almonds. She had no idea which version was correct. She was depressed. She would have loved a tasty dish at that point, even modern fare.

Zelda the researcher had had a streak of bad luck. She'd bought a new coat at Tsalke the Nose's ready-made clothing store. Not for herself, but for Rubinshteyn. She'd hoped it would occur to him to take her to one of Mr. Gershteyn's choir concerts. But what had happened? Rubinshteyn hadn't even glanced in her direction. They sat in the same room with their desks touching, but all he ever said was "Good morning." He walked from one room to the next with his lists of folklore, boasting about his treasures.

Everyone clucked over his findings and patted him on the back. Dr. Weinreich, the director of the Institute, congratulated him. Apparently Rubinshteyn had gotten to know some sort of fishwife, a backward element who'd supplied him with information. "If only he'd investigated scientifically, without mixing up his work with his personal feelings," Zelda thought. People in the Institute said that the pair had been seen sitting together near Castle Hill on Shabbes.

Zelda got up from her desk and walked across the room, nudging her molar with her tongue as she went. She sighed loudly. The final result of all her studying and rummaging around in books was that some simple woman got more pleasure from life than she did, even with all her knowledge. Rubinshteyn's notes lay on his desk. Zelda peeked furtively at them, like a hen at its oats. Rubinshteyn had written in florid handwriting on a large piece of white paper:

> Material from folklore investigation, taken from Mrs. Chana-Merka Solodukhin, a fish seller in the Vilna fish market.
>
> Sayings:
>
> You're already a dog, don't be a pig.
>
> When a shlimazl tries to kill a chicken, it's the chicken who walks away.
>
> Eating matzoh balls is better for your health than reading the Haggadah.
>
> From love she gets . . .

Reading the material had enflamed Zelda's sore tooth, but she still took a look at the list of curses.

> May they carry you and sing.
>
> May a weak balcony fall on your head.
>
> May they use your guts to hang laundry.

Zelda couldn't bear to read any further. She spat at the floor and returned to her desk to search for a source to explain *shleyskes*.

Chana-Merka started coming to the market in a clean apron. She didn't want to be embarrassed if Rubinshteyn showed up. She really wanted to please the folklorist. Her Shabbes meetings with him had unsettled her.

Chana-Merka had been a widow for close to two years. Orke the Net Caster had certainly been a good man, not a drinker. But what difference did that make now that he was no longer around? No one from Broslav could forget him. He'd been one of the best fishermen. His net casting was legendary. He'd brought in several nets full of fish every night, without fail.

To this day, no one knows exactly what happened. Did Krigude the blonde mermaid, who lives at the bottom of the lake and needs a different man each season, seduce him into her darkened chamber? Or did Orke's partner, Clumsy Iserke, argue with him and push him overboard while they were casting their nets? No one knows. The water failed to spit him out. Iser swore on his mother that Orke hadn't shown up that night to fish, but can you believe a clumsy oaf like Iser?

A number of the fishermen who'd been good friends with Orke spoke with the Broslav rabbi on Chana-Merka's behalf. The rabbi wanted to declare her an *agune*, rendering her ineligible for remarriage. Everyone in the trade had their eye on her, especially Iserke. But could anyone make her happy after Orke? Perhaps a man like Rubinshteyn. Everyone in the fish market knew that he was a real gentleman who wrote books.

Chana-Merka was in a tizzy. She walked around in a daze. "Even though he drags one of his legs, the folklorist is definitely not a repulsive man," she thought. "To say nothing of the honor." Her friends, the other fishwives, spoke to her differently than before.

"You should realize, Mr. Rubinshteyn, that everything that wriggles needs a place to hide. Just take a silly little fish like a minnow. Before she starts to have her fun and spawn, she clears out a spot in the river bottom, swishing her tail back and forth, back and forth. Then it's done. She has a humble home. All the more so with a person. Being alone doesn't even work in the bath. Who will rub your shoulders? I know an intellectual like you can obviously get—how can I say it—a woman with a tinch of the aristocratic in her blood. And just look at Clumsy Iserke. He's such a . . . I won't even say the word out loud."

The little park on Troker Street was deserted. Chana-Merka sat beside Rubinshteyn on a bench covered with yellow leaves that had fallen from the chestnut trees. She was all dressed up. He hung on her every word. The weather was cool, so Chana-Merka snuggled into her cat-hair coat.

The folklorist didn't even have the sense to move a little closer. Chana-Merka was beaming. She'd powdered her face and styled her hair with a little curl on her pale forehead. She smiled at Rubinshteyn and waited. Anyone else would have put an arm around her shoulder or tried something even naughtier. But Rubinshteyn was only worried about one thing: how to keep track of what she was saying so he didn't forget even the tiniest word that might contribute to his great collection. It was generally inappropriate to write things down on the spot. He stretched out his stiff leg like an impassable highway between himself and Chana-Merka.

Chana-Merka said, "Three things never hurt: a snooze, a bath, and a good piece of fish. I'm being blunt. What's the point of sitting in the park and freezing your ribs? I have goodies at home fit for a kaiser. I'll boil some tea and give you a piece of marinated pike."

Rubinshteyn tried to discourage her, "No, thank you. You really shouldn't put yourself out."

"I'm not putting myself out. Everything's ready. Our enemies should have bumps on their foreheads as large as the babka I baked yesterday. Come, Mr. Rubinshteyn, let's have a little something to eat. If you want to know what matters most, look at what's sitting on the dinner plate."

The folklorist hesitated another moment, but he was convinced by her juicy expression that it made perfect sense to go to her place for a piece of fish. For the sake of folklore, Rubinshteyn gave in and went home with Chana-Merka. She walked on his healthy side, taking his arm every so often. Rubinshteyn felt his heart open. He didn't look at her, nor did he hear what she said. An autumnal sadness accompanied him to Chana-Merka's.

★

Chana-Merka took on an air of gentility. She began to watch her language. The market women barely recognized her. She even started giving more accurate weights. All because of Rubinshteyn.

Ruzshke the Fishwife explained to Chana-Merka that if she wanted to please the folklorist, she should control her language in public. "Rubinshteyn is a refined man and you sometimes say things that are better left unsaid." All the fishwives knew that Rubinshteyn had become a regular guest at Chana-Merka's. Things like that happened in Vilna. Bizdun the actor got involved with one of Leybe the Chicken Seller's daughters.

Chana-Merka starting coming to the market with her hair combed, wearing a pair of pumps rather than Orke's boots. Everyone knew an engagement was in the offing. But Pale Tsirl wasn't impressed. She said that Rubinshteyn would, in time, turn into a frog. He was no fisherman. He never hung out at Itske's bar. He had to be in the business of sending women to Argentina. There was no other explanation.

Ruzshke went to the Institute to ask about Rubinshteyn. She returned looking radiant. "People didn't know what to do with me. Except for one woman," she added, "a dried up old maid. A long thin noodle of a woman who scowled all the time."

But Rubinshteyn stopped coming to the market. He hardly ever went to Chana-Merka's. He'd gathered enough material for the time being and spent his evenings working on his collection. Chana-Merka didn't understand. When she'd been covered in dirt from head to toe, the folklorist had shown up at her tub every day. Now that she'd started to wish every customer a healthy appetite and to add an extra fish to each purchase, Rubinshteyn was waxing cold.

She did what she could to appeal to the folklorist. She kept her house done up for Shabbes all week, with a tablecloth on the table and a flowered bedspread covering the bed. She bought a picture in the passageway of Adam and Eve being forced out of paradise, barefoot. But the more intelligent she tried to appear, the less interested Rubinshteyn was. She spent an entire evening at home. Each scrape of the door tore at her heart. She waited for him, but he didn't come.

The next day Rubinshteyn came upon Chana-Merka at the entrance to the Institute. She'd been embarrassed to go upstairs, so she'd stood outside for half a day waiting for him. Rubinshteyn was bewildered. Had he given Chana-Merka false hope?

"Mr. Rubinshteyn," Chana-Merka began, puffed up with anger, "Do you think that Chana-Merka is a sack of curses and sayings that you open, shove your hand in, and grab what you want for your books? Chana-Merka also has a heart." With that she indicated her full left breast. "This is not the way to treat a woman when you see she has a soft spot for you. If only you'd said at the beginning that all you wanted from this silly fishwife was her curses." Chana-Merka paused for a moment and then continued, "Forget it. Use them in good health."

Rubinshteyn had never felt the emptiness of his bachelor life so acutely. He wanted to tell Chana-Merka that she'd misunderstood, but before he could open his mouth, she disappeared behind the corner of Vivulske Street.

Rubinshteyn accepted his bitter fate, bought a green backpack, and limped away from Vilna to gather folklore in another city.

6

Chana-Merka the Fishwife

When Rubinshteyn the Folklorist left Vilna to gather folklore some-where else, the fish market was in turmoil. He'd been coming to the market regularly to collect curses, sayings, and aphorisms. Chana-Merka, whose tub of fish stood at the entrance to the market, was the main source for his merchandise. Rubinshteyn had spent so much time collecting material from Chana-Merka that a little romance had developed. She was smitten with the folklorist, even though one of his legs was a little shorter than the other. The other fishwives, especially Pale Tsirl, were expecting a wedding. But Rubinshteyn, the old bachelor, got scared. He went to the passageway where they sold secondhand things, bought himself a green backpack, and limped away from Vilna, planning never to return.

Chana-Merka took his disappearance very hard. Apart from the honor of someone like Rubinshteyn coming to visit her to polish off a bit of carp or to savor a glass of tea with a babka, he'd crawled into her very heart. A good few years had passed since her husband, Orke the Net Caster, had drowned in the Narotshe Lake, and she longed for the warmth of another body. Apart from his leg, Rubinshteyn the Folklorist was quite a present-able man. Chana-Merka was impressed by his refined manners, the way he sat at the table without trying to lay a hand on her.

But why had she bothered? It all came to nothing in the end anyway. Rubinshteyn left Vilna and nothing more was heard from him. Chana-Merka felt like a widow once again and tried drowning her sorrow in her tub of fish. Although she no longer let loose with humorous quips and curses, every so often she still blurted out a saying strong enough to pierce a person's seventh rib. Sadly, not even a good day's earnings could lift her spirits.

One winter Friday just before Shabbes, Chana-Merka was cleaning a heap of minnows from her tub. Instead of hollering and sending the water gushing through the market, she just let it quietly trickle under people's feet. This didn't compare with her exploits when she'd been in her full glory and the commander of the fish market.

The other fishwives understood her mood full well. Chana-Merka had dreamt a sweet dream, but it washed up on shore. Pale Tsirl, whose tub of fish stood next to Chana-Merka's, ranted and raved. She hissed that they should have shortened Rubinshteyn's other leg before he started coming to the market to collect curses.

Tsirl didn't know how to comfort Chana-Merka. Should she tell her that Osher the Clucker, from the trade after all, was pining after her? He was ready to take her exactly as she was, with only the shirt on her back. But Chana-Merka had experienced something better, a man who could hold a pen in his hand, so this would be no comfort to her. It's true that Osher the Clucker was a big shot in the fishing business, but he didn't compare to Rubinshteyn.

Pale Tsirl decided to have a talk with Chana-Merka. "It makes no sense to eat yourself up alive because of the folklorist, that cripple. He didn't appreciate the curses and little jokes you gave him. Or even a woman like yourself—you offered him his own plate and spoon and a good piece of fish. May he be well, but may he shit in his pants and have brown shoes at Passover."

The two women were walking home from the market one sunny Friday. Chana-Merka, who'd once been such a chatterbox, jabbering constantly, didn't utter a single word. Pale Tsirl tried to cheer her up. "Chana-Merka, a curse on men. There are a lot more fish in the sea. You aren't ugly. You can certainly still say, 'Good morning, mirror. Pretty one, don't despair.'"

Chana-Merka sighed. "I gave that saying to Rubinshteyn to record."

"You're still talking about Rubinshteyn? Can't you get that cripple out of your head? He used up all your expressions and went somewhere else in search of another pack of used odds and ends. A plague is what he'll find to record outside Vilna. He'll have to limp around the entire region for a year to land what you gave him in a single week. And it won't have that special Vilna flavor."

Chana-Merka sighed louder. "He once said that in Bialystok . . ."

Tsirl was furious. "What about Bialystok? How can Bialystok compare with Vilna? Here, you have the proof—that Institute, now what's it called?"

"The Yiddish Institute."

"See how easily you remember the name," Tsirl marveled at her friend's memory. "Exactly. They didn't build that Institute in Bialystok, or in Grodno, or Groys Vileyke, but in Vilna, obviously. Because Vilna is a city with curses, little jokes, and crazy people. It's unique. Vilna has what an institute like that needs."

"What of it? He took what he found here and left for another city to gather stuff for the Institute."

"So he left. You think the entire business will go under?" Here Tsirl came up with a plan for her friend. Thanks to this plan, YIVO, the Yiddish Scientific Institute in Vilna, was enriched with a collection of curses, little jokes, and sayings truly to be envied.

Tsirl urged Chana-Merka to do nothing less than to set off for the Institute and tell them where their folklore came from. "Everything Rubinshteyn brought them, he got from you. Why don't you offer to bring in the merchandise yourself and let Rubinshteyn bust a gut? There's no better way to take revenge on him."

Chana-Merka wasn't thinking about revenge. Her heart was broken. She'd grown accustomed to Rubinshteyn and then he'd taken off and left the city. Chana-Merka figured he didn't like her. Perhaps he thought she was beneath him. Why talk about revenge?

★

But Chana-Merka took up Tsirl's plan for an entirely different reason. During the few months she'd spent with the folklorist, she'd become infected with the folklore bug. At first she'd shrugged her shoulders, thinking, "What's the point of all this?" But gradually she'd come to understand that all the Vilna curses, insults, biting expressions, and aphorisms could easily be forgotten. In years to come, people might think that life in Vilna had been dry and humorless; without cutting words, without the hucksters who dragged customers into the shops from the street, without the *bobesnitzes* who sold boiled beans with a little saying and a tune, and without even the fish sellers in the Zaretshe market.

Chana-Merka was no simple peasant from the village. She'd managed to complete a few classes in the Devorah Kupershteyn Folk Shul for Girls. Thanks to her teacher, Gershon Pludermakher, she'd learned to hold a pen in her hand. Rubinshteyn the Folklorist had scratched off a bit of her crudeness, something a fishwife needs to earn her bit of bread. Some of the refinement that Chana-Merka had developed in school, particularly from Pludermakher's teaching, showed itself.

★

One beautiful morning, Chana-Merka set off for the Institute to discuss the delivery of goods. "I want to speak with the top boss," she said. The top boss of the Institute was Dr. Max Weinreich.

An ugly specimen known as Zelda the Researcher quivered and fretted, "Why do people come here and pester Dr. Weinreich?"

But Chana-Merka didn't give up. "Don't worry," she said. "I also have rights here in the Institute." One word followed another and soon people in the Institute realized that the woman with the gold front tooth was Rubinshteyn's folklore source. Her name did appear on his lists. When Rubinshteyn had been around, she'd been seen a few times standing outside the Institute. The first person to recognize her was Zelda the Researcher, who'd had her eye on Rubinshteyn even before Chana-Merka.

Dr. Weinreich was delighted with Chana-Merka. He saw in her a confirmation of his theory that research without the common people isn't worth a groschen. He'd recently written an article on that topic for the Institute journal. Dr. Weinreich sat Chana-Merka down opposite his desk, wiped his glasses, and got down to business. "Absolutely, you should bring in more material, on all topics. Here in the Institute, we'll file it where it belongs." He assured her that what she had given Rubinshteyn was more precious than gold. "Every curse and local expression is as sweet as sugar."

Chana-Merka left the Institute feeling elated. Dr. Weinreich had said to her, "Mrs. Solodukhin, you possess the ultimate charm. After a single conversation with you, a person can string together a strand of precious Yiddish pearls." It was true. Chana-Merka had presented Dr. Weinreich with language that warmed his soul.

★

The first list Chana-Merka supplied were Vilna curses. She didn't submit all of them because some were too crude to say out loud. But she collected a pack of curses that were far from Rosh Hashanah greetings. They are:

> May you get a piece of straw in your eye and a splinter in your ear and not know which one to pull out first.
>
> How long do they think she'll be sick?? If she's going to lie in bed with a fever for another month, let the month last five weeks.
>
> May a fish ball get stuck in your throat.
>
> They should call a doctor for you in an emergency and when he arrives, they should tell him he's no longer needed.
>
> May your teeth be pulled out on a winter night and may you give birth on a summer day.
>
> You should grow like an onion with your head in the ground.
>
> May all your teeth be pulled out except one, and in that one you should have a toothache.
>
> Doctors should know you and you should know doctors.
>
> May you speak so beautifully that only cats understand you.
>
> He should feel good. Good and dead.
>
> May you be lucky and go crazy in a more important city than Vilna.

Chana-Merka wanted to add, "You should swallow an umbrella and it should open in your stomach," but she remembered that everyone knew that curse. They'd even used it in the Yiddish theater. So she erased it.

★

During the evenings, Chana-Merka sat in her tiny room on Yatkever Street, preparing the lists for YIVO. Dr. Weinreich had told her to write everything down. It was all useful merchandise. He suggested she compile a list of words related to fishing. "What are the various tools called in Yiddish?" he asked. Filling his order, Chana-Merka wrote:

Words used in fishing, heard from my husband, Orke the Net Caster, who drowned in the Narotshe Lake:

a zavadnik: Someone who casts the nets.

tonyeven: To pull the net out of the water.

durkhshvenken di ozyere: To traverse the lake from shore to shore with a net. Literally, to rinse the lake.

When fish lay eggs, people say they're playing.

As an added treat, Chana-Merka wrote out the names of the different varieties of apples and pears:

Types of apples: *tulske, papinkes, olivne, siere, aportn, tshernohuzen.*

Types of pears: *margaratkes, sapeshankes, bures.*

Chana-Merka collected the fruit names at the lumber market. When she started asking questions and writing the answers on a little piece of paper, the market women looked at each other over the tops of their baskets. They all felt badly that some cripple, who'd also come around asking questions and jotting things down, had hurt Chana-Merka. Everyone in the Vilna markets knew the story of Chana-Merka and Rubinshteyn.

The Institute was abuzz. The researchers and visiting students were enjoying the latest list of aphorisms that Chana-Merka had provided. After each one was read aloud, the entire group exploded in laughter. Only Zelda the Researcher, the specialist in Jewish cuisine, made wry faces. She argued that Chana-Merka's collections were not scientifically sound and had not been collected with the appropriate methodology that proper ethnology demanded. But prattling on with fancy terminology didn't help her. Dr. Weinreich said that Chana-Merka's collections would be valued for their authenticity, specifically because they were taken directly from the mouths of the people. To acknowledge the importance of Chana-Merka's material, he took the list of aphorisms in hand and read them aloud to everyone present:

Everyone desires the nipple.

A wife known as a blessing can sometimes be the greatest curse.

In a fire, even the slop pail can help.

Of an ugly girl: She looks like a cross-eyed herring on heels that are too high to be flat and too flat to be high.

God pays honestly, but He takes His time.

A lowly boot also has ears.

Even a humble hut has windows.

A poor man complains when he has two weddings in one day. Where will he eat the next day?

Even a thief should maintain his honor.

If my grandmother had wheels, she'd be a locomotive.

At this, Dr. Weinreich doubled over with laughter and stopped reading from the collection of Vilna aphorisms and sayings.

One hot summer day Chana-Merka was standing next to her tub, waiting for a customer to come along and buy her last few barbels at a bargain price. She'd recently lost interest in the whole fishing business. Looking to switch to another line of work, she started hatching various plans.

Itske the Redhead had offered her a share in his bar on Yatkever Street, not far from her little room. Pale Tsirl warned Chana-Merka against it. "A tub of fish is an honest business. If you don't like a customer, just chase her away with the tail of a carp, saying, 'Madam, buy smelts instead. This fish isn't for you.' But all sorts of thugs come into a bar. You have to put on a sweet face, wiggle your bottom, and ask them what they'd like, when really you'd like to see the back of them. Here at the tubs, the entire city knows you, Chana-Merka, but at Itske the Redhead's, you'll be nothing more than Chana-Merka the waitress."

So Chana-Merka didn't take Itske up on his offer. But she no longer felt happy standing next to the tubs. When Rubinshteyn had spent time with her, she'd felt important. And in the Institute they'd treated her like an empress, fussing over her. Dr. Weinreich shook her hand. If only she could devote herself to folklore, like the young men and women who worked in the Institute. But they were so well-educated; she couldn't measure up to them. She had nothing but her tub of fish.

Heaving a sigh, Chana-Merka looked around for a customer. At one time, before she got involved with folklore, she'd lured her customers by yelling witty sayings, praising her merchandise to the sky. But now she ran a respectable business, which was no good for the tub of fish.

Pale Tsirl fretted. She watched her friend sink lower and lower. Chana-Merka just wasn't the same. Tsirl chastised her. "The only gleam left is from the gold tooth in your mouth. Pretty soon you'll be like Zelda the Researcher, that drab, old maid."

As Chana-Merka stood waiting for her final customer, she noticed off in the distance, at the edge of the market, a man walking toward her, dragging his stiff leg behind him. He stopped every ten or twelve steps, perhaps because of the heat. As the limping wanderer trudged toward the row of tubs, the green backpack hanging off one of his shoulders shone in the bright sunlight.

Chana-Merka stood at her tub, absolutely still. She couldn't be wrong. It had to be Rubinshteyn the Folklorist. He was too close for her to be just imagining him. He kept walking until he stood right next to her. She didn't know what to do. She stood still, leaving it to Rubinshteyn to limp the last step and take her hand that was clenched around the edge of her tub.

Rubinshteyn took the step. His hand clasped Chana-Merka's. They stood together, without saying a word. They left talking for later, when they sat at the table in Chana-Merka's tiny room and Rubinshteyn enjoyed a glass of tea and a piece of gefilte fish.

7

Lost and Found

Ortshik's eyes almost crawled out of his head before he managed to open his own barbershop. He'd been collecting equipment for a few years, one shaving knife at a time. Unfortunately, he couldn't just go to Kruk's daughter's warehouse and ask to have the barbershop supplies packed up. Had he been single, that might have been possible, but he'd just hitched up with Libke. And he'd barely stepped out from under the wedding canopy when she started to show.

Libke had to stop working. Itske the Redhead didn't, God forbid, force her to quit. He just told her she took up half the bar and the customers were afraid she'd go into labor and drop a plate of baby beets on them. Libke tried to tell Itske that she was only in her seventh month and still far from the big day, but it made no difference. He shouted that Vilna had never seen such a monstrous pregnancy. "Maybe you're carrying triplets."

Libke came home in tears. She hoped Itske's wife would bear him only black monsters. After all, she'd worked as a waitress in Itske's bar for ten years. Loyal as a dog, she'd ignored the pinches to her soft flesh so the customers would be happy and the business successful. And he'd dismissed her now, of all times, when they needed every groschen. In the past, she could always count on bringing home a few zlotys in tips, a piece of cheap udder, or a few stuffed chicken bellies from the bar. No longer.

Ortshik couldn't maintain the household and buy equipment on his wages. That was clear. He needed to open his own shop. As his grandmother used to say, "A door on the street is a window into heaven." He tightened the belt of his white housecoat, fighting off his doubts and hesitations.

Shabbes morning, before Ortshik got out of bed, he tallied up what he had and what he still needed. Libke lay next to him, her pointy belly covered with a cotton blanket like a cholent waiting for tardy guests. Poking him, she said, "Ortshik, stop counting the scissors." Ortshik ignored her. He peered over her mountainous belly into the distance, imagining the sign for his establishment, "Ortshik the Barber (Formerly at Bendel's)."

★

Libke had a boy. He came out of her belly with a real head of hair. He was just waiting for someone to sit him down and give him a good haircut. Everyone in Vilna came running to have a look at the amazing sight. Itsik the Redhead predicted the child would grow up to be an athlete and conquer the world.

The gangsters decided to hold the bris right there, in the bar, at their expense. They asked Itske to be the sandek. The chicken sellers from the lumber market contributed all their giblets. A few skinners threw in a side of meat. Itske provided whiskey. For a while Ortshik forgot his worries. His pals plied him with drink until he babbled that the bottle needed a shave. Embarrassed, Libke screamed that if Ortshik couldn't hold his liquor, he should stick to Yoshe's kvass. She was the first to leave for home, taking the child with her. Ortshik's pals dragged him home much later.

When Ortshik recovered from the bris, he began setting up his business. He heard that Avromke the Anarchist, who sold his wares in the passageway, had an assortment of barbering tools. A barber, a goy, had died in Rone-Pole. During his final years, the man had raised rabbits rather than cutting hair. His wife had shown up with a sack of equipment to sell.

Ortshik slipped away from Bendel's to look over the merchandise but there was almost nothing he wanted. Damaged razors, one with a cracked handle; moldy leather sharpening belts; a set of shears with missing teeth; worn-out brushes; and three yellowed shaving mugs. Of the many pairs of scissors, at most only one was worth taking. The *goye* offered to throw two faded mustache bandages from King Sobietski's time into the bargain. Ortshik spit at the ground and took off. Avromke the Anarchist wanted to call him back, but then he saw for himself that there was nothing worth buying. It was all just old junk. He grabbed everything, stuffed it back into the sack and escorted the *goye* out of the passageway, bidding her good riddance.

★

Things did not go well for Ortshik. He was plagued by bad luck. He leased a shop on Krupnitshe Street at a good rent. He was just about to hire someone to whitewash the place when a barbers' strike broke out in Vilna and wrecked all his plans. Altetshke had hired a barber who wasn't from Vilna, even though the barbershop bosses had agreed to only hire Vilna barbers. There were already enough locals. The barbers had sat in the union office on Zavalne Street with the bosses for many nights before they finally agreed to this point and signed it with a handshake and refreshments at Velfke's restaurant.

But Altetshke thought she was smarter than everyone else and claimed the man was a distant relative. The union decreed that Max and Liovke, who worked at Shirbe's on Daytshe Street, would go with Ortshik to remove the good-for-nothing from the barbershop. Ortshik was expected to maintain discipline until he was on his own. So he went.

The three men sat themselves down at Altetshke's and waited while the supposed relative shaved a customer. The guy dragged out the shave for as long as possible, going over the same cheek three times with the shaving knife and then getting rid of every little nose hair. To this day, no one knows who smashed Altetshke's mirror. However it happened, the customer ran into the street with the bib still under his chin and the fool from elsewhere went home with one eye a little smaller than the other.

The delegation didn't get off scot-free either. Ortshik suffered more than the others. Someone punched him from behind and twisted one of his sidelocks. Libke walked into the union office, holding the infant with the thick head of hair, and told the chairman, Yoske Geker, that in return for sending Ortshik into the flames, she hoped he choked on a fish dumpling. The chairman told Libke that her husband had to stand shoulder to shoulder on the barricades to defend the interests of the working class.

Altetshke submitted to the union's decree and gave up trying to be smarter than everyone else. Everyone in the trade was sure things would calm down. They would walk down Daytshe Street like heroes. But then it was the Days of Awe and time to negotiate a new contract. The bosses wouldn't budge. Strelnik from Gitke-Toybe's Lane wreaked havoc, insisting there would be no more overtime pay. "What God gives, He'll give, and no more. The workers have to share in the burden of turning a profit along with everyone else. They can't just throw their smocks at the wall when the clock strikes seven."

Ortshik didn't know where to turn. He stood at Bendel's with his shaving knife in hand, but his head was already in his own shop with his own garbage. And his heart was with his pals Yosl Pasovke, Shepske, and Max, who were all fired up and spent their time in the union hall, scheming about how to wage war against the enemies of the working class like Strelnik, Bendel and the other oppressors.

Ortshik used the few weeks of the barbers' strike to organize the cupboards in his barbershop. Libke told him to put a blue awning above the small white door so it didn't look like a medical clinic. When the neighbors showed up to offer their opinions, they said the place looked wonderful. The workers won the strike, but Ortshik didn't enjoy the victory. He took Libke's advice and didn't return to work. It had almost killed her when he went out onto the barricades.

Ortshik bought a few inexpensive mirrors and the shop started to look like something. It still needed chairs, a hair dryer, and a few hand implements. A friend of Libke's gave her a painting of a woman lying on a chaise lounge in a nightgown, with two chubby cherubs combing her bangs. Libke hung the painting where everyone would see it. She polished and scrubbed without standing still for a minute. By the time she finished, she had no feeling in her arms.

Friday evening, before the barbershop was scheduled to open, Libke barely had the strength to light the candles. She and Ortshik sat at the Shabbes table looking tired and bleary-eyed after a week of hard work. On Sunday morning, Ortshik would, with luck, stand in front of his own shop. Libke poured the chicken broth into a bowl and looked at her husband. Then she put down the ladle and burst out crying. Ortshik's sparse whiskers quivered. "Why are you crying?"

"Just look at you. You're half your normal size."

"What can I do? I've been rushing around to get everything ready."

"I know that. I also know the kind of brides they offered you. Girls with money and a place to live. You settled for a poor girl. Maybe you figure it wasn't worth it."

Ortshik smiled. "What are you thinking? There's a little one in the crib. We're an old couple now."

The Shabbes candles lit up Ortshik's smile. Libke's face was glowing. She walked over to her husband, ran her chubby fingers through the billows of his forelock, and revealed her naked breast. "Ortshik, my little tomcat. Are you still taken with me, like before?"

Ortshik smiled.

"So tell me the truth. Why did you choose me? Tell me."

Ortshik smoothed down his whiskers. "It was your good looks Libke. That's the only reason."

Early Sunday morning, Ortshik took his keys and went to open his barbershop. The short distance from Stephan Street to Krupnitshe felt like miles. He wanted to get there as quickly as possible and wish his first customer a hearty good morning. When he arrived at the shop, he looked at the sign with pleasure and then put his key into the hanging lock that held an iron bar. Carefully, so as not to damage the fresh paint, he moved the bar to one side, opened the door wide, and hurried into the business of his dreams.

Ortshik's face fell from shock. The barbershop was completely empty. There wasn't a single chair, a single mirror, or even the tiniest implement in the shop. Lonely hooks winked at Ortshik from the naked and embarrassed walls. He pulled out one drawer after the next, but found nothing. It was as though a demon had played a trick on Saturday evening and with one breath, blown the entire barbershop through the chimney. The new nickel chairs with headrests and hidden hinges were missing. Also the polished four-meter-high mirrors and the hair dryer with its bell-shaped attachment that Ortshik had bought for working on women's hair. Gone were the sets of shears, the shaving knives, the bone and steel combs, the soap mugs, and the brushes made from the best pig hair. Everything had disappeared. Even Ortshik's new smock with the small blue collar was missing. From Libke's picture, only the string remained.

Ortshik's felt his heart tighten. He stood absolutely still for a moment. Then he fell to the floor, stretched out to his full length. That's how his first customer, Hirshel the Canary, found him. Hirshel woke the entire street trying to revive Ortshik. Then he went off to find out who could have committed such a heinous act.

★

The people of Vilna were outraged when they heard that someone had cleaned out Ortshik's barbershop. The entire trade was fuming. Libke was so upset, her milk dried up. The boy clung with both hands to his mother's breast that was as big as a pumpkin, but he only managed to squeeze out a little sip. Ortshik lay in bed with his eyes closed. Libke begged him, "Orele, you have to be strong. The baby needs a father."

That evening Ortshik's friends came to comfort him. Yoske said they'd turn Vilna inside out to find Ortshik's things. He promised that, God willing, in the morning they would make contact with the shady elements in town and solve the crime. Yoske added that Ortshik shouldn't have betrayed the ranks and joined the petit bourgeoisie by opening his own barber shop. But still, when he found the bastards who'd robbed Ortshik, he'd personally shave them with a blunt shaving knife.

Hirshke the Canary wasn't sitting idle either. He'd experienced the robbery at Ortshik's barbershop as a personal insult. After all, he was the Emperor of Krupnitshe Street. No one dared lay their hands on a hair's worth of merchandise without his approval. And then, out of nowhere, some scoundrel showed up and robbed one of his neighbors. Hirshke informed Ortshik in no uncertain terms not to go to the police. Commissar Mayevski and his informers would just scare off the thief. Then Hirshke went to see the locksmith, Yanek the Grumbler, to find out whether anyone had recently ordered a skeleton key.

But there were no clues to the theft. Hirshke the Canary went to the criminal organization, the Golden Flag, to demand justice, but the president, Zelik the Benefactor, was in Lukishke prison, so there was no one to talk to. Zelik was due out any day. They had to wait.

When Libke saw that Ortshik's skin had turned as black as a cauldron from worry, she went looking for advice and the chance to unburden her heart. The pluckers in the chicken shed advised her to go see the yeshiva student who read palms. Maybe he'd be able to tell her where the contents of the barbershop had ended up. They explained that it wasn't only *agunes* who went to him, but also respectable people, merchants and the like. Everyone had their burden. The yeshiva student usually made his predictions from a lined piece of paper with horoscopes. For difficult situations, he consulted a book about the Kabbalah for the right combination of Hebrew letters and numbers.

Libke found the yeshiva student eating a herring with onions. Seeing her sad expression, he tried to calm her by pointing out that there wasn't a man on this earth who wouldn't eventually return home with his tail between his legs. He would explain everything in detail as soon as he finished the herring. Libke didn't wait for him to get to the herring's tail. She immediately corrected his mistake with a few sharp words. Wasting no time, the yeshiva student looked at his astrological chart for some hint to explain the disappearance of Ortshik's barbershop supplies. Then he did something with a little mirror. Finally, he looked at Libke's calloused palm and sent her home with a muddled explanation that because the theft was still fresh, she should sit tight for a little while. They would speak later. One thing was certain—the thief had whiskers.

Hirshke the Canary got his due. As soon as Zelik the Benefactor was released from prison, a meeting was organized. Rabbi Kivele, the rabbi for the profession, promised to attend. That evening, everyone with the slightest involvement in illegal activity showed up for the meeting at Itske the Redhead's bar. Itske closed the shutters against onlookers and told the waitresses to cut up two meters of roasted kishke for refreshments. Zelik the Benefactor sat at the head of the table with Prentsik and Zorukh the Double Boiler at his side to assist him. Further down the table, according to their rank, sat Avromke the Anarchist, Wise Melekh, Dodke the Ace, Elinke, Motke the Little Kaiser, both Squirrel brothers, and so on, all the way down to the little minnows at the end of the table.

Hirshke the Canary started by warbling in his high falsetto, "Dear brothers, we have come together to redress a wrong, but we don't know who the culprit is. Some crook with no ties to our organization had the nerve to clean out a business on my turf without my knowledge. If that isn't enough, he robbed Ortshik the Barber, who took one of our own, Libke the Waitress, to live an honest life with her. I have to inform everyone that as long as Hirshke the Canary walks down Krupnitshe Street, such behavior will not be tolerated. It's true that I don't know who to go after, but I swear to you, my dear brothers, in the name of my freedom, if I capture that scoundrel, he'll not only have to bring everything back at his own expense, he'll be carried out of Vilna in pieces."

Hirshke's lecture made an impression. The table shook under the banging of fists. Guys remembered old injustices and stirred up forgotten matters. Dodke the Ace threatened to pull a knife out of his bootleg. If it hadn't been for Zelik the Benefactor, the meeting would have ended in a bloodbath. Zelik asked Itske to bring a few more liters of whiskey to calm everyone down.

After the crowd settled down a little, Rabbi Kivele gave them a piece of his mind. "Even though God gave you this kind of work, you should still behave like decent human beings. There's a specific law in the *Shulchan aruch* about this matter. We have to make sure that the city of Vilna, the Jerusalem of Lithuania, is not disgraced. The thief had better return everything, down to the last thread. If not, we'll have to light black candles and call for the culprit's excommunication. At that point, the thief better not fault the all-powerful God if he burns his hands on whatever he touches. As long as God helps, the most difficult locks will open for you. But without Him, at some point you'll open a door to find a full slop pail." After warning them to keep God in their hearts, Rabbi Kivele downed a shot of whiskey and went home.

At dawn, Ortshik set off with a little ladder. He wanted to remove the sign over his barbershop before anyone was stirring in the streets, so no one would see him. The meeting of the underworld organization had upset everyone, but so far, nothing had come of it. Hirshke the Canary assured Ortshik that everything would be returned. He knew his people. "Even if my fraternal request doesn't help, do you think people will ignore Rabbi Kivele's warning? Excommunication with black candles is no laughing matter. The entire passageway is in turmoil."

With sad steps, Ortshik walked along Kleyn Stephan Street to Krupnitshe Street. The pre-Passover sun yawned, stretching its pink limbs over the Viliye. In the early morning light, shadows could be seen packing up their wares. Gradually it grew brighter. Puddles of melted snow captured the sun's rays, dragging them into the gutters. Ortshik jumped over the springtime rivulets. He felt no joy at the prospect of the days ahead when he would be able to put his baby in the buggy and take a Shabbes walk with his little family down Breyte Street to the Bernardine Garden.

Over the past few days, Ortshik had started to philosophize. He remembered one of his father's sayings. "It's a foolish world. A man hustles and bustles, fusses and frets, and what does he get? The devil comes along and takes everything. Then he's left high and dry. He could have lived it up with his few zlotys, eaten some udder, and gone to the theater." But what was past was past. When Ortshik reached his barbershop, he sighed deeply and resolved that from here on, he would know how to live on this earth.

Ortshik leaned his ladder against the wall above the window and was about to lift his foot up to the first step when a shudder went through his entire body. For a moment, he stood in front of the window like a stork, with one leg raised. Then he pinched himself, quickly freed the iron bar from the hanging lock, and pulled the door wide open.

The barbershop was ready to receive customers, as though nothing had happened. Everything was in place: the chairs, the mirrors, the hair dryer for women, and all the furniture. The shaving knives, scissors, soap mugs, and clippers were perfectly arranged on the shelves. The smock with the little blue collar was also there, without a speck. Libke's painting of the woman in her nightgown hung on the same nail from which it had been taken.

Dazed, Ortshik touched every tool and every screw. He opened one shaving knife after another and tried a comb on his own hair. Was this a dream or reality? Now he understood why Hirshke the Canary had told him, in no uncertain terms, that neither he nor Libke should leave home on Saturday evening, not even for a second.

Ortshik was about to lock the door and run home to tell Libke the good news when he noticed a brush lying in the corner by the doorway—a dark brown brush with short hair for a stiff beard. He'd bought the brush when he started at Bendel's as an apprentice. Ortshik held the brush in both hands as though it was a beloved little bird that had fallen from her nest. For the first time since he had entered the trade, Ortshik the Barber wet a brush with his own hot tears.

8

Vladek

I want to tell you about Vladek, one of Yusef the janitor's boys. Yusef was a goy who drank constantly and hit his wife and children whenever he felt like it. His son Vladek wasn't safe at home, so he grew up with us. The cellar where they lived was always dark. Yusef's wife had something on the boil all day long—either wash or cabbage. The steam only let up a little in the evenings.

Vladek hung out with us, the courtyard children. He didn't do too badly. Sometimes he got a piece of challah, other times a bit of buckwheat kugel—whatever one of our mothers had shoved into our hands. We didn't have much ourselves. The courtyard was full of poor, barefoot people, one poorer than the next. Seremetinke, the owner of the courtyard, was always fighting with his tenants about rent money. He was hardly a rich man himself.

When we were young, Vladek had somewhere to go. But when we got bigger, we were sent to a Talmud Torah, the Toras Emes School. Vladek was miserable. He had nothing to eat and no one to play with. In the afternoons, he stood watch, waiting for us to return.

We didn't walk to Toras Emes, we ran. They handed out American milk and wheat dumplings. We played cops and robbers in the large courtyard. No one pushed us very hard to study. Our teacher, Mr. Gershovitsh, knew who he was dealing with, so he gave up without a struggle. Tevke the Tapeworm, Orke the Lucky Seven, and Shmuel the Organ Grinder's Twin sat in the first row. They were already thugs by then. We had another teacher, the tiny Miss Funk, one of the daughters from Funk's bookstore. We called her by her first name, Chana-Bashka. She tried teaching us at first, but eventually she also let go of the reins.

Figure 2. "Vladek wasn't safe at home, so he grew up with us." By Yosl Bergner from Avrom Karpinovitsh, *Baym Vilner durkhhoyf* (Tel Aviv: I. L. Peretz, 1967). Courtesy of the artist.

If it hadn't been for the principal, Mr. Ayzikov, we would have looted the entire Talmud Torah, brick by brick. He barely talked to us but just gave us a look. Even if we were rolling on the ground and grabbing each other by the throat, one look from him was enough to send us crawling into the corners like wild animals in a circus. We sat quietly during his lessons. Sometimes he'd walk between the benches and stroke one of our heads, something that never happened at home. If we, hooligans that we were, left the school knowing how to write a letter from prison or give an accounting to a fence, we had only our teacher Mr. Ayzikov to thank.

Once Vladek asked his father to send him to school. Yusef was drunk. He beat Vladek badly and chased him out of the cellar. The only thing the janitor cared about was his bottle of whiskey. Vladek got tired of wandering around the courtyard on his own, so he started following us to the Talmud Torah in the mornings. One recess, Mr. Ayzikov noticed him and asked him what he was doing there. Vladek explained. Mr. Ayzikov was surprised to hear him speaking Yiddish. He told the other teachers to give him food along with the other children. Tevke started smuggling Vladek into class. Mr. Gershovitsh was ill and Chana-Bashka had no idea what to say. She was afraid if she walked through the classroom, one of us would grab the front of her dress. I got a pencil stub and a piece of paper for Vladek and he learned the *alef-beys* with the rest of us.

And so we grew up and went off, some earlier, some later. Every person at home was an extra mouth to feed. Lots of families didn't know where their next meal was coming from. The courtyard was in constant turmoil. Yusef died from drinking, and people started chopping up the bannisters to heat their ovens during the winter. Even Seremetinke stopped coming around to inspect his property. There was a brawl in the courtyard every single day.

We boys spread out through the city trying to find a way to earn a few groschen. Some of us managed to organize something. Zevke the Little Mirror started selling the *Ovnt-Kurier* newspaper. Shmuel, the Organ Grinder's elder son, had a good voice, so he sang and begged for money. One of the coachmen hired Tevke the Tapeworm. Vladek and I wrenched copper doorknobs off expensive doors and sold them for scrap. Before that, we'd tried working on the freight cars on Bunimovitsh's branch line going into Kinkulkin's mill, but it didn't pan out. One day there was work and ten days, nothing.

And so we got drawn into the profession. We stopped coming home to sleep. No one really cared. My father was ashamed of me. Even though our neighborhood was swarming with criminals, he never had anything to do with them. He collected rags for the Olkeniker paper factory until the day he died and never took so much as a thread for himself. My father even told my mother not to take money from me, but what choice did she have? Aside from letting her children go hungry. Vladek also used to toss a little something into the cellar. He wasn't a bad *sheygetz*.

★

Life went on. Before long, we'd served a few long sentences in Lukishke prison. I lost touch with Vladek a few times. He tried settling down outside the city. The life of a criminal just wasn't for him. Prison was really hard on him. As for me, after my last year in the clink, I also started to hate that life.

When people took off for the Soviet Union, I went looking for Vladek and said, "Let's go. We'll start over, get some training and live an honest life." Vladek was enthusiastic. We went to Hirshke the Canary, who took people across the border. Ten of us crossed into the Soviet Union at Radoshkovich. There was a long red banner with the words "A New Life Awaits You" hanging from the military outpost in Zaslov.

They took us to the Minsk prison. There was a famine in Russia and people were starving to death. In jail, we lived on two hundred grams of bread a day. We whittled pieces of wood from the bed planks for cigarettes. At that point, Lukishke was looking pretty good as far as prisons went. Vladek was going under. He didn't have the strength to stand up.

It was quite the new life. They interrogated us, hitting us everywhere. We told the truth: who we were and what we wanted. The officials wrote and erased. At one point, they took a group of detainees and ordered us into formation and onto a train. We had no idea where the train was taking us until the last minute. In the middle of the night, they ordered us to leave the heated freight car and told us they were sending us back to Poland. If we wanted a lighter sentence, we should tell the Polish border guard we were getting ready to cross into Russia. The Russian official told us we were being sent back to set up a Soviet government in Poland. In Mołodeczno we were convicted of trying to cross the border. We got off with a few months.

★

I want to talk about Vladek. We returned from Mołodeczno in rags, without a groschen. Vladek was so weak, he could barely speak. He went to stay with distant relatives in one of the villages to regain his strength. I asked Itsik the Buckwheat Pudding if I could keep score in the pool hall. It was a way to survive, at least in the short term. I got drawn into the world of the pool hall. There was no difference between day and night. Everything went by in a fog.

A good few months passed. One day the door of the pool hall opened and in walked Vladek, looking well fed and wearing a nice suit. He didn't rush over and throw his arms around me. He played a few games and then asked if I wanted to go to Velfke's restaurant with him for some liver with kishke.

Vladek was looking good. In our trade, you don't ask a person how they got their money; you wait to be told. But I was miserable and wanted out of the pool hall. So I broke the rule and asked Vladek if he'd snagged a once-in-a-lifetime opportunity or if he could bring a partner into the business. Vladek laughed so hard the glasses on the table shook. I was looking straight at him, but I couldn't make sense of what he was saying. When he calmed down a little, he said, "It's a business all right, but not for you."

I was insulted. "What do you mean, not for me? Haven't we broken enough locks together? You doubt my skill?"

"Well," he answered, "if you're ready to picket Khanovitsh's readymade clothing shop and make sure no goyim enter, then okay."

I couldn't believe it. "You? You've joined those hooligans? Do you realize they don't let Jews walk the streets?"

"We tell them not to carry sticks. Anyway, I do other things."

I got up from the table. Vladek called after me, "I'm done with being a criminal. No more jail for me."

Jewish students were being beaten up at Vilna University. And the anti-Semites hired guards to stand outside Jewish shops and stop Christian customers from entering. The threat of violence hung over the city and here Vladek was part of it.

I made for the exit. Here I'd thought he'd offered me whiskey to celebrate his success with a cashbox. But drinking to the money he was earning now? I left the restaurant without looking back.

To this very day, I don't understand what was going on with Vladek at that time. The *sheygetz* was raised in a Jewish courtyard. He knew the *alefbeys* as well as any of us. So well in fact that Zelik the Benefactor, a trustee for the small prison synagogue, once tried to include Vladek in a prayer minyan for a *yortzayt* service. I'd recruited Vladek into the profession and made something of him. And after all that, he went and joined the hooligans, the students with foxtails on their caps who beat up Jews. Had the Minsk prison broken his spirit? Quite possibly. After all, there were plenty of ways to earn money at that time. Mitsken was putting people to sleep on the trains and needed a helper to steal their suitcases. Handsome Mishke was looking for someone to travel to the fairs with him and sell fake lottery tickets. Vladek could have had any one of those jobs. He had a good reputation with us. But the gangsters decided the wolf had gone into the forest, and that was that.

I'd grown up with Vladek and knew him better than anyone. I remembered when we were boys and went swimming at the French mill. When the village louts attacked, Vladek was the first to grab a brick, even though they kept yelling they weren't after him.

The situation with Vladek really bothered me. I waited for an opportunity to talk to him. I knew the guys wanted to knife him. They said it was a short road from picketing to informing. I had to warn him. After all, he was no stranger.

The goons from the student associations used to sit in Sztral's Café. Behind the café there was a pool hall, one of the best in the city. That's where the party underlings, guys who earned their money breaking windows or causing a ruckus on market days, hung out. I knew Vladek spent his evenings there. I went to Sztral's, but I didn't go in. I didn't want the goyim to pick a fight with me and for Vladek to get pulled in. I asked Yane the Scorekeeper to tell Vladek I was waiting outside for him.

I remember our meeting like it was yesterday. It was a summer night. We sat on the grass next to the Viliye. The guys who pulled logs out of the water were baking potatoes on campfires at the river's edge. Some of the light from the fire reached us, and I saw Vladek's swollen face. He looked like he'd started drinking heavily. For a moment I thought about his father, our courtyard, and our childhood. I wanted to say something, to scold him like a younger brother and tell him to give up the whiskey, but before I could say a word, he stood up and said, "So, you want to pull a heist?"

I felt like he'd doused me with cold water. Can you believe it? Yusef's son Vladek had become honest and I was just a thief with nothing on my mind but breaking into a stranger's shop in the dead of night. Vladek obviously thought he was better than me, so who was I to tell him how to live his life? I just warned him that the guys were watching him. They'd figured him for an informer.

Vladek flew into a rage. He grabbed at his chest. "Let them stab me. Just let them, those dirty dogs. If it wasn't for me, Zevulin the Peach would have rotted away in Lukishke."

There was a story going around about Zevulin the Peach. He'd been a big shot in the gangster's organization, the Golden Flag, and some of the guys had questioned his authority. An argument broke out and Zevulin thrashed a few of them. He'd had to get out of Vilna quickly. Someone had definitely helped him get papers. Now Vladek was telling me he'd had a hand in it.

Vladek was standing with his face to the river, breathing heavily. I put a hand on his shoulder, "Vladek, maybe we're destined to be criminals. There are people like that."

"No. Not me. They promised me, when they take power, they'll give me a job on the trains. I want to work. I want to be like other people."

In the time I'd known Vladek, he'd never been a big-time crook. A real criminal loves the trade and the risks that come with it, but that just wasn't in Vladek's blood. He'd dreamt of becoming a machinist all his life. They'd promised him exactly that, so he was doing their bidding. Meanwhile his bosses were happy to look for Jewish children in the streets to crack their heads open.

Me and the other guys couldn't just do nothing. We walked around with knives, and blood flowed. I let it be known that Vladek had helped Zevulin. His good deeds protected him. Otherwise the guys would have gone after him. Vladek stopped coming into our territory. He and I grew apart.

The war broke out. People scattered in every direction. The year the Soviets were stationed in Vilna wasn't too bad at all. They harassed the rich but left everyone else alone. Almost everyone who was arrested and sent to Siberia returned after the war. When they were taken from their homes, everyone in Vilna was in tears except for Tsalel the Nose, who owned the big clothing store. He stood between two soldiers on a military truck, waving his cap and yelling, "Good luck, my fellow Jews. Soon you'll envy me."

A few of our guys found good work for themselves. Peretz the Diamond became the superintendent of the covered markets and Osherke the Bootmaker, a tannery manager. I could have gotten myself a job, but the trade in watches was brisk and guys were raking it in. I decided to stick with the watches for the time being. I didn't see Vladek in the city. I figured he was scared and lying low until things calmed down.

The celebration didn't last long. The Germans appeared in the city one fine morning. All year long, the Russians had bragged that if war broke out, they'd make mincemeat of their enemies. They had us convinced. And then suddenly there were Germans on Yatkever Street.

The Germans started grabbing people and taking them to Ponar. Everyone was stunned. We weren't used to violence like that. Even the gangsters were rattled. Our leaders were gone. There was no one to tell us what to do. People in the streets kept telling each other that things would change. They did change. They shoved all of us into three streets enclosed by a high fence. The Germans created a ghetto.

As luck would have it, I was already living on Shavelske Street with my Freydke, so I stayed in my apartment. Shavelske was part of the ghetto. They rounded up all the Jews from the other streets. They just stood on the cobblestones. I went down to the courtyard and saw Mr. Ayzikov with a bundle in his hand, staring at the sky. Of course, I took him and his wife up to my apartment. I gave them a room and informed Freydke that we would share everything.

Everyone in the ghetto worried about rustling up a crust of bread. Some people cozied up to the chimney sweeps—that trade was as good as gold. The sweeps moved freely through the city, so it was easier for them to find a little something to eat.

I was in bad shape in the ghetto. My mood was bad. The guys suggested I set up a table at my place with a slit in the boards to hide marked cards. I could lure in stiffs with money and cheat them at rummy. But I was no longer the same guy. The ghetto had broken me. I was also concerned about Mr. Ayzikov. I joined a brigade and went to work at the Poribaniker airfield.

★

In two roundups, everyone close to me was sent to Ponar. It was just me and Mr. Ayzikov left. His wife was sent to Ponar. He'd been in the ghetto hospital during the roundups, and the doctors kept him hidden. When people ask me how I managed to avoid death, I don't know what to say. Intelligence made no difference in that situation. Everyone played a stupid game of blackjack with their life and took whatever blind luck doled out.

Suddenly the apartment felt too big. I asked Tevke the Tapeworm to join us so I wouldn't feel so lonely. He was also alone.

One evening the three of us were sitting together, sharing a few smuggled potatoes, when Mr. Ayzikov said, "Children, you've got to get out of the ghetto. The Germans are going to kill us all."

Continuing to peal his potato, Tevke the Tapeworm asked, "What are you talking about? Where can we go? The Germans are everywhere. Things in the ghetto aren't so bad—we can still get by."

With the patience he developed over years of teaching, Mr. Ayzikov explained, "Tevele, the Germans are going to murder every single one of us. They've confined us in the ghetto to make it easier."

Mr. Ayzikov had been sitting all bent over. Suddenly he straightened up and began speaking harshly, almost shouting. "I'm telling you to escape! Fight back! Take revenge!" He was breathing heavily. Tevke and I sat there completely dumbfounded. We didn't dare say a word.

After he calmed down a little, Mr. Ayzikov walked over to his bed. He hoisted the mattress, took out a little pouch, and gave it to us. "Here's my wife's fortune—a few gold ten-ruble coins. To help you on your journey. If either of you survive the war, go see my son in Palestine. You'll find his address at the bottom of the pouch. Tell him that his father, the Jewish teacher, ordered his students to fight back. Don't forget to tell him."

Then Mr. Ayzikov stopped talking and buried his grey head in his hands. We found him dead a few days later. He'd poisoned himself. Life in the ghetto was hard for a gentleman like him, especially when he was on his own.

★

It was easy for Mr. Ayzikov to say, "Fight back." It's true that people were leaving the ghetto, but to get to Belarus. There was a rumor that things were calm there. Anyone with money made a deal with some wheeler-dealer and they went. The whole thing didn't appeal to me. I found out that Kozshik Stankevitsh was running the show. They'd called him Kozshik the Scythe in the pool hall because he held his stick on the oblique. In the good years, he couldn't go near the pool table until he put his money down. And now he was the big savior. We found out later what happened to the transports.

I started to think about Vladek. Maybe he could help me. After all, we'd once been like family. We'd grown up together and spent years in the same cell. Been through good and bad together. Had he forgotten everything? Was he watching the massacres and drinking whiskey with the Germans? Maybe. In times like that, anything was possible.

My fears were eating away at me. Eventually I said to myself, "What do I have to lose? If he helps me get where I need to go, good. If not, I'll wash my hands of him and live with whatever God sends my way."

In the meantime, Tevke and I got into an argument. He asked me for a few ten-ruble coins to play cards. Four-eyed Estherke had opened a gambling joint and was taking stakes. Tevke said she had a room full of suckers just waiting to be taken for everything they were worth. Of course I didn't give him anything. That money meant a lot to me. I'd stuck it under a beam in the attic and every night, when I shoved my hand into the crack to check if it was still there, the satin pouch stroked my fingers like it was alive. It felt like Mr. Ayzikov's order to leave the ghetto and fight the Germans was pulsing between the coins. Tevke said he was a full partner. I told him if he came with me, he'd get half. He was angry and went to help Esther with her business. He tried convincing me that it made no sense to escape and look for death. As if we had to go looking when everyone was carrying death on their shoulders. But what did Tevke know? He had a glass of whisky in one hand, a playing card in the other, and he'd even snagged a caress or two from Estherke. What else did he need?

I began to really look for Vladek. I asked everyone who worked in the city to find out what they could about him. One day Osherke the Chimney

Sweep had news for me. He'd seen Vladek near the post office lugging sacks of mail. I told him to let Vladek know I needed him. Osherke was afraid. I couldn't blame him, but I was determined. I reminded him that he owed me something.

Osherke showed up two days later, looking very pleased with himself. He took some cream cheese from his bucket, scraped off the coal dust, put it on a piece of bread, and handed it to me. Then he told me he'd managed to see Vladek and have a few words with him.

A week went by and Vladek didn't show. Whenever I returned from work, I craned my head in every direction. Maybe Vladek was lurking beyond some corner. I started to think Osherke had conned me about Vladek and brought the cheese to be done with the whole business.

In Lukishke prison, I'd once hatched a plan to saw one of the bars in two, but here in the ghetto I was at a complete loss. I'd given up. I felt I was betraying Mr. Ayzikov, and that really bothered me.

Vladek finally showed up. When I'd given up all hope of ever seeing him, he walked into the ghetto with a municipal work brigade so he could speak to me. I remember every detail of our meeting. I was sitting at the table, sunk in my depression, when the door opened and in walked Vladek. He had a determined look on his face—his jaws were working. I stood up and walked over to him. He put his arms around me. We hugged each other for several minutes without saying a word. Then he walked away and dabbed his eyes with his handkerchief. Finally he said, "Okay, so here we are."

I got to the point immediately. "Vladek, I want to leave the ghetto. If you can't or don't want to help me, there's no point staying."

Vladek got angry. "You think I risked my life coming here to listen to that? Sit down. Tell me everything."

"First you have to promise you'll help me."

"You don't trust me?"

"What can I say? You turned against us in the good years. What should I think now that your people are close relatives at the big celebration?"

Banging his fist on the table, Vladek yelled, "Shut up." He stood up, grabbed me by the lapels and hissed through clenched jaws, "We didn't ask the Germans to come." Then he stepped back and spoke in a calmer voice, "Those animals will die. Things will change. Everything has become clear."

I told him what was happening. When I mentioned Mr. Ayzikov, he shook his head and muttered to himself, "He was a decent guy. Looked out for me in those years."

We agreed that he'd wait for me three days later, next to the Ostra Broma Chapel. He'd show me when it was time to follow him by kneeling and crossing himself in front of the religious icon above the entrance gate. I gave him a few pieces of gold to get me a revolver and some bullets. We agreed he'd take me to his mother, Yusef's widow. She was staying with relatives in a little village. From there, it wasn't far to the forest.

The day I left the ghetto, Vilna was radiant. Summer had arrived. There were green leaves on the trees on both sides of the street, just like in other years. It was the first time I'd gone anywhere without the yellow patch. I felt like everyone was looking straight at me, thinking they were seeing things. I swallowed my fear and walked to the Ostra Brama Chapel dressed up in my Shabbes suit with Mr. Ayzikov's pouch sewn into my belt.

Vladek was standing with a group of men and women, praying silently. I walked over to one of the church pillars and stared at the picture of Mary with her child. The colorful ribbons hanging from the gilded frame made me dizzy. I waited for Vladek to kneel and cross himself. The ten minutes I stood there felt like a year. I was terrified. The ribbons looked like huge red tongues, dancing wildly. I found myself babbling, "God, have mercy. Show me a miracle." Just then Vladek got down on one knee.

The crowd turned their attention to God. Vladek saw me. For a second our eyes met. I waited for him to walk further and then I followed him. We left the city.

Vladek didn't live to see liberation. So many years have passed, but his cries still ring in my ears, "Berke, *antloyf*. Get going." He was lying in the street covered in blood, but still he yelled. From a distance, he'd seen the two Gestapo soldiers arrest me at the edge of Ruzele to take me back to the city. Another person would have pretended he'd seen nothing and kept going. But Vladek turned back to shoot at them. For a moment they didn't know what was happening. Vladek mowed one of them down, but the second soldier released a volley from his automatic. Meanwhile I ran back and forth in zigzags through a potato field.

After the war, I learned that Vladek had set up a Polish organization in the post office to pocket important letters. I don't know why he didn't tell me when he came to the ghetto. Maybe he'd been sworn to silence.

I gave Mr. Ayzikov's letter to his son in Palestine. The gold helped me get weapons in the forest. I never saw Yusef's widow. To tell the truth, I didn't look very hard for her. I wouldn't have been able to tell her that her son died because of me.

9

The Lineage of the
Vilna Underworld

When Mishke Napoleon was murdered, all of Vilna mourned. Mishke was the last of the dynasty and the pride of Gitke-Toybe's Lane and part of Yatkever Street. Mishke was famous. Unlike the French Napoleon, who was short in stature, Mishke had grown very tall. But he was still a Napoleon.

When Khaymke, Zelik the Benefactor's younger son, murdered Mishke, he wasn't thinking about lineage. Zelik certainly had reason to be angry with Mishke. Mishke ate kishke at Zelik's tavern on Glezer Street and then blew his money on whisky at Orke Big Bucks', Zelik's blood enemy. But that was just an excuse. People in Vilna didn't slit each other's throats over something like that. Zelik suspected that Mishke had spilled the beans about an illicit deal to Orke Big Bucks so he could look like a big shot and get free whiskey. A tavern has open eyes.

Zelik the Benefactor had treated Mishke like one of his own and even gotten him involved in a smuggling operation. Zelik took Mishke in, but he got nothing in return. Mishke's needs were huge—he ran from one gang to the next. He had to maintain his reputation. After all, he was a Napoleon. He dressed in brand-new clothes, played billiards for high stakes, and drank whiskey with gusto.

When Zelik's cronies mentioned that Mishke was carousing at Orke Big Bucks', Zelik's blood boiled, especially after an important deal was bungled because Orke had stuck his hand in. Mishke was the only outsider who'd known about the deal. Zelik decided not to let Mishke cross his threshold ever again. If Mishke showed up, he'd break his legs. But wiping him out, doing him in—that hadn't even occurred to Zelik. After all, Zelik the Benefactor had his own reputation that he worked hard to maintain. He'd earned his position as the first trustee in the Lukishke prison synagogue fair and square.

But Khaymke, Zelik's younger son, wasn't willing to ignore Mishke's behavior. He'd wanted to show Vilna who ran the city and use Mishke Napoleon to teach Orke Big Bucks' gang a lesson. So Khaymke had lured Mishke to Pospieshk, outside Vilna, with the promise of a shot of schnapps and a shiksa for dessert. He'd slit Mishke's throat at Oginski's Estate, right next to the Viliye, and thrown him into the river. Khaymke had expected the current to drag Mishke downstream, past the city, and all trace of him to disappear.

But the elegant Mishke Napoleon had shown up for his rendezvous with the shiksa wearing a flowered tie. The tie reduced Khaymke's calculations to nothing. Mishke had, indeed, floated downstream from Pospieshk, but only as far as the Green Bridge, where his tie got caught in the barbed wire on a raft in the river. The next day Mishke was found, stretched out to his full length, under the bridge that connected the city with Shnipishok.

If Mishke had floated a little further downstream and reached the brickyard, perhaps all trace of him would have disappeared in the waters of the Viliye and Khaymke could have avoided prison. But Commissar Rovinsky, who knew the Vilna underworld like the back of his hand, quickly found his way to Pospieshk and the shiksa who Khaymke gave to Mishke along with the whiskey. After only a little nudge from Rovinsky, she sang about her meeting with Mishke.

At that point, Vilna remembered Mishke Napoleon's lineage. Mishke was the great-great-grandson of Leybe the Fence. Leybe had had an inn in Shnipishok, right next to the city gate. The real Napoleon had stayed in Leybe's inn in 1812, when he'd fled from the burning city of Moscow. Leybe started out as a shingle carrier and laid the roofs at Count Huvald's estate near Mayshegole, not far from Vilna. A French immigrant named Monsieur Duval, a refugee from the French Revolution, insinuated himself into Count Huvald's estate. The strapping fellow became a big shot in the count's palace. The servants whispered that he was sleeping with the countess.

Duval stole everything in sight, particularly silverware. He needed to market the stolen goods, so he befriended Leybe and even taught him to speak French. When there was nothing left to steal, Duval read French newspapers and magazines to the countess. After all, he was no simple peasant.

Leybe marketed the stolen goods in the city. That's how he became a fence. All the thieves in Vilna trusted him with their loot. Over time, Leybe prospered and opened an inn. He stopped laying shingles for Count Huvald, but his friendship with Duval continued until the Frenchman closed his eyes for the last time.

Shortly before his death, Duval read Leybe an article from a French newspaper that said that during his campaign in Palestine, Napoleon had issued a manifesto stating that the Jews should be given their land back. When Leybe heard this, he grabbed the newspaper and went to see Rabbi Abraham Danzig, the author of the book *Chayei adam*. At that time, Danzig was a judge in the rabbinic court in Vilna.

Rabbi Danzig had arrived in Vilna after traveling the world. He knew many languages and was a learned scholar. He read the article and said quietly, "It could be. Maybe not now, but the time will definitely come when we'll get our state back."

Judge Danzig was very impressed that Leybe had rushed to inform him about Napoleon's manifesto. He trusted Leybe and asked for his help whenever a crime was committed, when a widow was robbed or some other heinous act took place. People in Shnipishok began to greet Leybe the Fence with a hearty "Good morning." His word carried weight. After all, Rabbi Abraham Danzig didn't associate with just anyone.

But it was later, after Napoleon stayed in his inn, that Leybe's prestige really soared. It was freezing when the defeated Napoleon retreated from Moscow. The emperor was sick: his bladder was weak, his hemorrhoids were torturing him, and he had stomach cramps from the terrible food. When he showed up at Leybe the Fence's inn, he was frozen stiff.

Leybe recognized the emperor immediately. He'd seen him the summer before when he'd marched through Vilna with his army on his way to Moscow. Napoleon was really taken with the city, especially the Church of the Holy Anna, which rose above the Vilenke. He told his entourage that he wanted to carry the church back to Paris on his own shoulders. But after his defeat in Moscow, Napoleon wasn't thinking about the beauty of Vilna. All he wanted was a soft bed and a hot glass of tea.

No one was supposed to know that Napoleon was in Vilna because the Cossack divisions, who were pursuing the retreating French army, had reached the city. Leybe sent the emperor's cavalrymen to various houses nearby, but Napoleon stayed with him. Aside from a few of Leybe's friends, no one knew that the French emperor was lying in a bedroom at Leybe's inn with a nightcap on his head and a hot water bottle next to his belly. Leybe tried to persuade the judge, Rabbi Abraham Danzig, to remind Napoleon about his manifesto calling for a Jewish state. Danzig explained to Leybe, "That's all yesterday's noodles. The emperor has lost his throne and no longer has a say in the world."

Leybe's wife saved the emperor. She cooked him chicken soup and gave him an herbal drink for his bladder. She also brought him a salve for his hemorrhoids. Napoleon stayed at Leybe the Fence's inn for a few days and regained his strength. When he left Vilna, he bade Leybe a friendly farewell and gave him a gold watch. He also promised Leybe that as soon as he got his throne back, he'd make him a marquis and give him an estate in southern France. Later, Leybe's heirs argued over the gold watch until it disappeared into the deep pocket of a distant relative, some scoundrel who wasn't from Vilna.

That's how Leybe got the nickname Napoleon. A pale reflection from the name landed on Leybe's great-great-grandson Mishke, who Zelik the Benefactor's son Khaymke had finished off. Because of Mishke's reputation, Zelik the Benefactor, the chairman of the underworld organization the Golden Flag, was furious about the murder. The other members of the Golden Flag were also angry. At Itsik the Redhead's bar, their regular hangout, Tovshe the Angel shouted, "Vilna is not Chicago!"

The younger guys were also enraged. Mishke Napoleon had his own reputation and didn't need to rely on his great-great-grandfather, Leybe of Shnipishok. Mishke knew how to read and write. He wrote court appeals in beautiful Polish for anyone who asked. Every Friday he could be seen at the Mefitsei Haskalah Library on Zavalne Street borrowing a book for Shabbes. Mishke played billiards like a gentleman, giving weaker opponents a few balls. He kept up appearances and was never seen with girls who were unkempt. He always conducted himself with dignity.

Everyone in the organization knew that Zelik would never approve of the murder. They remembered when Leybovitsh's son was kidnapped by a group of gangsters for a ransom. (Leybovitsh was a wealthy Jew who owned a tannery.) Zelik the Benefactor had gotten involved and issued an order that the boy be returned without them getting a groschen. The entire business was too crass for Vilna.

In the meantime, Zelik ran to Commissar Rovinsky and asked if he could book Khaymke on a lesser charge. "Not, God forbid, without getting something in return. Could you write in the police report that the murder happened during a drunken brawl over the shiksa?" But Rovinsky was nervous. Word of the incident had already spread far and wide.

"If Pilsudski were still alive," thought Zelik, "he would take care of everything." But Pilsudski, the founder of the Polish Republic, had already been in the ground for two years. Zelik had been very friendly with Marshal Jozef Pilsudski. Over the years, with Pilsudski's help, Zelik the Benefactor got off of dozens of charges that could have landed him in prison. Pilsudski simply wrote a few words to the district attorney's office and the matter was dropped.

Everyone at Belvedere Castle, Pilsudski's Warsaw residence, knew Zelik. He was a frequent visitor. They had plenty of problems at the castle: problems with smuggled tobacco or with the locks that had been pried open at Zalkind's jewelry store. The police bled Pilsudski dry, so he came to Zelik for help.

Jozef Pilsudski owed Zelik the Benefactor a debt from the years before Poland became Poland. Pilsudski had wanted to organize military units to take up arms against the tsar and win back Poland's independence. To do that, he needed money for guns, ammunition, and uniforms. Pilsudski was in contact with weapons merchants all over Europe. They were all ready to deliver the illegal merchandise immediately, as long as they were paid. But Pilsudski had no money.

Pilsudski found out that twice a week, a train traveling from Warsaw to Petersburg passed through Bezdan, a small train station near Vilna. As well as passengers, the train also carried sacks of money. Pilsudski decided to enlist his friends to help him rob the train. It had to be done during the summer, when the roads were dry and they could escape into the woods that ran beside the railway tracks. Pilsudski had been born in the area and knew it well.

The trouble was that all of Pilsudski's helpers were students from fine intellectual families, ill-suited to robbing rail cars guarded by Russian gendarmes. Pilsudski needed someone from the underworld. In Vilna, someone pointed out Zelik the Benefactor to Pilsudski. At that time Zelik was young and strong, the leader of the Vilna gangsters. Pilsudski confided his plan about Bezdan to Zelik and suggested that he apply his capable hands to the task.

Zelik agreed to lend a hand. This wasn't because he was mixed up with politics but because he was furious with the tsarist regime for hanging Hirshke Lekert after Lekert had tried to assassinate Von Wahl, the governor general of Vilna. Six years had passed since the assassination attempt, but the young people of Vilna were still determined to take revenge.

Whenever a charge was laid against Zelik the Benefactor, Pilsudski wrote to the judge and explained that the accused had done a great service to the Polish Republic and the Polish army. He was right. Simply put, Zelik had saved Pilsudski's life during the raid on the Bezdan train station. Pilsudski left the railcar carrying a sack of money, but two armed gendarmes blocked his way. There was chaos in the train station. Bullets were flying in every direction. Ignoring the danger, Zelik threw an iron bar at the two gendarmes and laid them flat. Then he grabbed the heavy sack of money from Pilsudski and hollered, "*Antloyf*, blockhead. Get moving." Pilsudski, who understood a little Yiddish, didn't wait around. He immediately fled to the appointed spot, where a horse and wagon were waiting.

★

"If Pilsudski were still alive," thought Zelik, "he would have taken care of everything." But because Pilsudski's body had already been lying in the ground for two years, Zelik couldn't find anyone to help his son Khaymke, who'd murdered Mishke Napoleon. Khaymke was sentenced to sit in prison until the end of time. He served his sentence in the Lukishke prison in Vilna, but he wasn't there long.

When the Germans attacked Poland in 1939, Khaymke escaped from prison and got to Bialystok in the Soviet Union. There, he worked as a skinner in a slaughterhouse and sold a few hides on the black market every once in a while. In 1941, when the Germans attacked Russia, Khaymke was mobilized into the Red Army. He was awarded the highest distinction for his service and attained the rank of captain. After the war, Khaymke left for America where he worked his way up doing respectable work, selling scrap metal for smelting and not, God forbid, by illegal means. His children became doctors and lawyers and Khaymke himself, the son of Zelik the Benefactor, raises money for the state of Israel.

Where on this wide earth is there an underworld with a lineage like the Vilna underworld? Gone are the likes of Leybe Napoleon, Zelik the Benefactor, and Orke Big Bucks. Mishke Napoleon is also gone, but to this very day he stands before my eyes.

The Vilna underworld was truly an exceptional world.

10

Jewish Money

There was a Jew who lived at number 12 Daytshe Street, where the gate opened into the synagogue courtyard. No one knew how the man survived. And even though the entire building lay open like a deck of cards for Vintsenti the janitor, he couldn't give Tsokh the landlord a clear accounting of who the man was or what he did. At some point, the landlord must have known how the tenant would pay the rent. Based on the janitor's reports, the landlord always knew who could pay regularly and who might be stuck for cash.

Vintsenti estimated each renter's situation based on the number of times the person arrived home late at night and had to pay ten groschen to have the gate opened. If the janitor got no money from someone for a period of time, he took it as a sign that the renter was down on his luck and had to cut back wherever possible. The landlord would show up in his carriage, pulled by a midget of a horse that had been rejected by Tsinizeli's circus, to talk with his tenant about the rent. He'd suggest the tenant look for a cheaper apartment.

But the man always paid his rent in advance; he was never a day late. And no matter how often Tsokh asked the janitor where the man got his money, the goy never had an answer.

The man lived alone in his garret apartment, without family. He spent more time sitting at home than walking around the synagogue courtyard. Once Vintsenti went up to his apartment with the excuse that he had to see whether the gutters had come loose from the wall. He found the man sitting at his kitchen table that was strewn with colored crayons and pieces of white paper cut in the shape of wine-bottle labels.

Vintsenti informed Tsokh that the man survived by preparing labels for Borovsky's vinegar or for Berger's lemonade. It made no sense to Tsokh to make labels by hand rather than ordering them from a printer. He concluded that even though Vilna didn't lack for lunatics, here was one more crackpot who figured he could compete with the printshops. As long as the man made no trouble and paid his rent, it was no concern of Tsokh's.

Vilna certainly didn't lack for lunatics. The entire synagogue courtyard was crawling with mixed-up characters. All year long, Yudke the Maid-Chaser ran after all the young ladies, married or single, who walked through the courtyard. People whispered that he wasn't the slightest bit crazy. The proof—he ignored the old women. Then there was Gedalke the Cantor who screamed that they wouldn't let him sing from the lectern in the City Synagogue because he didn't have patent leather shoes. Crazy Rokhl, who fancied herself a high-society lady, went around in a crinoline she'd gotten from the Yiddish theater. Iserson preached from the steps of the Gravedigger's Synagogue that the doors to the lunatic asylums should be opened because that's where the sane people were.

The lunatics gathered at Sheyndel's teahouse, under the window of the little Gaon's Synagogue. Sheyndel was the only one who could handle them. But the man didn't go to Sheyndel's teahouse. He had nothing to do with that crazy bunch. The only place in the synagogue courtyard where he went was the Strashun Library.

When Khaykl Lunski, the librarian, noticed a man standing in the library doorway and gazing forlornly at the bookshelves, he offered him a chair at the public reading table. The man sat at the edge of the table for almost an hour, strumming his fingers like a condemned person. Lunski walked up to him and quietly asked, "Can I help you?"

The man looked up at the librarian with a pair of dull black eyes that suited his thin, shriveled face. "I would like to know . . ." he mumbled and then clammed up.

Khaykl encouraged him, "Please, tell me what you'd like to know. Don't be embarrassed. Just ask."

The man plucked up his courage and answered quietly, "I want to know about Jewish money."

"About Jewish money? Certainly. What do you want to know?"

"Well, we once had a land of Israel. What kind of money did they use?"

Khaykl Lunski responded to the man's question as naturally as if he'd asked the time of day. He took the man to an out-of-the-way corner and explained that he'd have to consult many books to learn about Jewish money. But because he'd come to the library, Lunski would share a few key details with him. "It is written in the Torah, in the passage called 'The Life of Sarah,' that Abraham our Father paid four hundred shekels for a plot in the Cave of Machpelah to bury his wife. When the Jews fought a war against the Romans, they cast coins with the same name, shekel."

"Shekel," the man interrupted Khaykl's lecture. "Shekel is really a beautiful word. Don't you agree?"

Khaykl Lunski began to understand why the man was so preoccupied with Jewish money. The furniture in his head had been moved around a little. But he explained his obsession with such seriousness and enthusiasm that Khaykl's smile faded in a matter of minutes.

The man explained that he lived alone. His sister in Johannesburg sent him money to cover his expenses. "I figure there'll be a Jewish state one day. All our troubles point in that direction. I've decided to create money for that state. A state without money is nothing."

He'd thought about it for a long time, but hadn't known how to begin, in particular what to call the money. Now he knew. "I'll call them shekels." He would sign each bill himself, like a real state president and write "Yiddish gelt" on it so people would know it was Jewish money. "Everything will be written in Yiddish, even though they'll speak Hebrew in the future state. But Yiddish works better because people understand it. Soon I'll start buying things with Jewish money. Once a month, I'll exchange the Jewish currency for Polish zlotys. That way I'll get Vilna Jews used to their own money as a first step towards having their own state."

When the man spoke about the future Jewish state, Khaykl Lunski noticed that his dull eyes lit up with a flame fanned by a distant wind carrying his childlike dream.

★

And so the man introduced Jewish money into Vilna. It wasn't easy. At first people threw his bills back at him. He was ignored by the *bobesnitzes*, the women who walked around the city selling large pots of beans with the ditty, "Enjoy hot beans, good enough for the kaiser." But they wouldn't exchange a ladleful of goods for Jewish money. It made no difference to them when the man insisted that he guaranteed every groschen. "I'll buy out the Jewish capital with Polish money every month."

Sarah-Merah, the senior *bobesnitze*, asked, "What are you doing? You can pay with real money and be done with it."

"And Jewish money isn't money?" asked the man.

Sarah-Merah looked at the other women and then handed the man a ladleful of the moist fluffy beans that melt in your mouth. She carefully examined both sides of the shekel he gave her and then stuffed it into an inner pocket of her undergarment. The other women consoled her, "You've lost a ladleful of beans, but you've made some lunatic happy."

Little by little, the entire area from Yiddishe Street all the way to the lumber market on Zavalne Street started using the Jewish bills. The exchange rate was a shekel for ten groschen. Every month the man showed up to redeem his bills for state zlotys. Lots of people accepted the Jewish money: Probe from the bakery, Taleykinski with his salami, Frumkin's pharmacy, and even the stall where they sold half a herring and cottage cheese by the spoonful.

The man set up shop on the steps of the Tiferes Bachurim Society every Wednesday between *Minkhe* and *Ma'ariv*, the afternoon and evening prayers. He also did business in the synagogue courtyard, where working guys gathered in the evening to learn a little Torah from Shmerele Sharafan the Preacher. To increase the circulation of Jewish money, the man exchanged his money in the courtyard at a cheaper rate, for only eight groschen. The passageway where they sold secondhand merchandise as well as Yoshe's kvass stand and Itske the Buckwheat Pudding's bar all accepted the shekel as legitimate currency. The man was constantly surrounded by customers. To people who didn't balk at buying only the pickling brine, the salt water from the herring keg, two groschen was real money.

There were piles of shekels at Sheyndel's teahouse. Just like other state presidents, the man donated alms to the beggars from the bills he'd created himself. Sheyndel used these contributions to hand out tea and buttermilk. Once she even told Iserson, the chief lunatic, that her teahouse was the place to exchange shekels, not Bunimovitsh's bank.

The man never failed to pay his debts. Each month, like clockwork, he walked through the city redeeming his Jewish money. Even Avromke the Anarchist, the chief used clothing dealer in the passageway, who didn't believe in God, believed absolutely in Jewish money and sold the man a pair of trousers in exchange for shekels.

The man walked around the synagogue courtyard like a banker, wearing new trousers, carrying a briefcase, and supplying everyone with Jewish money. Gedalke the Cantor called him up to the synagogue lectern to receive a blessing for a long and healthy life, as befits a state president. Vilna Jews began grumbling that the time had come for them to live like everyone else. "Why not? Are the Poles entitled to a country and not us? Even if the guy's a little crazy, running around like a president with his Jewish money, still, he's got something to say."

A large part of Vilna happily participated in the man's dream about Jewish money. But then calamity struck and the entire business collapsed. Someone started counterfeiting the man's money. When the man went to Probe's bakery to settle accounts, she gave him a wad of bills that weren't his. He immediately fainted and would have breathed his last had someone not poured a can of water over him. When he came to, he started screaming that those weren't his shekels. "They've counterfeited my currency." That's exactly what had happened.

On each of his shekels, the man had drawn a pair of tamed lions sporting boyish faces and holding a blue and white flag with paws as thin as chair legs. On the counterfeit notes, someone had dashed off two shaved beasts without manes, like cats on a garbage can. The man's signature was nothing more than chicken scratches, rather than the ornate letters befitting a president. And the counterfeit bills were printed on second-rate paper.

The man soon discovered counterfeit shekels at Sheyndel's teahouse and at Itsik the Buckwheat Pudding's bar. Probe was the first to create a scene, demanding money. Then others followed. When the man berated them for not bothering to examine the shekels, they explained, "We thought you'd put out a new series of bills." The biggest tragedy of all took place at Zlatinke's stall at the corner of Yiddishe Street. With seven counterfeit shekels, they cleaned out her entire supply of herring and other goods.

Just a week earlier, the man had been the hero of the synagogue court-yard, and now everyone was railing against him. "Imagine. He made half of Vilna crazy with his Jewish money, with his buying and selling, the devil only knows why."

In a single instant, the good times were over. People fought, accusing each other of terrible things, all because this crazy guy had led everyone around by the nose. The story reached the policeman with the red beard who patrolled the Jewish area, ate cholent at Velfke's restaurant, and was on a first-name basis with everyone. He wasn't happy with the situation. "How can you have Jewish money in Poland? What are my Jews think-ing?" Avromke the Anarchist barely managed to appease the policeman with a gift for his wife. Then Avromke informed the man in no uncertain terms that he had to stop distributing Jewish money and close his bank.

★

The man's presidency came to an end. He struggled to pay his debts for the counterfeit shekels and was left without a groschen. No matter how much money his sister sent, it wasn't enough to silence all the scream-ing mouths. If Sheyndel from the teahouse hadn't given the man food, he would have collapsed in the street. He sat at the bare table in his garret apartment, waiting for Vintsenti the janitor to show up and tell him to come down to the courtyard to have a talk with Tsokh the landlord. The man trembled with fear that Tsokh would ask him to leave because he was behind with the rent.

One morning, just before Shevuos, Tsokh showed up in his carriage and told Vintsenti to ask the man to come down to the courtyard for a little conversation. The landlord stood next to the gate of number 12 Day-tshe Street with his tenant, the former president of a Jewish state he had financed out of his own pocket, almost losing his shirt in the process. Tsokh asked about the rent. The man began to stammer, making excuses. Tsokh listened. The man's words flowed from his mouth like drops of water off a goose's back. Finally he whispered in a muffled tone, "Believe me, Mr. Tsokh, I didn't drink away the money. Someone took me for a ride and counterfeited my Jewish money. One day there'll be a state and this wrong won't be forgotten."

Tsokh looked at his renter as though seeing him for the first time. "One day there'll be a Jewish state. Hmmm. The man says it with such conviction. Maybe he's right." And Tsokh, who would have demanded rent from the sparrows on the roof, smiled and said, "Bring down your shekels—all of them. I'll accept them as rent until your sister sends money."

The man brought down a bundle of bills. The janitor couldn't believe his eyes when the landlord put the colored pieces of paper into his pockets, got into his carriage, and with a lively giddy up, urged his midget of a pony down the length of Daytshe Street. Tsokh glided over the Vilna streets toward a distant place where Jewish money would be vindicated. But he never arrived there. The Germans wiped his building off the face of the earth, together with the synagogue courtyard. He and the man with the Jewish money went to their deaths at Ponar with all their Jewish neighbors.

Only the shekel survived. It arrived at a distant shore far, far from Vilna, in the Jewish state that the man with the Jewish money had imagined.

11

Tall Tamara

The trouble began at Stovepipe Berta's. Berta had a brothel on Yatkever Street. It was a well-established spot, a business truly to envy. Because of Tamara, the place was always packed. Vilna guys couldn't get enough of her. On Friday evenings, Tamara didn't have a free moment.

But Berta was greedy. She wanted to grab ahold of the entire world. She started screaming at Tamara, turning her days into a living hell. First, she accused Tamara of talking too much, then of laughing when she shouldn't and ignoring customers. Tamara would have swallowed these insults because, after all, Berta's brothel was warm and cozy, but one Friday evening Berta did something that was too much to bear. So Tamara waited until after Shabbes and the next morning, first thing, she took her little trunk, packed her few dresses and all the installments of the novel *Regina the Spy* that she bought every Friday, and left Berta's.

The other girls in the trade told Tamara not to leave. After all, they'd all swallowed plenty of insults from the madams. It's true that Tamara wasn't one of the grand ladies of Vilna. She didn't have a dacha in Volokumpie, the beautiful area just outside Vilna, or spend her days in the Griner Sztral Café. But still, she had her self-respect.

So why did Tamara leave Berta's? Here's the story.

Every Friday evening, all of Tamara's regular suitors came to see her. There was Itsik the Hare, One-eared Zorekhke, Sender the Stutterer from Yiddishe Street, Mendel the Fireman, and plenty of others. They all sat on a bench in the foyer waiting their turn. They'd prepared for Shabbes and were washed, clean-shaven, and wore clean shirts.

Hershele the Porter, a dwarf whose feet didn't reach the floor, stood out from the others. Tamara caressed him differently than the others. He didn't grab her like she was the kugel in the cholent or insult her with vulgar language. He had beautiful manners and even brought her a little bag of candy every so often.

Women tore each other to pieces over men like Hershele. With his virility, he really needed to stay the entire night, but he could barely afford one visit. Afterward he lay with Tamara, his short legs stretched out to her ankles and asked, "Tamarinke, let me lie next to you for another moment. I want to feel like a married man." Tamara didn't say a word. She took advantage of Hershele's fantasy to catch her breath with a glass of cold tea she'd prepared earlier but not had time all evening to drink.

Meanwhile, Berta noticed several guys get up from the bench, preparing to leave. She heard Sender the Stutterer suggest they pay a visit to Four-eyed Esther's brothel on Zavalne Street, next to the lumber market. Sender stuttered, "Wh-wh-why should w-w-we sit here like h-h-hens on our eggs?"

And so, while Hershele was lying next to Tamara, luxuriating in the moment, Stovepipe Berta began banging her fist on Tamara's cubicle door and screaming, "Hershele! May you burn . . . You know where? Guys like you shouldn't come Friday night. Come during the week. You're ruining my business!"

Tamara dragged her little trunk to her friend Black Leyke's rented room on Shkaplerne Street, behind the train station. As she made her way to Leyke's, Tamara's entire being raged against Berta. "That woman has completely forgotten that a girl from the trade is also a person with a heart and feelings, like they sing in the Yiddish theater. I'm not just putting holes in matzoh, where the oven's burning hot and you have to shove the merchandise in as quick as possible. And who did that gangster Berta pick on? Little Hershele, the loneliest guy in Vilna. He doesn't have a single soul to cuddle him."

At Leyke's, Tamara had a little time to open a book. She was better educated than any of the other women in the trade. She even exchanged books at the Mefitsei Haskalah Library on Zavalne Street where she depended on Krasni, the librarian, to tell her what to read. He recommended a book called *The Lady of the Camellias* by a certain Dumas.

Tamara read the story to her friend Black Leyke. They both had a good cry, especially at the end when the camellia lady, who was no lady at all but ate the same bitter fruit as they did, earned from lying in strangers' beds, went to her death.

When Siomke Kagan, the reporter for the *Vilner tog* newspaper, had tried to establish a professional union for Vilna streetwalkers, Tamara was the first to speak up. She'd raised the issue of overtime, which the brothel owners, the pimps, refused to recognize. Like many of Siomke's projects, nothing came of the professional union. But from that day on, Tamara used strange words like "exploitation," "class consciousness," and "general strike."

★

Tamara left the profession and lived with Leyke on Shkaplerne, pretty far from the center of the city. Leyke supported herself from the occasional guests she brought home, elderly Jews who weren't from Vilna. She was able to offer her friend a bowl of soup and a glass of tea.

Tamara felt badly about leaning on Leyke, so she looked for a way to earn a groschen but her efforts didn't lead to much. Stovepipe Berta wanted to take her back, but Tamara had her self-respect. Tamara still saw Hershele the Porter, who stopped by Leyke's every so often to see her. But she got more love than money from Hershele.

Siomke Kagan really wanted to help Tamara. He saw her as a victim of the brutal capitalist system, which he had fought so bitterly throughout his youth. He tried once again to open a school for love in Vilna and wrote a long article in the newspaper about the project, underlining its importance and the honor that such a school, the first in the world, would bring to Vilna. He pointed out that, to add to the bargain, Vilna had two highly qualified educators: Tamara Shimeliski and Leah Brener, known in professional circles as Tall Tamara and Black Leyke. That's how Siomke Kagan introduced his readers to Tamara and Leyke.

Tamara didn't put any stock in Siomke's plan. It had been tried once before. They'd even ordered a sign, but nothing had come of the plan. Siomke didn't give up on the idea and searched the city for teaching material. He rummaged in Funk's, the small bookshop on Daytshe Street, until it dawned on him that Khaykl Lunski, the librarian at the Strashun Library, would be able to help him.

So Siomke went to the library to see what Khaykl could do for him. Khaykl Lunski walked to an out-of-the-way cupboard and took out a pamphlet that precisely spelled out the rules for having sex with a woman as well as what to do to pleasure a man. He stroked the pamphlet, reprinted from a manuscript that had to be a good few hundred years old. The author's name wasn't given. The pamphlet, written in Hebrew, was called "Ahava be-ta'anugim," which in plain Yiddish means "Pleasure in Love."

Siomke asked Lunski to translate the pamphlet into Yiddish, but Lunski dismissed the suggestion. Smiling into his thick beard, he murmured, "Ah Siomke, our sages have already given us the knowledge you're thinking about bringing to Vilna. You won't discover America with this."

It didn't help Siomke to argue that his idea would be a huge success. "It'll stir up the entire world—a school for love in Vilna, using pedagogic material from original Jewish sources, literally from rabbinic literature." Khaykl Lunski patiently heard Siomke out. Then he put the pamphlet back in the cupboard with the other rare religious books.

Tamara wasn't counting on Siomke and his fantasies, so she searched around for a way to earn a living. She'd already tried standing in the market with a basket of chicken giblets, but the market women sent her away, claiming there were already too many women selling their wares. Tamara went to work in the chicken shed plucking poultry. There, the women readily accepted her. Before long, she brought Black Leyke to work. The two women sat with their legs buried in mountains of chicken and goose feathers, reminiscing about the old days when they had earned more from one client than from ten plucked chickens. Leyke's boy Elinke ran around the chicken shed, making all the pluckers happy. (Elinke was the product of a casual encounter with some unknown Jew, but Leyke insisted the father was Elijah the Prophet.)

Siomke did do one thing for Tamara. He got her involved in a group that met secretly in a garret in Ramayles Courtyard on Yiddishe Street. A pair of trouser stitchers, several journeymen tailors, a few seamstresses, and a glove maker sat together for hours in the evenings. A young man with hungry eyes praised life in the great Soviet Union under the sun of the Stalinist constitution. A life to envy. Everyone in the group knew about Tamara's former life. The skinny young man presented her as a former slave of the bourgeois order.

★

Tall Tamara plucked chickens, attended the group from time to time, and tried to be happy with her life. It wasn't easy. Sometimes she felt the urge to slip on a low-cut blouse and her skirt with the deep slit that showed off her long legs, take her patent leather bag in hand, and stand on Savitsher Street, beside the Piccadilly Cinema, winking at passersby. But what if someone from the group happened to walk by? What would they say? In the garret on Yiddishe Street, they treated her like she'd never worked for Stovepipe Berta. Tamara made do with the chicken shed and taking books from the library.

Once, Krasni the librarian hurriedly handed Tamara a book of stories called *Folktales,* written by someone named Peretz. Tamara wanted to ask for something else right away—a novel, a love story with duels. But it was Friday and readers were rushing around and pushing and shoving to get a book for Shabbes, so Tamara put the *Folktales* into her basket and went to Leyke's on Shkaplerne.

That evening, the two friends sat at the table without saying a word, like a pair of discharged soldiers. Elinke was already asleep. The candles, which Leyke had started lighting every Shabbes after Elinke, her kaddish, was born, flickered on the chest of drawers. It was autumn. A light rain tapped on the low window looking out on a small garden, in the style of the wooden houses in the neighborhood. Tamara leafed through the *Folktales,* her full lips frowning uncertainly while Leyke silently collected the challah crumbs from the Shabbes tablecloth. She resented Tamara who'd been so absorbed in her book that she hadn't said a word all evening. Finally Leyke couldn't stand it any longer. "Tell me what's so interesting," she grumbled.

Tamara lifted her chestnut cat's eyes whose glance had so warmed the blood of Stovepipe Berta's customers. She smiled. "These stories are hard to understand. There are a lot of Hebrew words. You have to be a rabbi to figure them out."

"So why knock yourself out?" Leyke asked. "On Sunday you can ask for a book you won't have to kill yourself to read."

Tamara thought for a moment. Then she said, "There is one story I did understand. It's very . . . very . . . well . . . about . . ."

Leyke prodded her, "So tell me. About this. About that. About what?"

"It has a deep thought."

"What's the thought?"

"I have to read it to you."

Leyke was impatient. "Just tell me what it's about."

Tamara cleared her throat and began, "It's a story about three gifts. A Jew dies, but he isn't allowed into Paradise until he brings three gifts to heaven."

"What? They need gifts in heaven?"

Tamara became annoyed. "If you ask stupid questions, you won't get to hear the story. A writer wrote it. Just listen!"

"What's the problem? I can't even ask a question?"

Tamara dismissed Leyke with a wave of her hand and continued. "He brought a pin to heaven as a gift."

Leyke was afraid to ask why they'd need a pin in heaven, so she kept quiet. Tamara continued, "The dead Jew brought two more gifts: a little sack of earth from Israel and a yarmulke. The story about the pin really touched me."

Tamara closed the book. "Here's what happened. The priests condemned a rabbi's daughter to death because she was out on the street when a church procession passed by. Years ago, Jews weren't allowed to be on the streets where goyim lived. To punish the rabbi's daughter, they tied her braid to the tail of a wild horse so the beast could drag her through the cobblestone streets.

"When the priests asked the rabbi's daughter for her last wish, she wanted a pin. She pinned her dress to the flesh of her legs. That way, her dress wouldn't lift up in the wind and people wouldn't see her female parts when the horse charged through the streets."

Leyke grabbed her head. "To her very flesh?"

"Just like you heard it."

This didn't sit well with Leyke. "She was going to her death. Didn't she have other things to worry about? At that point, what difference did it make?"

Tamara disagreed. "That's exactly the point. She went to her death as a rabbi's daughter, not a shameless woman." Leyke shrugged and frowned, not convinced that the rabbi's daughter in Peretz's story had done the right thing.

The two friends, who regularly removed their clothes for strange men, went to bed, each drawing her own conclusion about the story.

★

Tamara stayed in the chicken shed surrounded by feathers until the war broke out. The Germans and Russians divided up Poland. On the nineteenth of September 1939, on a beautiful morning at the beginning of autumn, tanks with red five-pointed stars on their steel sides appeared on the streets of Vilna. Tamara shook the down feathers from her apron and ran along with everyone else to see the miracle. The entire group from the garret in Ramayles Courtyard on Yiddishe Street danced around the tanks like close relatives at a long-anticipated wedding.

But the party didn't last long. In total, six weeks. Then the Russians gave the city to the Lithuanians as a gift. The Russian tanks, looking like well-fed turtles, snuck out of Vilna in the middle of the night. The *klumpes*, as the Lithuanians were called in Vilna, enjoyed the gift for eight months, until the Soviets decided to return and free them from the problems of running their own state. This took place on the fifteenth of June 1940.

That's when the members of the group that met in Ramayles Courtyard really came to life. Shayke Eykher, who lost an arm in the Spanish Civil War, became the director of the city buses. Lam, a men's hat cleaner, was appointed manager of a movie theater. Brayke the trouser tailor took over Berger's soda water plant. Vilna was drenched in the odor of the dictatorship of the proletariat. Everyone said that Tamara had had leftist sympathies from way back. The new regime installed her in a meat cooperative warehouse.

Black Leyke did better than anyone else. She ensnared a lieutenant from the Red Army, a fine *sheygetz*. Not a big drinker. He immediately bought her a white shawl, the type worn by the lieutenant's wives, and even went to live with her on Shkaplerne Street. The shawl lay on Leyke's locks like snow on a hill of smoldering coals. It was a pleasure to look at her.

Leyke fit right in with the other garrison wives. She quickly picked up bits of Russian, enough to explain to her cronies the difference between a long nightgown and a formal gown. The ladies, who'd just arrived in Vilna, were sure you could go dancing in the officer's club in a nightgown. With the lieutenant, Leyke became more refined and took on style. Vilna didn't recognize her.

Tamara was seen with various officers, but nothing stuck. She found herself a tiny room on Shavelske Street so she wouldn't interfere with her friend's good fortune. It really was good fortune. Thanks to the lieutenant, Leyke and her son were saved. During the Soviet retreat from Vilna in 1941, the lieutenant placed them on a military truck that took them deep into the hinterland. Leyke wanted to take Tamara with them, but because of the urgency of the situation and the general turmoil, it didn't happen. The lieutenant cursed in the name of his mother, screaming that the German troops could show up at any moment.

And Tall Tamara? She didn't have to suffer under the Germans for long. On Wednesday, the seventeenth of September 1941, only ten days after the Jews of Vilna were driven into the ghetto, Tamara stood with almost 1,300 Jews on the field at Ponar—the place not far from the city where the Germans murdered the Vilna Jews.

Tamara had had her own special luck. They didn't drive her into the ghetto; she was already there. Shavelske Street lay in the heart of the Vilna ghetto.

During the first months of the brutal German rule of Vilna, Tamara tried her hand at various things. She sold chicken giblets and got what she could from Hershele the Porter. Until she fell, as if into a whirlpool, between the evil decrees stipulating that to stay alive she needed a certificate from the Germans, called a *Schein*, allowing her to work and stay alive.

Tamara stood with the other women on the field at Ponar, gazing into the distance. Who could she have been thinking about? She was absolutely alone. She had no one. She'd been abandoned as a child and was raised in an orphanage. She'd earned her living as a waitress for Zuske the Professor in his bar on Konske Street, until he told her that with her legs, she could make good money if she stood on a street corner.

★

The order was given to undress.

Tamara did not undress. She dug her fingernails into the soft flesh of her plump arms without giving any indication that she would undo even a button. Tamara refused to obey the German who stood opposite her with his machine gun. She was taller than him. Standing in her cotton dress with its red and blue flowers, she looked him straight in the eye without reacting to his shouting. He didn't shout for long. A moment later Tamara lay in the sand, felled by a hail of bullets.

That's how Tall Tamara, the last Jewish streetwalker in Vilna, met her death.

A woman who was wounded and managed to crawl out of the pit at Ponar during the night and return to the ghetto told us what had happened.

12

The Great Love
of Mr. Gershteyn

After Siomke Kagan drove the flirtatious actress Regina Tsuker out of town with his review in the *Vilner tog* newspaper, the theater curtain stayed closed. Siomke was a harsh reviewer. He didn't tolerate any hanky-panky. If a touring actor in Vilna dared utter a coarse word on stage, he found himself impaled on the tip of Siomke's pen. And the clever bastard had quite the pen, a veritable sword.

No one was surprised when Dina Halperin came within a hair's breadth of suffering the same fate as Regina Tsuker had.

When Dina Halperin and her partner Sam Bronetsky came to Vilna to save the season, the troupe came back to life. Had their situation lasted any longer, the actors wouldn't have been able to buy what they needed for Passover. Even Velfke Usian, with his restaurant on Yiddishe Street, had started to grumble: "How long should I keep feeding the actors on credit?"

During Passover the theater revived. Dina Halperin and Sam Bronetsky staged a melodrama with singing and dancing. It was a hit—the public bought tickets. Dina danced and sang, and Sam played the seducer. But Siomke Kagan screwed up his nose, especially at a few of the lines from one of Dina's songs. She sang,

> Sometimes when I see a redhead,
> Seems to me his pencil lacks lead.
> I don't want a man with hair bright red,
> But a swarthy black-haired man instead.

At first Siomke planned to submit a review tearing the performance to shreds. He wrote the sentences: "Songs containing double entendres that are an affront to good taste and to all redheads shouldn't be sung in Vilna. Everyone understands precisely what is meant by 'his pencil lacks lead.'"

But Siomke decided to take another look at the performance. He watched Dina Halperin perform with so much charm, sharing her smile with each and every person in the dark hall. So Siomke went to speak with the visiting actress about changing the lyrics of the song before he gave his review to the *Vilner tog*.

The next day Dina Halperin sang,

> "I quickly grow tired of a redhead.
> Looks like *tsimmes* in a pan of lead.
> No, I don't want no redhead,
> But a swarthy black-haired man instead."

Siomke Kagan had toned down the original. He tore up his previous review.

Siomke became a regular backstage visitor. He was really taken with Dina Halperin. She had a beautiful alabaster face and black almond-shaped eyes with a dewy radiance like the waters of the Viliye at dawn on a summer morning. She was also well-read, often with a book in hand.

There was no lack of beautiful girls in Vilna. You could fill a second city with them. Siomke, a slender youth with an eagle nose, only had to stretch out his hand, and one of them would happily climb the Hill of the Crosses in the late evening with him. But Siomke ignored them all. He was only interested in spending time with Dina.

Bronetsky wasn't very happy with this situation. He muttered, "Some fool shows up before every performance and drives us all crazy." It was true that Siomke had written a very good review, but he'd noted that an actress like Dina Halperin deserved a better repertoire. Bronetsky took this as a personal affront. He only knew how to sing ditties and tap dance, but not how to play King Lear. Mendke the stage manager, who understood more about the theater than the actors, told Bronetsky not to interfere. "Just let Siomke run around between the sets. Don't start up with the press."

Siomke brought his friend, Mr. Gershteyn the teacher, to a performance. Usually, Mr. Gershteyn only attended the theater when the Yung-teyater Company from Warsaw performed *Cry Out, China*. He ignored shows like *With Open Eyes* and *The Model*. But Siomke really wanted to introduce Mr. Gershteyn to Dina. Afterward, Mendke joked that Siomke had brought a tomcat to pass judgment on a bowl of sour cream.

Siomke was a good few years younger than the teacher, but this in no way interfered with their friendship. However, standing beside Mr. Gershteyn, Siomke looked like a rooster beside a pheasant. Dina Halperin took one look at Mr. Gershteyn and completely forgot that Siomke, her admirer, was standing right next to the teacher. Dina had good taste. Even though Siomke Kagan was well-built, Mr. Gershteyn, with his aristocratic mustache and his thick head of hair that was graying at the temples, completely outshone him. It took only an instant for Siomke to feel completely extraneous. He really regretted dragging the teacher to meet Dina, but there was no turning back.

Dina struck up a conversation with Mr. Gershteyn and completely forgot about Siomke. Mr. Gershteyn was infatuated with the actress. If Bombe, the assistant director, hadn't shouted that the curtain was about to go up, Dina and Mr. Gershteyn would have kept right on talking. They decided to get together at Velfke Usian's restaurant after the performance to celebrate their meeting with tea and a frying pan of latkes.

★

Siomke didn't do Mr. Gershteyn any great favor when he introduced him to Dina Halperin. The teacher was smitten with the actress from the first handshake. It wasn't surprising. Dina Halperin's smile, her pearly Yiddish with a hint of a Warsaw accent, and everything about her appearance disturbed the bachelor's emotions.

Dina became a regular visitor at the Re'al Gymnasium where Mr. Gershteyn taught and conducted the student choir. Mr. Sher, the drawing teacher, said that Dina Halperin didn't have a single unnecessary gram of flesh on her. "Every part of her body is perfectly shaped. She carries herself like a mature woman only recently emerged from her youth."

Siomke saw that there wasn't even a crack left for him between Dina Halperin and Mr. Gershteyn. He took his knapsack and set out for Trok where the Gypsy camp stood next to the lake. Siomke fit right in there. He knew the Gypsy language and even drank with Kviek the Gypsy king. Siomke also had a special relationship with Kviek's daughter. At night, she taught him to whisper in her language.

Mr. Gershteyn was completely infatuated with Dina Halperin, so he had no regrets about his friend's departure. There was only one problem—the pair had no place to be alone. The teacher lived on Literatzke Lane with his spinster sister. Like her brother, she'd given up on ever getting together with anyone. She ran his modest home and the teacher couldn't imagine anything else.

Sam Bronetsky watched their every move. He kept badgering Dina with the same questions. "Where were you? Why are you running around the city? What business do you have at the Re'al Gymnasium? You want to be a teacher? Being an actress isn't good enough for you?"

Dina was drawn to Mr. Gershteyn like to a magnet. This wasn't because of his masculinity, nor his sturdy gait with his walking stick, nor his gentle touch. Rather, his conversations that had no connection to premieres, successful theater box offices, or plans for a new musical comedy transported her to imaginary worlds where songs are everywhere and children reign.

Everyone in Vilna had their eyes on Mr. Gershteyn and Dina Halperin. The students at the Re'al Gymnasium watched Dina Halperin stroll around the schoolyard during recess time, hanging on Mr. Gershteyn's arm and talking passionately. They knew their teacher doted on the actress. He wouldn't spend time with just any woman. That's precisely why he'd remained a bachelor: he was too picky.

★

Mr. Gershteyn and Dina Halperin walked down Daytshe Street toward Velfke Usian's restaurant. The troupe had decided to eat there. Mr. Gershteyn really wanted to go home, but Dina urged him to go to Velfke's with her and he couldn't deny her wishes. The pair walked down an aisle formed by the hucksters, the guys who lure customers into the ready-made clothing stores. Winking at each other, the jokers lined up on both sides of the street. Sarah Klok left her sewing notions shop, swelling the crowd with her little group of salesgirls. Everyone was enamored with the couple. Tsalel the Nose, the biggest ready-to-wear clothing merchant, said the pair was made to measure. "You can't do better." Only Sarah Klok, who was no great beauty (people said she needed to shave), grumbled about the romance.

Mr. Gershteyn and Dina Halperin walked together. No one on Daytshe Street begrudged the teacher his choice. They knew him from the choir concerts he conducted of the Society of Friends of the Re'al Gymnasium. For a beautiful piece of music or a lovely song, people in Vilna were willing to walk all the way to Lipuvke at the edge of the city.

There was someone else who was unhappy with the romance: Sam Bronetsky. He happened to be leaving Bendel's barbershop next to the German church when he noticed the couple on the other side of the street. Dina and the teacher didn't see him. They were too wrapped up with each other.

Daytshe Street was bustling. It was Tuesday, a market day. People were buying and selling trousers, nails, rope, and calico dresses. There was plenty to buy on Daytshe Street, especially because the day had turned out sunny and clear, typical of the weeks after Passover. The recent rain had washed all the signs clean, and the Yiddish letters and the pictures of gloves, corsets, and double-breasted suits were glowing. People were running around in the courtyards on their way to dentists, dressmakers, shoemakers, and tinsmiths. Business was brisk. Customers searching for bargains pushed and shoved each other at every cart laden with merchandise and at every corner stall.

In the midst of this din, Sam Bronetsky searched for the right words to say to Dina. He was furious. He'd already told her a number of times to stop. Dina had explained to him that Vilna was no ordinary town. "It's important to get involved with a little culture here. Mr. Yankev Gershteyn (this is how she referred to him, using his full name) is well respected in Vilna. He's a musician and a conductor. My involvement with him brings honor to our entire troupe."

Sam Bronetsky would have gladly forgone the honor, but he didn't want to provoke Dina. After all, she drew the audiences, not him. "She's young and there are no children. She could easily say to me, 'Good-bye and good luck.' Things like that have happened in the theater world." But the entire business with Gershteyn was more than Bronetsky could bear. He would have to speak with Dina. This could not continue.

Bronetsky made his decision and then crossed the street. On his way to the restaurant, he nearly got caught in the shaft of Shimon the Coachman's carriage. The horse whinnied as if to make fun of the actor. If that wasn't enough, from his coach box Shimon cursed people who don't bother to look where they're going.

Sam Bronetsky arrived at the restaurant feeling more upset than he would have liked. But there was no arguing at Velfke's. The actors slipped Bronetsky a few shots of whisky. They toasted Dina Halperin's success. They didn't forget Bronetsky. The troupe had made money and treated themselves to a second round of chopped liver with *griven*. The restaurant was hopping, and Bronetsky's anger subsided. Mr. Gershteyn was sipping a glass of wine and enjoying himself. He didn't get too chummy with the actors, who also behaved themselves. They looked up to Mr. Gershteyn, so they were careful to watch their tongues and not let fly with words better left unsaid.

Mr. Gershteyn walked toward his home on Literatzke Lane, brooding over the situation with Dina. "It's true that Sam Bronetsky didn't say anything at Velfke's restaurant, but his eyes spoke volumes. And no wonder. What man would want to suffer that? But really, what's the big sin? After all, nothing's going on."

Mr. Gershteyn didn't want to fool himself. Deep in his heart he knew full well this wasn't "nothing." He was completely focused on Dina and thought of nothing else.

Acknowledging the situation did nothing to ease the teacher's mind. He knew his involvement with the actress had become a major topic of conversation in Vilna. As he walked home, he went over these thoughts in his mind. At the corner of Literatzke Lane he berated himself: "You old goat, you're making a complete fool of yourself. Why are your thoughts so muddled?" But his heart refused to listen. The slightest reminder of Dina Halperin set it pounding madly, driving away all reason.

★

The theater took a few days break. Sam Bronetsky left for Warsaw to arrange a tour of Romania. The director of the Bucharest theatre was waiting for him there. At first, Sam Bronetsky had insisted Dina go with him, but she'd said she didn't have the strength. "I deserve a little rest after performing night after night." So Bronetsky relented and traveled on his own. He figured nothing could happen in just a few days. "I'll be back before she does anything with the teacher."

Mr. Gershteyn and Dina were both in the city. He was hoping to take her to Verek, outside of Vilna. It was just before Shevuos and everything was green. The sun was shining, but it wasn't too hot. Everyone in the city was enthralled with the scent of the blooming lilacs adorning the treetops on every street. "Imagine what it's like now in Verek," Mr. Gershteyn said to Dina, hoping she'd go with him.

The teacher rescheduled all his lessons to the morning. During the long recess, he strode off with his walking stick in hand to get Dina. She was wearing a white dress with a low-cut neckline and a straw hat with a wide brim. Her beauty took the teacher's breath away. They walked to the Viliye and boarded the steamship Smigly for the trip upstream to Verek.

Standing on the upper deck of the steamship, the pair leaned over the railing to watch the water pour out from under the paddlewheel. Dina was delighted watching the roiling water and the shore of the Viliye, where the willows, bent like old men, struggled for a piece of ground among the proud white birches. She breathed deeply, exhilarated by the breeze that opened up the folds of her dress like a sail on a sunny outing. Dina realized how good it felt to take a break from performing and escape to sunny freedom. She quietly pressed Mr. Gershteyn's hand to thank him for his invitation.

When they arrived in Verek, Mr. Gershteyn wanted to take Dina to the local palace. From the lovely terrace in the palace park you could see all of the surrounding area. But Dina just wanted to walk along a path by the water that led to the edge of the forest. She sat under the first tree they encountered. But first, Mr. Gershteyn spread his jacket out on the mossy ground to protect her white dress. They sat there without speaking, watching a ladybug crawl lazily towards one of Dina's knees.

There wasn't another soul in sight. The teacher didn't know what to do. Should he take her hand? Dare he place a kiss on her blushing cheek? He was inexperienced with the opposite sex and his bachelor ways encased him like the bark of a tree. He and Dina were absorbed in a conversation whose thread kept breaking. Finally Dina laughed and said, "How about something to eat?" They walked to the inn to get potatoes with buttermilk and fresh radishes.

The sun began to set. Mr. Gershteyn and Dina Halperin sat on the balcony of the inn and watched the shadows snuggling into the vines and climbing the wall of their refuge. The innkeeper had recognized Mr. Gershteyn from his field trips with the gymnasium students. She'd sent him and his lady friend up to the second floor where there were rooms for rent. The worldly *goye*, who could recognize a couple in love from kilometers away, assumed they'd stay the night. But they simply sat on the balcony as though nothing was going on between them and said nothing to the innkeeper.

They failed to notice the moon replace the sun and bathe the balcony in a pale light that nestled up to the window. Nightingales began singing as though at the command of an invisible conductor. When one bird became silent, another started up. "In the area around Vilna," the teacher explained to Dina, "the nightingales have always sung beautifully, especially in Verek, on the roof of the Slomyanke Inn."

Dina Halperin's dress blended with the milky white moonlight. Her low-cut neckline made it impossible for the teacher to collect his thoughts. Wanting to stretch her limbs a little, Dina arched backwards with her arms extended. A strap from her brassiere slipped off her shoulder. Mr. Gershteyn moved towards her, nestling his face in the valley between her breasts. A few minutes passed before he was able to whisper, "Dina, my love. You are my great love." Dina pressed his body to her. They were frozen in the theatrical glow of the moonlight with the nightingales singing on the roof of the inn.

They just managed to catch the last steamship back to Vilna. They were met by a city in deep darkness.

Sam Bronetsky found out about Dina Halperin's outing with Mr. Gershteyn. The actors said that Zisel, the hotel porter, supplied Bronetsky with the information. In her innocence, Dina had announced that she was going to Verek. If anyone asked about her, she wanted them to know where she was and that there was no reason to worry because she wasn't alone.

However it happened, when Sam Bronetsky found out, he was furious. People heard shouts coming from their hotel room. Bronetsky had summoned all his strength and restrained himself at Velfke's restaurant, but he was now determined to put an end to the romance.

One school day during the long recess, the students spotted Sam Bronetsky standing in one corner of the large schoolyard, speaking with Mr. Gershteyn. The yard was instantly quiet. All the playing, the shouting, the running, and the jousting stopped immediately.

Mr. Gershteyn didn't say a single word to interrupt Sam Bronetsky's tirade. He just nodded his head. The students from his class stood on the other side of the yard, squeezed against each other like a legion, watching to make sure the lowbrow actor didn't try to hurt their beloved teacher. They knew full well what Sam Bronetsky was talking about. They saw the actor's hands shake. They also saw how distressed Mr. Gershteyn was. Every so often he stroked his mustache and looked around, as though searching for someone to rescue him from the unpleasant discussion.

After talking for a good few minutes, Sam Bronetsky left the schoolyard. Mr. Gershteyn stood by himself until the bell rang. None of his students dared approach their teacher whose pat on the head could sweeten a day of study.

After his conversation with Sam Bronetsky, Mr. Gershteyn stopped seeing Dina Halperin. Meanwhile, the theatrical run came to an end and the couple prepared to leave Vilna. The night of the final performance, Velfke Usian's restaurant was bustling, with one toast after the next. The actors were having a very good time. Sam Bronetsky bought a round of whiskey. There were plenty of speeches.

Only Mr. Gershteyn was missing; he had stayed home. After Dina Halperin and Sam Bronetsky left the city, Mr. Gershteyn confided to his friend Siomke Kagan that he'd promised Bronetsky to stop seeing Dina. To soothe his aching heart, Mr. Gershteyn had only a note that his sister had found under the entry door of their little home on Literatzke Lane. The note read,

> Dear Yankev (Mr. Gershteyn):
>
> I do not take the beauty of the city with me, nor the warm reception I received here. I take nothing with me except your breath on my naked breast in Verek. I will carry that with me through the entire world.
> Farewell,
> Dina.

The June evening erased all memory of rain and cold. The trees on Literatzke Lane held their breath, listening to the silence. Summer slumbered on the cool stones at the entrance to the Church of the Holy Anna.

Mr. Gershteyn took his concertina out of its case, sat down on his narrow bed, and from the inner recesses of his instrument, drew the melody of a song he'd prepared for the choir. The words of the song expressed his own painful feelings. "Autumn has arrived, the trees and flowers wither."

Translator's Note

In December 2008, I spoke with Liba Augenfeld, a native of Vilna. When the Nazis invaded Vilna in June 1941, Liba was about to graduate from the Re'al Gymnasium. Mr. Gershteyn was one of her teachers. "I was in his student choir. He had two choirs, one for students in the Re'al Gymnasium and one for people who were no longer in school." Liba told me that she and the other students had heard their teacher was having a romance with Dina Halperin. "He used to conduct us kids in a song that went, 'Di netsn in shifl' [the nets in the little boat]. To tease him, we used to sing, 'Di ne-e-e-e- Hal-per-in.'"

13

The Tree beside the Theater

For years, my mother complained that Regina Tsunzer had destroyed the business. My mother was actually jealous of the actress. Regina Tsunzer called my father the Caucasus Count because of his trimmed beard and burning black eyes. And if that wasn't enough, when she spoke to him, she brushed against him like a kitten after her little saucer of milk.

Aside from full-blooded talent, Regina Tsunzer also possessed a full bosom and was generously endowed in her other limbs. It wasn't surprising that my mother thought the actress was nothing but trouble. She warned my father, "Moyshe, when that woman wiggles her rear end on stage, respectable people turn up their noses."

Things turned out exactly as my mother had predicted. Not only did Regina Tsunzer show off her assets, she also sang the following song:

> Though you've come in such haste,
> And sharpened your knife—'twas a waste.
> The seeds were already well placed,
> And your timing, so badly paced.

Regina Tsunzer also winked lewdly at the audience. The people in the balcony were delighted. They clapped their hands and begged for more. Those in the parterre were, however, not impressed. That's where Siomke Kagan, the theater critic from the *Vilner tog* newspaper, sat. He decided the song wasn't appropriate for Vilna. Immediately after the performance, he went to the editorial offices of the newspaper and wrote a damning review, claiming the performance flirted with debauchery. "The shameless song severs the audience from their social problems. Moreover, the verse about the sharpened knife appeals to people's basest instincts. The entire performance is a threat to Yiddish culture, which has its organizational center in Vilna."

If that wasn't enough, the next morning Siomke went to the Re'al Gymnasium and asked his friend, Mr. Gershteyn, to bring his entire class to the theater and have the children shout in unison, "Down with trashy theater."

Zeyben the chimney sweep wrote a letter to the editor threatening to bury Siomke in soot. "Regina Tsunzer is a world-class dish. We should kiss every one of her limbs. Because of her, the audience managed to recover after the Yung-teyater Company's play, *Cry Out, China.* Who is Siomke anyways to measure the level of people's instincts?"

Zeyben wasn't the only one to stand up for Regina Tsunzer, but it made no difference. The actress was driven out of the city. High culture had triumphed. My mother forgot her jealousy. She hoped Siomke would grow a wart on the tip of his pen for ruining the theater season.

The theater had no female lead. My father sat at the edge of the sofa, stroking his beard, rubbing one of his eyebrows, and trying to figure out how to get the theater going again. Unable to think of anything, he went to Velfke's restaurant on Yiddishe Street, where actors got together and ate on credit.

Kuznietsov, the classical actor who always played a banker dressed in a Shabbes suit, was the first to intercept him. When he saw my father's forlorn look, Kuznietsov said, "I propose a drink before we try to solve your problems." The ragtag gang of actors unanimously agreed. They took over one of the tables and told Velfke to bring some spleen and soldier's kasha from the kitchen.

After the first glass, the actors began suggesting plays to get the box office open again. *Khashie the Orphan* had already been staged. They couldn't revive *Pauperson and Hungryman* because Shtraytman the comic had left Vilna to try his luck in Argentina. *Where Are My Children?* was certainly a good play, but it needed music and the musicians were refusing to perform until they were paid what they were owed from Regina Tsunzer's run. Stufel, the conductor and first violin, announced that he would no longer draw his bow simply for the sake of art. Orliek stood up and asked to have his say. He suggested they stage a play with national themes. "Lately there's been pressure from all sides and no way for people to earn a living. We have to provide people with hope."

Orliek was a very intelligent actor. He wore glasses, and his word carried weight. People in the theater knew he was a Zionist who dreamt about the state of Israel. Orliek proposed they remount *Bar-Kochba*. My father agreed immediately. They wouldn't have to lay out any money. The cardboard mountains were still lying around from the opera, *Shulamit*. Zakovitsh, the prop manager, would only have to get wooden lances for the Jewish army and they'd be set.

There was one thing bothering my father. Orliek wanted to play the role of Bar-Kochba and he wore glasses. If Siomke Kagan had criticized Regina Tsunzer for a silly little song, what would he do when he saw Bar-Kochba in glasses? He'd heap scorn on the entire theater. But Orliek needed his glasses. Without them, he couldn't see a centimeter in front of himself. He'd tried removing his glasses during the love scene in *The Rose of Istanbul* and almost killed himself when he tripped over a set of stairs Mendke the stagehand had left lying around.

My father had no choice. He had to let Orliek play the lead. The theater was dark and deserted in the middle of the season. The actors were wandering around without a groschen and threatening to dissolve the troupe.

Then Bombe, a longtime member of Father's troupe and a loyal soul, spoke to Father. He complained that he wasn't feeling well. Dr. Yedvabnik had told him to take a little holiday and get a change of air. He wanted an advance. My father looked at Bombe with sad black eyes and shook his head. He didn't know what to say. The cashbox was empty, cleaned out to the last groschen. Then my father had an idea. He said to Bombe, "An advance would rob you of your dignity. You know full well that the season has collapsed. But we'll take care of your need for a change of air in the best possible way. You've been performing in *The Yeshiva Student* and sitting in a tiny synagogue for four acts. Now you'll perform in the mountains and fields of *Bar-Kochba*. You'll get a change of air and recover quickly."

Acting the imp, my father got Bombe to tell everybody at Velfke's the story. They split their sides laughing. For years, the actors would tease Bombe, "You want a change of air? There's a great play with lots of forests."

★

They produced *Bar-Kochba*. Orliek wiped his glasses on his red cape and dispatched the people, two pale extras wearing short tunics and armed with lances, to save Jerusalem. Siomke Kagan didn't write anything. After the previous catastrophe, he decided to do nothing, but it didn't help. Orliek couldn't carry the play. The audiences just didn't believe he was Bar-Kochba. They didn't applaud, not even at the Shabbes matinee performances. Children cried in the middle of the play, frightened by the hullabaloo on stage. By Sunday, everyone in the lumber market knew there was no singing or dancing in *Bar-Kochba*, just talking.

For years, Orliek had played the elegant seducer who got a girl pregnant by the end of the second act and then walked out on her. Now he was running around on stage with sandals on his hairy legs and a helmet decorated with a little broom. It just wasn't Orliek. The play didn't work.

My father sat alone in the theater early one morning. He looked at the empty seats and thought about his situation. A permanent bulb burned on the stage, throwing more shadow than light onto the pile of props. A rare smile lost itself between my father's beard and mustache. Here was his entire fortune, a few pieces of wood and painted canvas. If he'd stayed in the print shop, he'd be a rich man. My mother reminded him of this every time she couldn't cover expenses. But everything in the print shop, including the machines and the letters, was black, and everything in the theater was colorful, even the poverty.

My father so loved sunny colors. He created the posters himself—he knew the printing trade better than any of the printers. He'd worked for a number of years in fine art print shops in Frankfurt am Main. Every Friday, he'd stood at the type cases and dreamt up announcements from his imagination. The printers had admired his work, but they'd failed to see the point of a poster that didn't bring in an audience. Now my father had to maintain a home with a wife, six children, and an entire troupe. In the early mornings, sitting alone in the theater, my father had decided more than once to give it all up.

Even my mother grew weary and stopped complaining. She just sighed from time to time and mumbled, "The theater should burn to the ground." She didn't notice that the theater burned despite her sighs.

It burned in Father's eyes with a silent flame. But instead of devouring the theater, the flame nurtured his theatrical dreams that could never be realized.

My mother hated the theater. Not so much the theater as the actors. She maintained that the only people who entered the trade were lazy good-for-nothings who didn't want to wake up early for work like everyone else in the world. She also said acting wasn't a real trade because anyone could do it.

When my mother began to bear children, my father sold his print shop. She never forgave him. The print shop had produced steady income, but the income from the theater was unreliable.

To ease his mind, my father went to Velfke's to discuss theater. Avrom Morevski was there, his chair pushed far back from the table to make room for his belly. Tearing pieces from a duck, he hollered hoarsely, "Velfke, I'm hungry."

Morevski was the richest actor in Vilna. He owned his own building with four floors, but it wasn't big enough to satisfy his appetite. For that, he would have needed half the city. Even though Morevski and my father were good friends, it was hard for my father to talk to the actor about mounting a show. To satisfy his appetite, Morevski had to earn a lot. He needed the entire box office take. My father tried anyway. Morevski chewed on the thigh of a duck and grumbled, "Moyshe, it's difficult. I've eaten almost the entire fourth floor." He was talking about his building that he no longer owned because of his debts to the bank.

The other actors ate beets and potatoes and glanced respectfully at Morevski's duck. They took it for granted that Morevski would eat duck. Aside from his quickly disappearing fortune, Morevski was the eternal star, the jewel of every troupe, the intellectual with stage charisma.

My father announced that he'd worked something out with Morevski. The actors cheered. Kuznietsov immediately proposed a toast, but they were a long way from drinking. First Morevski had to hold forth. He'd earned this right when he played the Miropol *tsadik* in *The Dybbuk* and shook up the entire theater world. The troupe sat down at the actor's table and immediately became a family: a theater family with quarrels over roles, jealousy over applause, and love for one another, just like any family.

Morevski discussed various aspects of the play and the different roles, offering theater doctrine. "Goethe said that the one thing demanded from a genius is the love of truth. Rolland said the objective of art is not the dream, but reality. Stanislavsky said. . . ."

The actors hung on Morevski's every word, treating his utterances like truth from above. Even Bombe, who'd long believed you couldn't produce theater without dancing and singing, listened closely. My father sat in a corner with his glasses on the tip of his nose, scribbling his calculations on his cigarette package. He listed his estimates for expenses with tiny numbers and saw that even with full houses, he wouldn't get out of the red. But did that matter? The main thing was, they'd produce theater. Morevski would mount a play. Siomke Kagan would be stunned. So would the audiences.

Siomke Kagan was indeed stunned. He couldn't believe his eyes. After the fiasco with Regina Tsunzer, Morevski chose *The Duke* by Alter Kacyzne. The stage was bustling; the boards shook. The director told Ruden, the carpenter, to build an entire castle. Zakovitsh, the prop manager, turned in a requisition long enough for ten plays. Bombe, the assistant director, chose costumes for the Polish nobility, who had to parade around the stage. Efron, the artist, painted a nobleman's courtyard in gold and silver.

Morevski played the duke, the capricious landowner dressed in bouffant pants with a nobleman's mustache stuck to his face. In a hoarse voice he demanded that his lease-holding *arrendar*, played by Shloyme Kutner, dance the bear dance at the great ball he would host for his prominent guests. The bear dance wasn't in the script, but Morevski's directorial ambition pushed him to add it. He didn't realize what his artistic whim would cost him.

My father combed the city for a bearskin. There wasn't one among Zakovitsh's props. Father suggested they revise the script. "Why doesn't Kutner dance wrapped in a sheet? Everyone will laugh and the run'll go on forever. Kutner can tap-dance like a real Steppe dancer. It'll be something to see."

When Morevski heard about Father's suggestion, he got so upset, he completely lost his voice. He threatened to cancel the play if they didn't find a bearskin. My father remembered seeing a brown bearskin with a full head, including bared teeth, in Bunimovitsh the banker's living room on Pohulanke Street. Father went to the bank and explained what he wanted. Everyone in Vilna had a weakness for theater, even bankers. My father didn't have to say much. Bunimovitsh immediately gave orders for the bearskin to be taken to the theater.

Shloyme Kutner danced the famous bear dance wrapped in the bearskin. He took heavy steps, imitating a bear in a thick forest. Kutner poured the desperation of the Jewish condition into his dancing. Each of his crude steps expressed a helpless protest against humiliation. Kutner, the eternal clown in all the heartbreaking musical melodramas, took his role so seriously that with each step he took, he moaned bitterly. The sound rang out from the stage to the heavens above.

The audience was stunned. People talked of nothing but the bear dance. It was difficult to silence the ovations after the scene.

Morevski was in a rage. Nothing satisfied him. The actors shot each other knowing glances. Kutner was stealing the show. When Siomke Kagan wrote more in his review about Kutner than about Morevski, the theater was in an uproar. Siomke wrote, "Shloyme Kutner has elevated himself from the swamp of lowbrow theater and created a figure who can serve as a symbol of the small shop owner's protest against the powerful capitalist system. His bear dance brings a salutation from the state that buried the landowners and now brightens the world with proletarian art." About Morevski, Siomke wrote that his tycoon mustache impressed no one.

One fine day, Morevski informed my father that he was done with the play. "Kutner's bear is more like a raccoon. He's just not used to serious roles."

My father understood perfectly well that the actor's words were simply a cover for his jealousy. So he said to his star actor, "Avrom, the play is going so well. It's sold out every night. They're writing about the show in all the newspapers."

Morevski looked at my father with the eyes of a Tatar bandit. "Oh sure, they're writing about the play." He wanted to add something, probably to mention Siomke's review, but he just rasped hoarsely. Annoyed, he went off to Velfke's to polish off a tasty piece of sirloin in gravy.

Meanwhile Kutner became ill. Each time he finished the bear dance, he went directly into the chilly change room drenched in sweat and ended up catching a cold. They had to interrupt the run. My father asked Morevski to go to Warsaw and find someone in the artists' union to play the lease-holding *arrendar*. Getting up from his chair, Morevski said, "No, no one is going anywhere. We're not getting anybody to replace Kutner. He isn't, God forbid, dangerously ill. The audience will wait a week for him to recover."

Morevski could wait. He still had his building. My father had only debts. He couldn't wait a single day. People were fighting for tickets. Dovidke the Epileptic, the chief scalper, speculated on the tickets for every hit show, selling them at the closed box office in the evenings for a profit. He begged my father, "Mr. Moyshe, I'll give you money in advance for ten performances!"

Of all times for Morevski to refuse to perform. My father reminded him gently, "Avrom, you told me you can't act with Kutner, that he ruins entire scenes. Now you're telling me to wait for him to recover." This conversation took place at Velfke's restaurant. Morevski moved away from the table to make room for his belly, wiped his mouth, and thought for a moment. Then he coughed, trying to clear his voice, but it didn't help—he was still hoarse. He stopped coughing and rasped, "Moyshe, I can't believe you've been involved in the theater for so many years and you still don't understand that as long as Kutner is on stage and people clap for him, he's my mortal enemy. But when he's lying in bed sick, he's my friend, and more than that, a talented friend."

My father and Morevski went to visit Kutner on his sickbed.

★

A fire broke out in Zalkind's building where the Palace Theater had made its home. Only a few embers remained from the entire theater. Everything had gone up in smoke. The sets burned like kindling. The chairs didn't fare any better. Only the tacks that Mendke had used to fasten the curtains survived. They lay scattered around the wet stage like worms after a rainfall.

My mother raised her eyes to heaven. "Good riddance to the theater. He'll have to do real work now." But before very long my father came home with a schmaltz herring, two Spanish onions, and good news. First, he had the herring killed. Then he announced at the table that he was going to take over Tsinizeli's circus on Ludvizarske Street. He'd already spoken with Krengel, the owner. My mother peeled the onions and said nothing. My father tried to convince himself that her tears were from the onion. He thought she should be happy. They were setting up another theater. When he finished eating, he filled both sides of a cigarette pack with tiny numbers and passed it to my mother so she could see for herself how successful the business would be. My mother pushed the cigarette pack away and groaned, "Oh, Meyshe, you're getting into a whole new set of problems."

My mother only went to Tsinizeli's circus once, to watch Zishe Breitbart bend an iron bar over his knee. Her face was flushed when she arrived home. This wasn't because Breitbart had wrapped the iron bar around his arm like a leather tefillin strap, but because of the way he'd rode into the arena in a chariot, flinging his cape from his shoulders. "If Orliek had looked like that in *Bar-Kochba*," she told Father, "the box office would also have looked very different." Breitbart was a well-built man, and the women in Vilna appreciated masculine beauty.

Once, the handsome Ben-Tsion Vitler played a gentleman bandit. He put on his pajamas and went to bed at the beginning of the first act. All on stage. The women in the theater poked each other with their elbows and whispered, "Oh my, look at that body." My father also wanted to please the women, his best customers, so he had his beard trimmed every two weeks at Bendel the Barber's.

My mother didn't understand how they would be able to put on plays in the circus, but my father had a vivid imagination. The circus had gone bankrupt, and the few remaining animals were given to the zoo for a song. My father decided he would dismantle the arena, build a stage, and put out chairs. That's exactly what happened.

My father hurried to see Ruden, the theater carpenter. Ruden had dragged wooden stakes around behind the closed curtains during intermission for years. He was angry with God for giving him night work, so he pounded his hammer so hard you could hear it throughout the hall. Like my mother, Ruden hated the theater. He'd left the theater countless times and returned each time. He insisted that someone had cast a spell on him. Even though he hated the theater, an evil force kept dragging him back.

When Ruden heard my father's plans, he grumbled, "Mr. Meyshe, I refuse to climb on the circus rafters. I want to live out the few gloomy years left to me in the theater with my legs intact. For work like that, look for goyim."

My father did exactly that. He went to Novishviot where the Starovyern, the Old Believers who'd left the Greek Orthodox Church, lived. They were known throughout the region for their carpentry skills. It wasn't long before bearded Russians sat astride wooden logs, chopping beams for the theater with axes that were as sharp as razors. My father walked from one to the other, telling them how to do their work.

There was a theater again. Elaborate performances with extras and choruses took place on Ludvizarske Street. A live horse even appeared on the stage once. Rudolf Zoslovski insisted that he come on stage with a horse and wagon, exactly as Sholem Aleichem wrote in *Tevye the Dairyman*. My father liked the idea, so he went to the lumber market and brought back a horse and wagon. All evening the potato farmer who owned the team of horses sat behind the curtains bent over, waiting for Tevye to have it out with God and leave the stage.

On Saturday evenings, the balcony almost caved in from the crush of people. One woman took the play so much to heart that she fainted when our sister Dveyrke and another girl sang, "We will remember you" after their father was seized for forty years of hard labor. The housewives from Kalvareyske Street left the theater with swollen red eyes, cursing the evil seducer.

The entire city knew the theater. Everyone attended the performances—from young to old, from poor to rich, from the upper crust to the underworld. Sashke the Count had his regular seat for every premiere. He behaved himself in the theater and didn't try to enrich himself from anyone else's wallet.

My father only had a problem with Sashke once. A Jew from America complained to my father that someone had stolen his passport with a hundred dollars in it during the performance. He demanded compensation. My father immediately went to see Sashke, ostensibly to ask for advice. Sashke the Count straightened his necktie and returned the passport with great dignity. Then he said, "Mr. Meyshe, here's the passport. I hope that fool appreciates the city of Vilna and particularly, this theater. And I hope you realize the American is a swindler. He'd steal the whites from your eyes. He bamboozled you. There was only twenty dollars in his passport, not a hundred. You should rake him over the coals for that lie."

What was a Jew with a beard and a Gemara hoping to find in the theater? What dream did he hope to fulfill among the paper flowers and the green leaves cut from sack linen? A dream of riches? Definitely not. A magnificent performance that would turn the world upside down? He didn't have the money for that. Then what? The simple truth is that my father loved the theater. He loved the constant talk; the anticipation; the actors, that gang of jokers; the colorful world that shimmered with lights of every color.

Once my mother went to the theater courtyard and saw some goyim putting up a fence around the bare earth in front of the foyer door. When she asked what they were doing, they explained that my father had hired them to create a garden. My mother yelled at him, "You thief! You're throwing away even more money."

My father calmly explained that the garden would draw visitors to the theater, especially during the summer, the dead season. He explained his plans. He wanted bushes around the edge of the garden with a tree in the middle. My mother looked at him with glassy eyes, as though he'd just shown up from another planet. She asked him worriedly, "Meyshe, are you all right? For years you've run around between trees made from veneer. Have you suddenly remembered that a tree is something you plant, not something you bang together from boards?"

My father sighed, "Whatever I do, it's never right. You're always yelling that I should get involved with real work. Now I have."

The tree bore shiny brown chestnuts. The courtyard children collected them in their little caps and boiled them for ink. Sitting under the tree, the actors bargained with each other for cigarettes that they used as collateral for their card games. My father walked through the garden, searching between the bushes for inspiration for the next hit to keep the theater going.

The theater disappeared into eternity along with my father.

The tree remained.

14

Memories of a Decimated Theater Home

When my mother got to the end of her rope because no one was attending the performances in Father's theater and there was no money coming in, she'd rail at him, "I hope the miserable business burns to the ground."

Father would look at her, his smoldering black eyes filled with reproach, and sigh, "Rokhl, Rokhl what are you saying?"

Out of respect, my mother wouldn't respond. She'd dismiss his question with a wave of her hand and go into the kitchen to prepare a simple meal. If she'd held my father's gaze for even an instant, she would have suffered the fate of her own curse. The theater burned in Father's eyes. It burned, but it didn't go up in flames.

My father's father was a rabbi in a poor neighborhood outside of Minsk, in White Russia. Father left home very young. Two forces drove him away: need and imagination. He studied at the Ramayles Yeshiva in Vilna for a while but was thrown out after a Russian grammar was discovered under his Gemara. After that, he learned the printing trade in the Vilna print shop of Rozenkrantz and Shriftzetser. They printed religious books in Hebrew and the Yiddish storybooks that brought so much joy to Jewish homes.

There was another apprentice in the print shop who was related to Shriftzetser, one of the owners. The two young men became close friends. Stooped over the printing plates for the Mishnah, they transported each other to brighter and more interesting worlds than the leaden gray print shop. My father's friend, Leyb Shriftzetser, later became famous for his dramatic interpretations of Sholem Aleichem's characters.

When my father and Shriftzetser were well on in years, they were still sharing stories from their youth. Father often described how Shriftzetser disguised himself as a devil and frightened everyone in the print shop half to death. Shriftzetser, in turn, told us that they once found Father hanging upside down from the beams in the attic. He had fainted. My father simply wanted to know how long a person could survive hanging upside down. He hoped to train as a circus acrobat, so he needed this information.

Shriftzetser's path to the theater was shorter than my father's. Shriftzetser was an actor in body and soul, but Father wasn't. A whole world bubbled up in my father, but he couldn't bring it to the surface. The quiet upbringing of his rabbinic home weighed on him.

My father only tested his ability on the stage once, and that was in an emergency. Isaac Samberg, one of the most acclaimed actors on the Yiddish stage between the two world wars, became ill. He was playing the messenger in Ansky's *The Dybbuk*. The play was a great success in Poland during the 1930s. It ran in my father's Vilna theater for an entire season with full houses. Even my mother was happy. But bad luck struck. Isaac Samberg fell ill, and it looked like they'd have to cancel some performances. My father was adamant; they couldn't cancel any of the performances that were drawing such crowds. He couldn't afford to lose the income he needed to keep the theater going.

My father met with the actor's collective, headed by Avrom Morevski, who was playing the Miropol *tsadik* in *The Dybbuk*. My father convinced them that he could replace Isaac Samberg until the actor recovered. "I have a little beard." (Father started growing a beard when he was a very young man.) "I'll put on a long coat and recite the few words."

My father's first and last appearance as the messenger took place at a Shabbes matinee. He came on stage dressed in a long coat with his own beard, and quietly whispered the well-known line, "The groom will arrive in good time."

Someone from the audience recognized him and yelled, "Karpinowitz, speak louder."

My father answered the heckler, "I'm not an actor. I'm just replacing Samberg. I don't have to speak louder."

With that performance, my father bade farewell to the stage forever. He wasn't willing to replace anyone, not even if it meant continuing a run and keeping the box office open.

My father came to the theater after a little detour. When his friend Shriftzetser was already traveling through Russia with various theater ensembles, my father was still working in the print shop. He fell in love with a young woman and tried his skill at journalism. His romance lasted longer than his passion for the pen. The young woman became his wife and bore him six children, but the newspaper he founded, the *Vilne vokhnblat*, bore no fruit. For years, my mother argued that if my father paid more attention to the print shop rather than organizing concerts for the singing duet of Kipnes-Zeligfeld, his business might have a chance. But just a chance.

World War I broke out. There was nothing but hunger in my mother's cast iron pot. Father spent his days running around the city in search of food for his family. He benefited from the good deeds of his ancestors. The Shnipishok rabbi, a close friend of my grandfather's, asked my father to speak to the city commander about starting a soup kitchen for the poor Jews from the neighborhood of Novogorod. My father put on his holiday overcoat, smoothed down his black Herzl beard, and went to see the German general.

In 1915 and 1916, Vilna was occupied by the Germans. Why did the Shnipishok rabbi choose my father to speak to the commander? Because my father knew German. When he'd worked for Rozenkrantz and Shriftzetser, they'd recognized his ability and sent him to Frankfurt am Main to learn the art of color printing. He'd worked for a few years in a large company that printed books in color. My father returned to Vilna enamored with German culture. He even brought back a few parcels of books that adorned our house until the Nazis arrived in 1941 and obliterated our home along with the admirer of German literature.

My father managed to convince the German commander to provide food for the kitchen. Father received help from a soldier who worked in the commander's office. The soldier was Arnold Zweig, who later wrote the famous book *The Case of Sergeant Grischa*, based on a situation he encountered during his military service in Vilna. Even though Zweig was assimilated and estranged from Judaism, he felt moved by my father's request to save Jews from starvation. When I think of the Novogorod kitchen, with its large black cauldrons of potato and oat groats soup, it's as though I'm still peering through thick steam. Years later, the line of hungry Jews seeking food was transformed into a line of well-fed people wanting theater tickets.

My father was apparently destined for the theater. A bit of theater whirled around the kitchen cauldrons in the form of a beautiful girl with a dark complexion. She used to rub her body against Father's legs, like a kitten. Her mother worked in the kitchen peeling potatoes. The girl later appeared on theater posters as Khayele Kushner. She performed in the Yiddish theater in Riga, the capital of Latvia, where she was murdered with all her fans.

The war ended, and actors gathered in Vilna from the far reaches of Russia. They showed up wearing military boots and cloaks without buttons, smelling like freight trains and moldy bread. Yitzkhok Nozshik, his wife, Shtraytman, and Maksimov were among the first to arrive. At that time, the actress Franye Vinter was singing at the Shtremer Cinema. During the intermission, she came onstage dressed like a young Hasid and performed two songs.

The kitchen closed. Dr. Yakov Vigodski, one of the leaders of the Vilna Jewish community, said they shouldn't let a man like my father slip through their fingers. "The community needs people like him." But my father didn't go to work for the Vilna Jewish community. As soon as an actor's union was formed in Vilna, he became the secretary. Yitskhok Nozshik, who later became the director of the Israeli satirical theater *Hamatatei* (The Broom), got my father involved in the actors' union.

My father followed his heart. My mother wept and cursed her bitter fate. Only a month earlier, she'd seen Father in a black top hat and a snow-white shirt at a Jewish community meeting with the finest gentlemen in the city, and now he was running around with a bunch of paupers. My mother didn't like actors. She didn't even like her own son-in-law, Leybl Vayner, the son of a successful furrier. Instead of following in his father's footsteps, Leybl wanted to become an actor. My mother thought of her children going into the theater as an evil decree from above, dooming them to a life without peace and quiet.

Foreign armies made their final attempts to wrest the city of Vilna from each other. Meanwhile, my father rented a theater to stage Sholem Aleichem's *Stempenyu*. He had adapted the story for the stage himself. My father had immense respect and admiration for our classic Yiddish writer, Sholem Aleichem.

In 1914, a few months before the outbreak of the first world war, my father had organized an evening for Sholem Aleichem in Vilna. The street around the hall where the event was to take place had been black with people. The performance was an enormous success.

My father often spoke with admiration about Sholem Aleichem's talent as a reader of his own work. A postcard Sholem Aleichem sent my father was displayed in our home like a holy relic. I am certain that when my father walked the final road to his death, he had Sholem Aleichem's postcard in his breast pocket.

It was 1918, and there was no established authority in Vilna. People were afraid to stick their noses outside in the evening. The actors predicted that not even a dog would show up for the performance. My father stood his ground. "We have to give it a try," he insisted. So they gave it a try and people came. A lot of people. The hall was full. My father didn't, God forbid, gloat over his success. He just stroked his beard with pleasure and murmured quietly, as though to himself, "Jews need theater. They love it."

Father took over the Eden Cinema and converted it into a theater. Nozshik directed *The Rabbi's Reyzele* with Yokheved Zilberg as Reyzele. After that, a play called *The Yeshiva Student* premiered. Standing in front of an open coffin, Zubak the actor talked to his dead father. The critics said Shakespeare's *Hamlet* didn't hold a candle to *The Yeshiva Student*. In another performance, the handsome young Motl Hilsberg played Bar-Kochba. Standing half-naked on the mountains of Palestine, he ripped off the chains of foreign oppression. The chains were paper and the sword made of wood, but Hilsberg's acting was the real thing. Ignoring the cardboard mountains, the audience believed every word and kept coming back for more.

And so a generation of theatergoers was groomed. Later, a troupe that could grace any world stage, including Zigmund Turkow, Jonas Turkow, Ida Kaminski, Moyshe Lipman, and Isaac Samberg, performed at the city concert hall. Night after night, the building teemed with mature audiences who knew exactly what they wanted.

Even my mother got used to the commotion. She wore a black silk dress and a lambskin coat to the premieres. In truth, she still looked on everything with critical eyes, but she stopped berating my father when he got carried away during a successful run. Once, she even experienced the theater's lofty possibilities. This was when Mr. Khayim Gordon, one of Vilna's religious leaders, came to a performance for the first time in his life. *The Dybbuk* was playing, as I mentioned earlier. The Gordons were our neighbors. They also lived in the synagogue courtyard in the center of the city, at number 12 Daytshe Street. When he had a free moment, my father used to visit Mr. Gordon to study a page of Gemara with him. Ramayles Yeshiva had left a deep impression on my father's soul.

Father convinced Khayim Gordon to attend a performance of *The Dybbuk*. My father kept his guest in a separate room until the hall became dark. As the curtain went up, Mr. Gordon slipped quietly into the hall and sat down on a chair that had been placed behind the last row for him. A moment before each intermission, my father led the observant Jew back to his hiding place. For weeks afterward, Khayim Gordon made no mention of his visit to Father's theater. But one day, during a chance encounter in the synagogue courtyard, he said, "Mr. Moyshe, I'm sure you realize that I'll never go back to the theater. But I want you to know that the Divine Presence actually resided for a moment in the Miropol *tsadik*. I congratulate you for bringing the Divine Presence onto the stage of your theater, if only for a moment."

My mother figured that if Father could persuade Mr. Khayim Gordon to watch Avrom Morevski play the Miropol *tsadik*, then the theater couldn't be so crass. There had to be something about it that couldn't be grasped with simple common sense. She stopped criticizing Father when he spent a few hours after a performance with the actors at Velfke's restaurant on Yiddishe Street. That's where the devotees of Yiddish went to eat broiled kishke and chopped liver. Coachmen, who drove passengers around the city in their horse-drawn carriages, sat in one area. The hucksters, who dragged customers into the ready-made clothing shops on Daytshe Street, sat with them. The actors and writers sat in another area with the patrons who helped out in a pinch, during a bad theater season or by providing whiskey for theater celebrations. Shapely girls, fans of various artists, adorned the tables. Itsik Manger imparted wisdom over a glass of slivovitz. Shimson Kagan, the reviewer for the *Vilner tog* newspaper, thundered against performing trashy plays. Avrom Morevski, who had a huge appetite, tore pieces of meat from a duck and shouted hoarsely, "Velfke, I'm hungry." A frying pan of latkes with *griven* immediately appeared.

Behind the restaurant, there was a little walled-in courtyard where the actors gathered on summer evenings with my father. A linden tree grew there. The branches of the tree peered over the wall at Velfke's guests, offering them its honey scent while they ate cold beets with slices of white cheese, the cheapest dish on Velfke's menu. My father stroked his beard and declared the tree to be a symbol of the blossoming Yiddish theater. In 1944, when the Germans retreated from the city, the crown of the linden lay buried under a heap of debris. All that remained of Velfke's sanctuary was a broken piece of wall.

My father achieved a degree of security. He had his own theater, the Palace Theater, and he was renowned in the theater world. Zelverovitsh, the director of the Polish Theater in Vilna, had enormous admiration for Father's accomplishments, particularly given his modest resources and the fact that he had no state support. Even my mother was happy. Thank God, the business was doing well. But my father wasn't satisfied. He kept imagining building a theater with a balcony that would have as many seats as the parterre, so the common people could also afford to buy tickets. "What's a Yiddish theater without the common people?" he'd ask. The Palace Theater didn't have a balcony, and from my father's point of view, this had to be rectified.

The actors often marveled at how my father produced financial reports on the covers of cigarette packages. He wrote out the tiny figures like little mosquitos and, rubbing his hands together with glee, slid the pack over to my mother so she could look at his calculations. "Rokhl, it's as good as gold. One evening from the balcony will cover expenses for an entire week."

My mother pushed the pack away and groaned, "Meyshe, you're just looking for trouble."

My father went to see the former home of Tzinizeli's circus on Ludvizarske Street and decided it was the perfect place to build a theater. He chose the circus for one very important reason: it already had a balcony for the common people. My father decided to put the parterre in the arena.

Elaborate performances took place in the Folk Theater. Morris Liampe played *A Heart That Yearned*. Women were so moved by the play, they used to come to the box office very early to get cheap tickets. The balcony was full and my father walked around the theater like a conqueror striding across the battlefield.

On Saturday nights, the balcony was so packed it almost collapsed. A woman once fainted during the scene in *A Heart That Yearned* when two children sing the sad refrain, "I'll remember you. I'll always yearn for you." The loyal women from Father's theater audience left the performances with swollen red eyes, cursing the seducers with deadly insults and taking a lesson from the melodrama for their own lives. Men crinkled up their noses and quietly wiped away a tear.

And so my father gave the Folk Theater to the common people to whom he was so attached. The theater tickets didn't lie in a lacquer purse but in a basket amid a heap of greens, a piece of lean meat, and a small carp for Shabbes.

One day, when my father came home from the theater, instead of busying himself with his collection of cigarette lighters (he had a weakness for all kinds of fire-producing paraphernalia), he just sat on the edge of the couch, rubbing his eyebrow. He used to rub his right eyebrow when he was deep in thought—this was an old habit from his yeshiva days. He often sat like that at night after a performance, but this was the middle of the day. When Mother came out of the kitchen with a plate of chopped herring and saw father rubbing his eyebrow, she felt a twinge in her heart. "No doubt he's thinking about something new for the theater," she thought. "He's bothered by the few groschen he earns."

Sure enough, when we sat down to eat, my father said, "You know, Rokhl? I've been talking with people. There are complaints about the theater." My mother didn't ask about the complaints. She just looked at Father with the chestnut-colored eyes he loved so much. My father explained. "The problem is that the Jewish intelligentsia goes to the Polish theater. We have to lure them away."

My mother cut the Spanish onion, my father's favorite appetizer, and mumbled under her breath, "The intelligentsia. Hmm. How much do we get from them anyway?"

To satisfy the Jewish intelligentsia in Vilna, my father traveled to Warsaw and hired the famous Vilna Troupe as guest performers. Expenses were huge. The troupe set difficult conditions. My father realized that the honors from the visit wouldn't go to him, but to Mazo, the director of the Vilna Troupe. But none of this affected his decision to bring the troupe that bore its name to Vilna.

Mazo did, in fact, take the honors for himself. At the gala premiere, he stood at the door greeting all the important guests. He also gave interviews to journalists and spoke at all the banquets. But my father had his satisfaction. During the intermissions, the Vilna upper crust paraded around the foyer of the Folk Theater praising the play in the Polish language with Jewish enthusiasm.

The troupe performed Shakespeare's *Shylock*. Vayslitz played Shylock and Yakor Mansdorf, Bassanio. Mansdorf strolled gracefully across the stage, dressed in short velvet breeches, with stockings covering his young muscular legs, and a little velvet jacket tossed over his powerful shoulders. Zakovitsh, the prop master, girded Mansdorf's hips with a rapier. The actor smiled with his full lips and beautiful white teeth. The audience really enjoyed his youthful appearance. They also enjoyed the fresh new tone the Vilna troupe brought to the Yiddish theater.

What happened to that world?

The Germans converted my father's Folk Theater into a garage for military tanks. They tore down the balcony. Before they left the city in

1944, they destroyed the theater, tearing it down to the ground. Not a single one of the beams that my father had so lovingly placed in the building remained intact. He went to the mass grave at Ponar with his audience, the loyal Vilna theatergoers.

My father walked the last road alone, without my mother, the love of his youth. The Germans had already taken her and my sister Devorah, a gifted actress, to Ponar to be murdered. Devorah's husband, the actor Leyb Vayner, went with them.

My father's dream about a theater, actors, performances, scenery, the stage, and special effects: about the entire colorful world that gave him so much joy went up in flames. The ash from that dream still smolders in my memories of my decimated home.

Translator's Note

There is some repetition in the original version of this story, "Zikhroynes fun a farshnitiner teyater heym" from the book *Vilna mayn Vilna*, and the story entitled "Der boym nebn teyater" from the book *Auf Vilner vegn*, translated here as "The Tree beside the Theater." To avoid this repetition in this collection, three paragraphs from the original Yiddish of this story have been omitted in this translation.

15

Vilna, Vilna, Our Native City

For years, a Jew with blue spectacles stood on Daytshe Street begging, "Take me across to the other side." His plea was so heartrending that, rather than asking to be taken across the few cobblestones separating Gitke Toybe's Lane from Yiddishe Street, he sounded like he needed to cross a deep and dangerous abyss. Maybe he was the first Jew in Vilna with a premonition about the Holocaust. Just the name of the street, *Daytshe Gas*, German Street, drove him from one side to the other. We could all see the little water pump and Yoshe's kvass stall on the other side of the street, but through his dark spectacles, that Jew saw farther. Fate didn't take him to the safer side. He ended up in the abyss at Ponar with everyone else.

When I think of that man, who can serve as a symbol of our fate, what comes to mind is the decimated beauty of Vilna.

I must confess in the name of the survivors, in the name of the small group of Vilna Jews who managed to travel to the other side and escape their native city when it was converted by the murderers into one bloody Daytshe Street; in the name of all those who escaped from the hellfire through ghettoes, through forests, through camps, combat zones, and battlefronts; in the name of them all, I must confess that we were in love with Vilna. To this very day that love pierces our hearts like a broken arrow that can't be removed without taking part of us with it.

Vilna gave us every opportunity to dream exalted dreams about bringing happiness to the world, about creating a better future, about bringing all people closer to the beauty that surrounded us. Vilna possessed youthful joys that couldn't be purchased with money. Because none of us had very much, the joys of Vilna were all the sweeter.

The Viliye River brought us greetings from vast, distant waters. We cooled our feverish fantasies in the Zakrete forest. From the Shishkin hills, we pined after distant, unknown worlds.

It's not surprising that people walked through Vilna who couldn't be seen anywhere else in the world. Take, for example, a Jew like Khaykl Lunski, the librarian at the Strashun Library. His gentle gaze reflected the naïveté of the hundreds of children who came to the library, like sheep to a spring, to imbibe knowledge. Or Gedalke the Cantor. For years, he stood in the courtyard next to the Great Synagogue and sang. He chose that spot so the echoes of prayers that were once sung with such flourish by Hershman, Sirota, and Koussevitzky, the greatest cantors of our time, would reach their highest expression in him.

Where else in the world could you find jokers like the guys in Vilna? The hucksters on Daytshe Street with their expressions, their jokes, and their ridiculing of the entire respectable world. They could convince a peasant to buy a tuxedo jacket to match a pair of striped pants. Only in Vilna could those oddballs have paraded around in all their outlandishness. Every Vilna Jew possessed their own peculiarities, so they could understand the fantasies of others. The Jews of Vilna didn't only relish the tasty meals at Usian's restaurant and Taleykinski's peppered salami but also their own wild and expansive dreams.

On Yatkever Street, Kive the Locksmith tinkered with a lock shaped like a nightingale that sang when the door opened. The carpenters in the production cooperative on Troker Street tried to figure out how to make a sofa that would also work as a desk.

Siomke Kagan decided to translate Gypsy songs into Yiddish, so he went to Trok to live in the Gypsy camp and learn their language. Gedalke, the crazy cantor, didn't sit around with his arms folded. During the winter, he would freeze religious melodies by singing them into a teapot of water in the synagogue courtyard so they wouldn't be forgotten by springtime.

Our restlessness drove us to wander in search of traces of yesteryear's snows in the summer shallows of the Narotshe Lake.

Was there anything the Jews of Vilna didn't think of? Even about buying a plot of land in some corner of the world and creating a Jewish republic where everyone from the street cleaners to the president would speak Yiddish. A Jew created bills for that republic in a garret in Leyzer's Courtyard on Yiddishe Street. He made sure to draw a Star of David at the center of each bill.

The criminal organization the Golden Flag spoke about loyalty and friendship in their constitution. "Our members should behave properly and not forget that even though we are who we are, we are still Jews." There was a directive for the general treasury to provide dowries for poor brides. The organization bought all the tickets for Shriftzetser's jubilee performance so their beloved actor would come away with funds.

It's difficult to figure out where all that dreaming, all that yearning for better and more beautiful things, came from. We had very little. Few of us came from wealthy homes. And yet, hardworking youths strode through Vilna with clear and open faces. Far from feeling depressed, we were full of life and at peace with ourselves.

We should be careful not to idealize Vilna. We shouldn't turn all the outlandish Vilna notions, the fantastic ideas and the perfectly crafted expressions into moral virtues. As well as light, there was plenty of shadow. There were poor, hopeless days. That hopelessness drove hundreds over the border to a great snow-covered land in search of a better life. Let us remember the pure souls who believed, with true Vilna faith, in the lofty slogans. Let us remember those who crossed the border with open hearts and naïve faith and who were murdered in prisons and camps. They were the forerunners of Ponar. They, the believers in a just world under the red flag, were the first to be murdered.

In Vilna, we lived a full-bodied Jewish life. Despite the alien surroundings, despite our poverty, despite the pressure from all sides, we contributed with creativity and enthusiasm to Jewish culture and to Jewish continuity.

Vilna left her mark on her inhabitants. The narrow Vilna alleys possessed a magic that inspired boundless effort. You find yourself walking down a vaulted street. You feel there is no way out. The old walls press in on you, trying to merge over your very head. Just when you are about to turn back, a little garden and the Vilenke, a happy rushing stream, opens up before you. You want to take off your shoes, roll your pant legs up to your knees, and stand on the shore with a fishing rod in hand.

Figure 3. "You find yourself walking down a vaulted street." By Yosl Bergner from Avrom Karpinovitsh, *Baym Vilner durkhhoyf* (Tel Aviv: I. L. Peretz, 1967). Courtesy of the artist.

We were spread out through Vilna from one city gate to the other, from Lipuvke, Ruzele, and Novogorod, all the way up to Shnipishok. We, city folk, were drawn to Shnipishok. Crossing the Viliye over the Green Bridge always held the promise of entering another world. There were many interesting characters in Shnipishok to listen to your thoughts. You could also share a kiss and a first embrace beside a closed wooden gate in the summer moonlight.

Sometimes, in a foreign place, you get a hint of Vilna. You open a window and a chestnut tree, like the trees in Talyatnik Park, thrusts its disheveled crown towards you. It reminds you of your childhood, when people made ink from its shiny fruit. We no longer use the ink of our childhoods to write cheerful letters. We use it instead to extinguish our burning sorrow over our native city. Now, when we are so far from Vilna, so very far that there is no longer any place for longing, now everyone and everything appears more clearly. And when the string of memory is plucked, that world sings for us as though still pulsing, as though it hadn't been taken from us forever.

We moved through Vilna with a longing for faraway places without names. We were content to lose ourselves in a feathery cloud and swim across the blue sky. We didn't know that a day would come when we would be flung across the globe, forlorn and orphaned individuals from entire families, and that from all of Vilna, only a pale memory would remain. When we swam in the waters of the Viliye, when our dreams knocked up against every tree in Volokumpie, when we lay on the soft moss trying to capture a bit of sun in our squinting eyes, we didn't know that one day all this would no longer bring us joy but instead, only sorrow.

We cut walking sticks and whittled secret youthful symbols into their fresh bark. We went out into the world in open shirts with buttons undone. How could we have known that the world of our youth would one day be soaked in the blood of those closest to us?

What remains of our memories of Vilna? They bind us to the city. Despite everything, we are still intoxicated by the perfumed poison of the Vilna forests, by the fresh snow on the Hill of the Crosses, by the quiet song of the Viliye. We are bound by one longing and one sadness.

May all of us, the last Jews of Vilna, throw a green bridge over everything that has disappeared, so that our children will one day be able to set foot there and understand our past lives, our past joys. About our suffering they know enough. May they taste the water from the spring in Pospieshk. May they cool their spirits in the hidden shadows of the trees in the Bernardine Garden.

And in years to come, may they continue to sing, "Vilna, Vilna, Our Native City," the song of their mothers and fathers.

Maps

∙

Glossary of People,
Places, Terms, and Events

∙

Story List

∙

Bibliography

These maps provide a conceptual framework for the urban geography of Jewish Vilna during the 1930s as depicted in Abraham Karpinowitz's stories. We have transliterated the place names used by Karpinowitz's characters, rather than using the place names on contemporary maps. Because accurate records of the urban geography of 1930s Vilna are not readily available, we have estimated some locations. There are some locations we could not find.

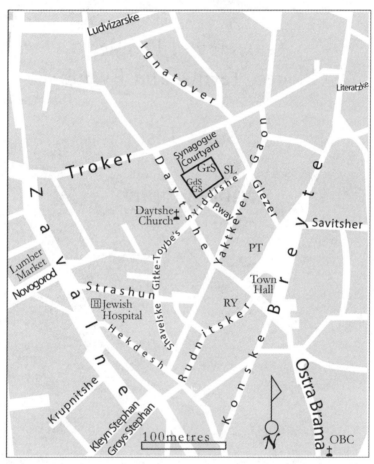

Key Features

GrS	– Great Synagogue	SL	– Strashun Library
GS	– Gaon's Synagogue	OBC ‡	– Ostra Brama Chapel
GdS	– Gravediggers' Synagogue	Pway	– Passageway

Map 1. The synagogue courtyard and surrounding streets. Map prepared by Michael More, Department of Geography, University of British Columbia, Vancouver, Canada.

Key Buildings

BM	= Bernardine Monastary	RS	= Railway Station
CS	= Cathedral Square	RG	= Re'al Gymnasium
CHA	= Church of the Holy Anna	RY	= Ramayles Yeshiva
LP	= Lukishke Prison	ZC	= Zaretshe Cemetery
YH	= YIVO Headquarters	ZM	= Zaretshe Market

Vilna neighborhoods (e.g. Antokl)

Outlying towns and communities (e.g. **Bezdan**)

Map 2. Vilna and the surrounding area. Map prepared by Michael More, Department of Geography, University of British Columbia, Vancouver, Canada.

Glossary of People, Places, Terms, and Events

agune: A woman whose husband has disappeared. If she is unable to provide proof of his death, under Jewish law, she will not be granted a divorce and is not permitted to remarry.

alef-beys: The first two letters of the Hebrew alphabet are *alef* and *beys*. To "know the *alef-beys*" means to know how to read.

amcha: In Biblical Hebrew, literally, "your people." Similar in connotation to "the masses," it refers to the poor, uneducated people.

arrendar: A Jew who leased an inn or estate from a Polish or Ukrainian land-owner. An *arrendar* could also be a tax collector or holder of the "lease" on liquor or kosher meat.

Bar-Kochba: Written in 1883 by Avrom Goldfadn (1840–1908), considered the father of professional Yiddish theater, the play is "a stirring spectacle about the hero of the last revolt of the Jews against their Roman conquerors in the year 137" (Sandrow, *Vagabond Stars*, 61).

Bernardine Garden: The Bernardine Garden is the oldest public park in Vilnius, located between Cathedral Square and the Bernardine Monastery. During the interwar period, when it also included Talyatnik (see below), it was the only interconnected stretch of greenery in the city and a favorite spot for Shabbes strolls (Briedis, interview).

black candles: Black candles were lit in the synagogue during a ceremony of excommunication.

Breitbart, Zishe (1883–1925): A Polish-Jewish performer, Breitbart was admired both for his strength and his physical beauty. Known as the "strongest man in the world," Breitbart "bridged sports and entertainment by offering up athletic feats in an artistic format" (Gillerman, "Strongman Siegmund Breitbart and Interpretations of the Jewish Body," 62). In the early 1920s, he had a mass following both in Europe and the United States.

Breyte Street: Broad Street.

bris: Ritual circumcision of a Jewish male, traditionally performed when the infant is eight days old.

Bronetsky, Sam (1894–?): Bronetsky began his career in the Polish theater, where he achieved considerable box office success. Because of the anti-Semitism of both the other actors and the Polish press after World War I, he switched to the Yiddish theater. By his own account, "I started by speaking Yiddish like a goy. The audience was more amused by my Yiddish than by my acting" (Zilbertsvayg, *Der leksikon fun yidishn teyater*, 6: 5119). Bronetsky mastered the Yiddish language and worked in Yiddish theaters in Warsaw, London, Paris, Riga, and Vilna. He married Dina Halperin (see below) in 1931. They formed their own theater troupe and traveled for a year through the towns and cities of Poland, performing his musical adaptations. In 1938, the couple moved to the United States, where the press lambasted Bronetsky for the lowbrow, burlesque quality of his performances. He left the theater to work as a hairdresser (Zilbertsvayg, *Der leksikon*, 6: 5118–21).

Bunimovitsh: Uri Miller writes that he feels "duty bound" to share his memories of "the people among whom I was born and raised." The Bunimovitsh bank was founded by Israel Bunimovitsh (1848?–1929) and taken over by his son Tobiash 1867– or 1881–1938) who committed suicide just before the bank was declared bankrupt. Both father and son were very involved in charitable works (Miller, "Family Story"; Cohen, *Vilna*, 396).

Casimir fair: "A large annual Lithuanian folk arts and crafts fair dating to the beginning of the 17th century . . . originally held at the two main markets in Vilnius as well as in the city streets" (Visit Lithuania, "St. Casimir's Fair Weekend").

Cave of Machpelah: According to the Torah (Genesis 23:1–25:18), Abraham paid to buy the field where the cave in Hebron was located so that he could bury his wife Sarah there (see "The Life of Sarah" below).

***Chayei adam*:** This work, written by Abraham Danzig (see below), called *The Life of Man* in English, is an abridged summary of the laws found in the section of the *Shulchan aruch* (see below) dealing with prayer and synagogue, Shabbes, and holidays. "It was written for both Torah scholars and ordinary Jews" (Brown, "Danzig, Avraham ben Yeḥi'el Mikhl," 393).

chests of old prayer books and Mishnahs: Any Jewish book or page that has God's name printed on it is considered holy and must be buried in a Jewish cemetery, not simply discarded. Such items are held in a repository until the community buries them.

cholent: A baked dish of meat, potatoes, legumes, and sometimes kugel. Served on Shabbes, it is traditionally kept warm from the day before in the communal oven.

City Synagogue: see Great Synagogue, below.

Cry Out, China: Revolutionary play about China written by the Soviet writer Sergei Tretyakov. "The rebels turn on their tormentors" (Zable, *Wanderers and Dreamers*, 31).

Danzig, Rabbi Abraham (1748–1820): Halachic authority and author, Abraham Danzig was born in Gdansk and moved to Vilna where he was appointed a rabbinic judge. His most notable work is *Chayei adam*.

Days of Awe: The start of the new year, the period from the beginning of Rosh Hashanah (see "Rosh Hashanah greetings," below) to Yom Kippur (see below) is known as the Days of Awe.

Daytsh: German.

Devorah Kupershteyn Folk Shul for Girls: In 1912, Devorah Kupershteyn, known as "the blind disseminator of knowledge" founded this Yiddish language school for poor females in Vilna. "The school became so popular, that it quickly became the largest school in Vilna, with overcrowded classes" (Abramowicz, "Pludermakher, Gershon," 320-21).

The Duke: This play by Alter Kacyzne (see below) was first produced in Warsaw in 1925 and achieved considerable success in Poland, Romania, and Argentina. The play "is based on the legend of Count Walentyn Potocki, known as the Ger Tsedek of Vilna, who supposedly converted to Judaism and paid with his life for his loyalty to the Jewish faith" (Gliksman, "Kacyzne, Alter-Sholem"; Y. Niborski, "Kacyzne, Alter-Sholem").

The Dybbuk: Written by S. Anski (Shloyme-Zanvl Rappoport), this play about betrayed marriage vows and the resulting spirit (*dybbuk* in Hebrew and Yiddish) possession is based on material the writer uncovered during ethnographic expeditions in Ukraine between 1911 and 1914.

-ele: The suffix -ele appended to a name, as in *Orele* or *Tevele*, is an affectionate diminutive in Yiddish, similar in meaning to –ke (see below) and -y in English as in *Bobby* or *Billy*. Characters are frequently known by more than one name. For example, Orele is also called Ortshik and Tevele, Tevke.

Elijah the Prophet: A popular figure in Jewish folklore, Elijah excelled in miracles. "He helps those in need, especially the poor and pious. . . . His chameleon-like disguises are marvelously clever and numerous" (Schram, *Tales of Elijah the Prophet*, xxiv).

famine in Russia: "The most conservative estimate of the number of famine victims, from either starvation or disease related to malnutrition" in Soviet Ukraine during the Great Famine or the Holodomar of 1933 "is 4.8 million people. This figure represents 15 percent of Ukraine's population at the time" (Magocsi, *A History of the Ukraine*, 563).

Freeland League: Founded in London in 1935, the Freeland League hoped "to procure a sizable tract of land . . . where East European Jews could settle. . . . Its members . . . aimed to build a secure foundation for the continuity of their economic and cultural life (including the Yiddish language)" (Salant, "Frayland-lige," 545; see Tshernikhov below).

Funk's: Funk was the name of a Jewish family in Vilna who owned a bookstore with that name on Daytshe Street (Brancovskaja, interview).

Gaon's Synagogue: The Gaon's Synagogue was located in the Vilna synagogue courtyard on the site where the Vilna Gaon (see below) had once lived.

Gemara: The rabbinical analysis of and commentary on the Mishnah (see below). Sometimes the entire Talmud (see below) is referred to as the Gemara.

Gershteyn, Yankev (1904–1943): A devoted Yiddishist, Yankev Gershteyn was active in TSYSHO (see below). He taught music at the Re'al Gymnasium (see below), and conducted two choirs, one for Re'al Gymnasium students and one for adults (Augenfeld, interview). Gershteyn was a colorful personality and an excellent teacher. His students loved him. He died in the Vilna ghetto hospital (Katcherginski and Pupko, "Gershteyn, Yakov," 109–11).

Giligitsh, Yoysef (1891–1979): The principal of the Re'al Gymnasium (see below) where he taught Yiddish literature, Giligitsh also taught natural science at the Yiddish Technical School in Vilna. In 1937, he traveled to Australia to raise money for secular Yiddish schools in Poland and remained in Melbourne. Giligitsh wrote scholarly works about zoology and botany (I. Pat, ed., "Giligitsh, Yosef," 2: 213).

Glezer Street: This street, Glazier Street in English, was in the original Jewish quarter in Vilna during the sixteenth and seventeenth centuries, when many of the streets were named after the trade of the people who lived and worked there. By the interwar period, these streets no longer housed the shops of the tradespeople for whom the streets had been originally named (Augenfeld, interview).

Khayim Gordon: Khayim-Meyer Gordon, the shammes of the Great Synagogue, is described in *The Last Days of the Jerusalem of Lithuania* as "a big, tall Jew with a white beard." On July 4, 1941, he was charged by the Nazis with setting up a

"Jewish representative body" and given one day to complete the task (Kruk, *The Last Days of the Jerusalem of Lithuania*, 52).

goy: A non-Jew. Although in English the word *goy* has negative connotations, in Yiddish the connotations are sometimes negative, sometimes simply descriptive, and sometimes ambiguous.

goye: A non-Jewish female.

goyim: Plural of goy.

Gravedigger's Synagogue: In pre–World War II Vilna, many of the trades had their own small synagogues. The Gravedigger's Synagogue was located in the synagogue courtyard (see below).

Great Synagogue (also known as the City Synagogue): Originally built in 1573 and remodeled and restored a number of times, the synagogue had "the overwhelming grandeur of an edifice in the style of the Italian Renaissance and an awe-inspiring atmosphere" (Cohen, *Vilna*, 105). The building could accommodate between 3,000 and 5,000 people. "As its construction was subject to the law forbidding it to tower above the neighboring buildings, its foundations had to be dug deep so as to give it a distinguished altitude within" (ibid., 104). Damaged by the Nazis during World War II, the synagogue was destroyed by the Soviet authorities after the war (Venclova, *Vilnius*, 155).

Green Bridge: A bridge over the Viliye (now called the Neris) River, it is the oldest bridge in Vilnius, connecting the city with the suburb of Shnipishok.

griven: Fried goose skin. In other words, straight cholesterol.

Grodzenski, A. I. (1891–1941): Aaron Yitzkhok Grodzenski was born in the Kovno (Kaunas) area. The loss of both his legs in a tramway accident when he was a young man did not interfere with his prolific output as a poet, novelist, and translator. He worked on various newspapers, first in Western Europe—in Denmark, Belgium, and the Netherlands—and then in the Soviet Union. In 1924 he began to publish the *Ovnt kurier* (see below). Grodzenski was murdered by the Nazis at Ponar (Kharlash, *Der leksikon fun der yidisher literatur*, 2: 333–35).

groschen: A Polish coin (grosz), worth 1/100 of a zloty (see below).

Groys Vileyke: The Large Vileyke (see Vileyke below).

gymnasium: European high school.

Halperin (Halpern) Dina (1909–1989): Born in Poland, Halperin first appeared on the Yiddish stage at the age of 15 as a ballet dancer under the choreographic direction of Sam Bronetsky (see above) who she married in 1931.

They formed their own theater company and traveled through the towns and cities of Poland. In 1938, Halperin left for America where she had a successful career as both a theater and film actor, touring widely throughout the world, and as an artistic director. She divorced Sam Bronetsky and married Daniel Newman, a theater and opera press agent (Melamed, email; Zilbertsvayg, *Der leksikon fun yidishn teyater*, 4: 3167–73).

Hekdesh Street: Poorhouse Street.

Herzl beard: Theodore Herzl (1860–1904), considered the founder of modern Zionism, had a full beard, cropped just below his neckline.

Hill of the Crosses: The three large white crosses at the top of a hill in the center of the city were a distinctive feature of the interwar Vilna skyline. They can be seen in contemporary Vilnius.

Kabbalah: Esoteric Jewish teachings that form the foundation of mystical religious interpretation.

Kacyzne, Alter-Sholem (1885–1941): Born in Vilna, Kacyzne was a literary disciple of Isaac Leib Peretz (see below). He wrote dramatic poems, plays (including *The Duke* [see above]), and novels. He was also an accomplished photographer who was commissioned in 1921 by HIAS (Hebrew Immigrant Aid Society) to document the deplorable conditions of Polish Jews. Kacyzne and his wife and only daughter were murdered by the Nazis at Tarnopol (Gliksman, "Kacyzne, Alter-Sholem"; Y. Niborski, "Kacyzne, Alter-Sholem," 839–41).

kaddish: Kaddish is a prayer recited by a close relative daily for a year following someone's death and on the anniversary of their death (see *yortzayt* below). Traditionally, this prayer was recited only by males. The son who is expected to say this prayer is sometimes referred to as the parent's kaddish.

Kagan, Siomke (Shimshon Kahan, Shimshon Kagan): A reporter and later editor for the *Vilner tog* newspaper (see below) (Jewish Telegraphic Agency 1935). According to Liba Augenfeld, a native of Vilna, he was "a poet and a real character. He lived with the Gypsies [Roma—translator], learned their language, and translated some of their songs into Yiddish (Augenfeld, interview).

Kalvareyske Street: Probably refers to Kalvareyska (Kalvariju, in Lithuanian) Street, the main street in Shnipishok. During the interwar period, poor and uneducated working class and tradespeople lived in this neighborhood (Briedis, interview).

Karpinowitz, Moyshe (1882–1941): Father of Abraham Karpinowitz, Moyshe Karpinowitz (known affectionately as Meyshe) was "a writer, critic, printer, typesetter, lithographer, painter, and even an actor" (Turkow, *Farloshene*

Shtern, 1: 188). In 1905, he started a Jewish print shop in Vilna and briefly produced the *Vilna vokhnblat*, a weekly Yiddish paper for which he wrote theatrical reviews. After organizing a tour of White Russia and Lithuania for Sholem Aleichem, Karpinowitz began producing Yiddish theater. Between 1919 and 1939, he was the director, manager, and administrator of various theater groups and performances, both in Vilna and in others towns and cities. In Vilna, he created and managed the Palace Theater and then the Folk Theater. According to Hirsz Abramowicz, "The Yiddish theaters that managed to survive . . . in the cities of Poland in the difficult years between the two world wars, owe no small measure of thanks to Moyshe Karpinovitch" (Zilbertsvayg, *Der leksikon fun yidishn teyater*, 5: 3929). Karpinowitz's dramatization of *Stempenyu* (see below) by Sholom Aleichem (see below) was produced by Yiddish theater companies throughout Eastern Europe. Moyshe Karpinowitz was murdered by the Nazis at Ponar.

-ke: The suffix -ke appended to a name as in *Estherke* (also known as Esther), *Hirshke* (also known as Hirshel), *Iserke* (also known as Iser), and *Itske* (also known as Itsik), is an affectionate diminutive in Yiddish, similar in meaning to -ele (see above) and -y in English as in *Bobby* or *Billy*. See entry on –ele.

kishke: A Jewish dish traditionally made from beef intestine stuffed with flour or matzoh meal, fried onion, fat, and spices.

Kleyn Stephan Street: Little Stephan Street.

klumpes: A Lithuanian word meaning "clogs," the wooden shoes worn by Lithuanian peasants. When referring to Lithuanian people, the word is derisive and is similar in meaning to "hick" or "country bumpkin" (Briedis, interview).

Krasni, Fayvush (date of birth and death unknown): In 1918, Fayvush Krasni took over the directorship of the library and thanks to his tireless work, Mefitsei Haskalah (see below) became the largest Jewish library in Vilna (Kruk, "Library and Reading Room in the Vilna Ghetto, Strashun Street 6").

kugel: A pudding. A kugel can be either savory or sweet (filled with raisins and lots of sugar). As a special treat, kugel was sometimes added to cholent (see above).

kvass: A fermented beverage made from black or regular rye bread.

Kviek the Gypsy King: "In 1930 Michal Kwiek . . . emerged . . . as the 'King of Polish Gypsies' and established a 'royal dynasty' that was to survive until 1961. . . . The high point in the life of the royal court was the coronation of the last pre–World War II king, Janusz Kwiek . . . in 1937" (Barany, *The East European Gypsies, 102*). Because the story "The Great Love of Mr. Gershteyn" is not precisely dated, it is not clear whether Siomke Kagan drank with Michal Kwiek or Janusz Kwiek.

The Lady of the Camellias: Written by Alexandre Dumas *fils* (1824–1895), who adapted the novel into a play known in English as *Camille*. Dumas *fils*, who was the child of one of his father's affairs, "devoted his plays to sermons on the sanctity of the family and of marriage" (Britannica Reference Centre, "Alexandre Dumas fils").

Lekert, Hirsh (c. 1879–1902): On May Day of 1902, Lekert, a Jewish shoemaker, participated in an illegal demonstration in Vilna. "The demonstrators were chased through the streets and beaten mercilessly" (Abramowicz, *Profiles of a Lost World*, 134). Many were arrested and further brutalized under direct supervision of Governor von Wahl (see below). In response, Lekert shot and wounded von Wahl and was sentenced to death by hanging. For many years afterward, Lekert remained a hero to large numbers of Jewish workers (Levin, "Hirsh Lekert").

"The Life of Sarah": Chayei Sarah in Genesis 23:1–25:18, one of the weekly Torah readings (see Cave of Machpelah above and Torah below).

Lunski, Khaykl (1881–1942 or 1943): A self-taught librarian, Lunski was the librarian and manager of the Strashun Library (see below) from 1895 until 1941. Most of the material in the library collection was not catalogued. "Lunski knew by heart the names of all the books . . . and their location, and could immediately locate the appropriate book that provided the answer to each question" (Shavit, *Hunger for the Printed Word*, 27; Abramowicz, *Profiles of a Lost World*, 260–64). Lunski was murdered by the Nazis at Treblinka.

Manger, Itsik (1901–1969): Best known as a Yiddish poet, Manger used traditional folk forms like the ballad to express contemporary themes. "A lifelong enfant terrible" (Howe, Wisse, and Shmeruk, *The Penguin Book of Modern Yiddish Verse*, 561).

Mazo, Mordechai (1889–1943): One of the founders, organizers, and managers of the Vilna Troupe, Mazo was "a man of great intelligence, considerable knowledge of both Yiddish and world literature, and a fanatic commitment to highbrow Yiddish theater" (Turkow, *Farloshene Shtern*, 1: 64). After engaging in ongoing disputes with other Vilna Troupe members, he eventually resigned from the company not long before its demise. He was killed during the Warsaw ghetto uprising.

Mefitsei Haskalah Library: In English translation, the Society to Spread Enlightenment Library, it was established in 1910 and "became the largest Jewish library in Vilna, in terms of both the number of volumes in its collections and the quantity of books circulated to readers. . . . The 45,000 volumes included in the library in September 1939 were as follows: Yiddish, 10,000 volumes; Hebrew, 5,500 volumes; Polish, 10,000 volumes; Russian, 18,000 volumes; Lithuanian, German, French, and English, 2,000 volumes" (Kruk, "Library and Reading Room," 174).

minyan: Ten adult men, comprising a minyan, are required for certain Jewish religious obligations, notably communal prayer.

Mishnah: One of the two components of the Talmud (see below), the Mishnah was the first written compendium of Judaism's oral law, c. 100 CE.

Mitchurin, Professor Ivan Vladimirovich (1855–1935): According to the Encyclopedia Britannica, Mitchurin was a Russian horticulturist who developed "more than 300 new types of fruit trees and berries in an attempt to prove the inheritance of acquired characteristics. . . . [His] theories of hybridization . . . were adopted as the official science of genetics by the Soviet regime, despite the nearly universal rejection of this doctrine by scientists throughout the world" (Joravsky, "Mitchurin, Ivan Vladimirovich").

The Model: Sam Bronetsky's musical adaptation of George Bernard Shaw's play *Pygmalion.*

moyel: A ritual circumciser trained in both circumcision and in the Jewish rituals and laws surrounding the event.

Napoleon's manifesto: "In May 1799, during the campaign in Palestine, the French government newspaper *Moniteur* published an article stating that Napoleon had issued a manifesto promising the Jews their return to their country. Many European newspapers reproduced this information, although today scholars question whether Napoleon ever really issued such a declaration" (Mevorah, Brawer, and Shapiro, "Napoleon Bonaparte," 777–78).

Oginski: Old Lithuanian noble family.

Ovnt kurier: A Yiddish afternoon newspaper edited by Aaron Yitskhok Grodzenski (see above) and published in Vilna from 1924 to 1939. The paper, which was "lively and not too serious," had a circulation of between 4,500 and 5,000 readers (Kharlash, "Grodzenski, Aaron-Yitzkokh," 2: 334).

Peretz, Isaac Leyb: (1851–1915): Peretz was considered, along with Mendele Moykher Sforim and Sholem Aleichem (see below) to be one of the classic authors of modern Yiddish literature. "More than any other Jewish intellectual, Peretz expressed and represented the hope that Jewish cultural leaders could take over from rabbis the function of inspirational authority" (Wisse,

"Peretz"). Peretz wrote in both Hebrew and Yiddish (and briefly in Polish), inspiring a number of Yiddish writers including Anski, creator of the play *The Dybbuk* (see above). After 1899, when he was arrested and imprisoned for three months for socialist activities (which included writings that attacked economic and social exploitation), Peretz altered his writing style and began to "adapt traditional folk motifs to modern tales 'in the folk manner'" (ibid., 1341) in works like *Folkstimlekhe Geshikhtn/Folktales*.

Pilsudski, Marshal Jozef (1867–1935): Polish revolutionary and statesman, he was the first chief of state (1918–1922) of the newly formed country of Poland. In 1908, determined to form a Polish army to fight the Russians, he created a secret Union of Military Action "financed with a sum of money stolen from a Russian mail train by an armed band led by Pilsudski himself." In 1910 Pilsudski converted this secret union into a legal Union of Riflemen, actually a school to train Polish officers to lead the Polish Legion (Smogorzewski, "Jozef Pilsudski").

Pludermakher, Gershon (1876–1942): An activist and leader in TSYSHO (see below), Pludermakher worked with Devorah Kupershteyn to organize and develop the curriculum for the Devorah Kupershteyn Folkshul for Girls (see above), where he served first as a teacher and later as principal. Pludermakher wrote extensively on pedagogical subjects both in the press, for example, in the *Vilner tog* newspaper (see below), and in pedagogical journals. He perished in the Vilna ghetto (Abramowicz, "Pludermakher, Gershon").

Ponar: "A wooded area . . . some ten kilometers southwest of [Vilna]. . . . Once it served as a holiday resort for the people of [that city]. . . . [It] became the site of the mass murder of 50,000 to 60,000 men, women, and children who were shot on the edge of the pit and then buried within it. The vast majority of (these victims) were Jews from the [Vilna] ghetto and environs" (Arad, preface, xiii).

Psalm reciters: Psalms are traditionally recited to pray for those who are ill or otherwise in danger. In Jewish Vilna, the families of those who wanted these Psalms recited paid (poorly) for this service thus providing an extremely meager living for the Psalm reciters.

Ramayles Yeshiva: "Ramayles, the first well-known yeshiva in Vilna, was founded in the mid-1820s and continued to operate until World War II" (Zalkin, "Vilnius").

Re'al Gymnasium: The Re'al Gymnasium, also called the Mathematics and Sciences Gymnasium, opened in 1918 and operated until 1941 under the direction of TSYSHO, the Central Yiddish School Organization (see below). It was the first Yiddish-speaking high school in Vilna. "Besides regular studies as prescribed by the Polish government, Yiddish, Jewish history, and Hebrew were taught. Emphasis was placed on the establishment of student clubs and on self-government among the students. After much effort, the gymnasium acquired government status in 1933" (Guide to the Records of the TSYSHO [Tsentrale Yidishe Shul Organizatsye] 1919–1940).

Rosh Hashanah greetings: Rosh Hashanah marks the start of the new year in the Hebrew calendar. According to Jewish liturgy, this is the beginning of the period of judgment, when God decides who will live and who will die during the coming year. It is customary on the first night of the holiday for Jews to extend greetings to each other, wishing that the recipient be inscribed in the Book of Life for a good year.

sandek: An honorary function at a bris (see above) ceremony, the sandek holds the male infant while the bris is performed.

sending women to Argentina: "Fear of Jewish white slavery, the sexual traffic in immigrant Jewish refugee women, often conducted by Jewish men . . . was a topic that preoccupied Jewish communities in Europe . . . from the 1880s until the outbreak of World War II." Buenos Aires was considered "a haven for white slavers because it had a system of municipally regulated prostitution from 1875 until 1936." When Samuel Cohen, secretary of the London-based Jewish Association for the Protection of Girls and Women, went to South America in 1913 to look at the situation of Jewish women, he found a considerable number of Jewish women living in brothels in deplorable conditions throughout South America (Guy, "Argentina: Jewish White Slavery").

Shabbes: The Jewish Sabbath, which begins just before sunset on Friday evening and ends just after sundown on Saturday evening, is a day of rest. Jews are encouraged to mark a separation between Shabbes and the rest of the week, between the holy and the profane. Jews are encouraged to clean themselves of the remnants of weekly toil and to exchange their workday garments for special Shabbes clothing. Among the activities that are encouraged on Shabbes are marital relations between husband and wife. Tamara's clients in the story, "Tall Tamara," interpret this in accordance with their own situation.

Shabbes candles: It is a *mitzvah* (commandment from God) for Jewish women to light Shabbes candles on Friday evening to usher in the Sabbath.

shammes: Synagogue caretaker.

Shevuos: A Jewish holy day seven weeks after Passover, commemorating the receiving of the Torah (see below) at Mount Sinai.

sheygetz: A non-Jewish boy or young man. The term can be a neutral descriptor, but it also often has the connotation of a ruffian.

shiksa: A non-Jewish woman. The word can be a neutral descriptor or it can have the connotation of easy sexual availability.

shlimazl: Someone who, depending on your point of view, is either the constant victim of bad luck or who constantly makes a mess of things.

Sholem Aleichem (Shalom Rabinovitz 1859–1916): Considered, along with Mendele Moykher Sforim (S. Y. Abramovitsh) and Isaac Leyb Peretz (see above), to be one of the classic authors of modern Yiddish literature, Sholem Aleichem "resolved to elevate Yiddish literature to the role of a Jewish national literature." Best known for his short pieces, many of them monologues, Sholem Aleichem used an ironic humor to describe the disintegration of small-town Jewish life in Eastern Europe. He is best known for his Tevye stories (see "Tevye the Dairyman" below). He also wrote plays and novels including the novel *Stempenyu* (see below) in 1888 (Miron, "Sholem Aleichem"; see also Moyshe Karpinowitz above).

Shriftzetser, Leyb (1886–1941 or 1942): Born in White Russia, Shriftzetser moved to Vilna to work in the print shop of Shriftzetser and Rozenkrantz. He soon began reciting and performing the works of Sholem Aleichem in amateur productions and came to the attention of the professional theater world. Over the course of his career, Shriftzetser was a member of various prestigious Yiddish theater companies including the Peretz Hirshbein Company (which included Esther-Rokhl Kaminski). He settled in Vilna in 1922 but continued to tour. Whenever his salary in the professional theater fell, he traveled through villages and small towns with his evenings of Yiddish humor, impersonating the characters in the stories of Sholem Aleichem, Mendele, and other Yiddish writers. Shriftzetser and his family were murdered at Ponar (Zilbertsvayg, *Der leksikon fun yidishn teyater*, 4: 4738–44).

Shulchan aruch: Authored in 1563 and known as the Code of Jewish Law, the *Shulchan aruch* is the most authoritative legal code of Judaism.

King Sobietski's time: Jan III Sobietski (1629–1696) was king of Poland and Grand Duke of Lithuania from 1674 until his death.

soldier's kasha: A cereal grain (usually buckwheat or millet) cooked slowly with the addition of meat or chicken.

Stempenyu: A novel, written in 1888 by Sholem Aleichem (see above), about a klezmer violinist.

Strashun Library: Mathias (Mattisyahu) Strashun of Vilna (1819–1885), a renowned philanthropist, communal leader, and scholar, bequeathed an extensive library of 5,700 books to the Vilna Jewish community. This was supplemented by donations from other Jewish scholars and book lovers as well as by the University of Vilna, which, from 1928 onward, sent a copy of every book published in Poland in either Hebrew or Yiddish to the Strashun Library. The reading room, with seating for 200 readers, was so popular that two readers often shared one chair. These readers included both pious Jews and secular scholars (Abramowicz, *Profiles of a Lost World*, 260–63; Shavit, *Hunger for the Printed Word*, 25–27).

students with foxtails on their caps: During the 1930s, some Polish students formed various anti-Semitic organizations that were distinguished by the shape and color of their hats. In Vilna alone, there were five or six such student associations (E. Niborski, interview).

spleen: The spleen pulp is removed from the spleen, chopped, and then mixed with chopped onion, bread crumbs, eggs, salt and pepper, and sometimes meat. The mixture is fried and then stuffed into the spleen and baked.

synagogue courtyard: The synagogue courtyard surrounding the Vilna Great Synagogue (see above) contained more than ten different prayer houses (Lempertas, *Musu Vilne/Our Vilne*), the Vilna Jewish community library, the Strashun library, and a number of Jewish religious schools. (Cohen, *Vilna*, 107–13). By the thirties, various low-level criminals and other marginal people hung out there.

Sztral's Café: In her memoir about Vilna during 1938, Lucy S. Dawidowicz writes that Sztral's Café was located on the elegant Adam Mickiewica Street. "With umbrella-covered tables on a large terrace, [it] was one of the poshest cafes I'd ever seen. . . . [However] Sztral's . . . used to turn Jews away and consequently most Jews boycotted the place" (Dawidowicz, *From That Place and Time*, 56). According to Fanya Brancovskaja, "The Sztral family owned three different restaurants: the White Sztral Café, the Red Sztral Café, and the Green Sztral Café (Brancovskaja, interview).

Talmud Torah: Free traditional religious Jewish elementary school for orphaned and poor boys, supported by the community.

Talyatnik Park: Part of a continuous stretch of greenery located between the foot of Castle Hill and the Bernardine monastery, it was closer to the cathedral and more open to the city than the rest of the Bernardine Garden (see above; Briedis, interview).

tefillin: A pair of small, black leather boxes containing scrolls of parchment inscribed with verses from the Torah. Observant Jewish males bind these small boxes to their foreheads and arms with leather straps during weekday morning prayers.

Tevye the Dairyman: Sholem Aleichem (see above) is best known for his series of sardonically humorous stories narrated by Tevye der Milkhiker (Tevye the Dairyman). These stories have been dramatized in theatrical productions (including as the Broadway musical *Fiddler on the Roof*) and in films throughout the world.

Tiferes Bachurim Society: "Founded in 1902 for the propagation of religious education and knowledge among the working class" (Cohen, *Vilna*, 514).

Torah scroll: A scroll on which the Torah has been handwritten. This scroll is kept in a special cabinet in the front of the synagogue and ritually removed each week for the reading of a prescribed section or *parsha*. Over the course of a year, the Torah is read in its entirety.

Toras Emes School: Literally "the Truth of the Torah School," it was a religious school with seven grades for boys from poor and working families (Augenfeld, interview).

Trok: Now known as Trakai, the town, situated 28 kilometers west of Vilnius, is surrounded by lakes.

tsadik: A righteous man. Also, the leader of a Hasidic group.

Tshernikhov, Joseph (1882–1941): One of the organizers and leaders of the Freeland League (see above) in Poland during the interwar period, Tshernikhov was active in all aspects of the Vilna Jewish community, including serving as the chairman of the Vilna Jewish community. He also a well-respected lawyer in Vilna who specialized in political cases. According to Abramowicsz, "Thanks to his aggressive militancy, a number of Polish-Jewish communists were saved from police 'justice' and, in some instances, from the gallows." Tshernikhov "frequently conversed audibly in Yiddish with his clients and others, something that was previously unheard of in court" (Abramowicz, *Profiles of a Lost World*, 285–87).

tsimmes: A stew made from a variety of vegetables and legumes, usually combined with dried fruit and sometimes with meat.

Tsuker, Regina (1899–1943): Born in Poland, Tsuker married the actor Karl Tsimbalist, joined his theatrical troupe, and played the starring role in performances in Warsaw and the provinces of Galicia. Yiddish actor and director Janos Turkow wrote of her, "Regina Tsuker was an enormously talented actress, possessing limitless charm and simplicity. . . . She was, however, not always capable of distinguishing between what was and was not appropriate . . . (Turkow, *Farloshene shtern*, 1:117). Her popularity stemmed not only from the joy her performances provided, but also from the constant attacks by the Yiddish press in Poland against low-brow, trashy theater. These attacks were often directed against Regina Tsuker personally. When Tsuker came to Vilna as a guest performer, the welcome she received from the local Yiddish press forced her to terminate her performance and leave Vilna. The city remained forever closed to her" (ibid., 116–21; Zilbertsvayg, *Der leksikon fun yidishn teyater*, 5: 3853–57).

Tsunzer, Regina: The librarians at the Jewish Public Library in Montreal, whose skills at research go beyond the highly competent into the magical, have been unable to find any mention of Regina Tsunzer. Everything that Karpinowitz writes about Regina Tsunzer in "The Tree beside the Theater" coincides with what we know about Regina Tsuker (see above). Did this actress perhaps go by two different family names?

TSYSHO: The aim of the Tsentrale Yidishe Shul Organizatsye (Central Yiddish School Organization) was to create a secular Yiddish school system in Poland that promoted socialist ideals.

Velfke's restaurant: "Volf Usian owned a restaurant on Daytshe Street . . . which served as the meeting place for the entire [Yiddish] literary and artistic world" (Turkow, *Farloshene shtern*, 1: 192). He regularly fed various actors on credit and loaned them money.

Vilenke River: A tributary of the Viliye River (see below).

Vilna Gaon (1720–1797): Eliyahu ben Shlomo Zalman Kremer, known as the Vilna Gaon, was an extraordinary Torah scholar, a prolific author, and one of the most influential Rabbinic authorities since the Middle Ages.

Vilna Troupe: The Yiddish theater troupe, founded in Vilna in 1915, relocated to Warsaw in 1917. Known for ensemble work, the Vilna Troupe presented literary and artistic theater as opposed to lowbrow vaudeville productions. After 1927, members of the troupe split off into different theater companies, all calling themselves the Vilna Troupe. A small group of actors under the management of Mordechai Mazo (see above) returned to Warsaw where they recruited new members (Bulat, "Vilner trupe"; Sandrow, *Vagabond Stars*).

"Vilna, Vilna, Our Native City" (*Vilne, Vilne, undzer heymshtot*)**:** This song of longing for the city of Vilna was written by L. Wolfson for the *Vilne zamelbukh*, published in New York in 1935, and set to music by Alexander Olshanetsk. It begins,

Vilne, Vilne, undzer heymshotot

Undzer benkshaft un bager.

Akh, vi oft es ruft dayn nomen

Fun mayn oyg aroys a trer.

Vilna, Vilna, our native city

The source of our longing and our desire.

Oh how often your name

calls forth tears from my eyes.

> (Lipphardt, "Vilne Vilne undzer heymshtot";
>
> Wolfson, "Vilne, Vilne, undzer heymshtot")

Vilna vokhnblat: Vilna Weekly.

Vilner tog: The Vilna Day/Daily, a Yiddish newspaper that was published from 1920 to 1939. To deal with the problems resulting from censorship by the Polish authorities, the newspaper often changed its name, but always maintained the word *tog*/day (Yad Vashem, "The Interwar Period—Cultural Life"). As well as covering the news, the *Vilner tog*, which had an intellectual readership, published the work of local Yiddish writers and reviews of Yiddish theater.

Viliye: A river running through Vilna. On contemporary maps, it is called the Neris.

von Wahl, Victor (1840–1915): Sent to Vilna in 1901 as governor, in his first year, von Wahl ordered the Vilna police to severely beat and torture any workers who participated in May Day activities. He was also personally present for some of the beatings. "The entire Jewish population [of Vilna] was very disturbed about the punishment inflicted on the . . . demonstrators" (Abramowicz, *Profiles of a Lost World*, 140). "A shoemaker named Lekert [see above] fired two shots at the governor, wounding him slightly" (ibid., 141). Lekert was condemned to death by hanging. After Lekert was hanged, von Wahl received a decoration by "order of the tsar and later, a higher office" (ibid., 142).

Weinreich, Dr. Max (1894–1969): A Yiddish linguist, literary scholar, and social and political activist, Weinreich was "the driving force" behind the *Yidish visnshaftlekher institut* (Yiddish Research Institute) or YIVO (see below) from 1925 until his death. Weinreich's four-volume *Geshikhte fun der yiddisher shprakh* (*History of the Yiddish Language*), completed just before his death, remains the "benchmark" study of Yiddish linguistics (Glasser, "Weinreich, Max").

With Open Eyes: A drama in three acts written by Leyb Malach, a Yiddish poet, playwright, and cultural worker. Malach was born in Poland in 1894 and died in Paris in 1936 (Baker, "The Lawrence Marwick Collection of Copyrighted Yiddish Plays at the Library of Congress").

Yatkever Street: *Yatke* means "butcher" in Yiddish. The street was in the original Jewish quarter in Vilna (see Glezer Street).

Yiddish: In the Yiddish language, the word *yidish* can mean "Yiddish," referring to the language, or "Jewish," referring to the religion or culture.

Yiddish gelt: Jewish money.

Yiddish Institute, Yiddish Scientific Institute, YIVO: The YIVO Institute was founded in 1925 and centered in Vilna, Poland, from 1929 until 1941, when the institute relocated to New York. YIVO "became the leading institution for scholarship in Yiddish and about the history and culture of East European Jews" (Kuznitz, "YIVO," 2090). The work of the organization depended on volunteer *zamlers* (collectors), "ordinary men and women who gathered documents, data, and funds for YIVO in their local communities throughout Eastern Europe" (ibid., 2091). As well as preserving language, songs, and stories, YIVO also "recruited *zamlers* to record Yiddish terms from various professions and technical fields" (ibid., 2091; Kuznitz, "YIVO"; see Weinreich, Dr. Max above).

YIVO Institute journal: YIVO published a number of periodicals, both popular and academic. When the narrator of the story "Chana-Merka the Fishwife" refers to "the Institute journal," s/he is probably speaking about YIVO's general academic journal *YIVO-bleter*/YIVO Pages, although s/he may be referring to YIVO's short-lived popular linguistic journal *Yidish far ale*/Yiddish for Everyone (Glasser, "Weinreich, Max").

Yizkor service: A communal memorial service held in the synagogue four times a year, including on Yom Kippur, for all those who have lost loved ones.

yortzayt: Literally means anniversary. On the anniversary of the death of a loved one, a memorial service is held. This service includes the lighting of a candle and the recitation of a memorial prayer.

Yung-teyater (1932–1939): An avant-garde Yiddish theater company in Poland that believed in theater as an agent of progressive social change (Steinlauf, "*Yung-teater*").

zloty: A Polish coin. In the interwar years, one U.S. dollar was worth roughly five zloty ("Zloty," Internet Encyclopedia of Ukraine, http://www.encyclopedia ofukraine.com/display.asp?linkPath=pages/Z/L/Zloty.html, accessed September 9, 2015).

Story List with Original Publication

Karpinowitz, Abraham [Karpinovitsh, Avrom]. *Baym Vilner durkhhoyf.* Tel Aviv: I. — L. Peretz Publishing House, 1967.
- — "Der folklorist" (The Folklorist)
- — "Vladek"

Karpinowitz, Abraham [Karpinovitsh, Avrom]. *Auf Vilner gasn.* Tel Aviv: Di goldene keyt, 1981.
- — "Di vunderlekh teyorie fun shuster prentsik" (The Amazing Theory of Prentsik the Shoemaker)
- — "Shibeles loterie-tsetl" (Shibele's Lottery Ticket)
- — "Hashoves-aveyde" (Lost and Found)
- — "Der boym nebn teyater" (The Tree beside the Theater)
- — "Di royte fon" (The Red Flag)
- — "Vilne, Vilne, undzer heymshtot" (Vilna, Vilna, Our Native City)

Karpinowitz, Abraham [Karpinovitsh, Avrom]. *Vilna mayn Vilne.* Tel Aviv: I. L. Peretz Publishing House, 1993.
- — "Vilna on Vilna" (Vilna without Vilna)
- — "Di groyse libe fun lerer gershteyn" (The Great Love of Mr. Gershteyn)
- — "Yidish gelt" (Jewish Money)
- — "Yikhes fun der Vilner untervelt" (The Lineage of the Vilna Underworld)
- — "Tamare di hoykhe" (Tall Tamara)
- — "Zikhroynes fun a farshnitener teyater heym" (Memories of a Decimated Theater Home)
- — "Khane-Merke fun di fish" (Chane-Merka the Fishwife)

Bibliography

The following sources were referenced in the translation of the stories and in the preparation of the forward, the introduction, and the notes. I have listed special topic Yiddish dictionaries but not the standard Yiddish dictionaries and thesauruses. A separate bibliography of sources used for the maps is to be found after the main bibliography.

Abramowicz, Hirsz. "Pludermakher, Gershon." In *Lerer yizkor bukh, di umkegumene lerer fun TSYSHO in Poyln*, ed. Y. Pat, Y. Rotenberg, B. Tabatshinski, and S. Gilinski. New York: Martin Press, 1952–54.

———. *Profiles of a Lost World: Memoirs of East European Jewish Life before World War Two*, ed. Dina Abramowicz and Jeffrey Shandler. Translated by Eva Zeitlin Dobkin. Detroit: Wayne State University Press, 1999.

Arad, Yitzhak. *Ghetto in Flames: The Struggle and Destruction of the Jews in Vilna in the Holocaust*. Jerusalem: Ahva Cooperative Printing Press, 1980.

———. Preface to *Ponary Diary, July 1941–November 1943: A Bystander's Account of Mass Murder* by Kazimierz Sakowicz, xiii–xvi. Translated by Laurence Weinbaum. New Haven, CT: Yale University Press, 2005.

Augenfeld, Liba. Interview by Helen Mintz, Montreal, Que., December 2008.

Baker, Zachary M. "The Lawrence Marwick Collection of Copyrighted Yiddish Plays at the Library of Congress: An Annotated Bibliography." Library of Congress, Washington, DC, 2004.

Barany, Zoltan B. *The East European Gypsies: Regime Change, Marginality and Ethnopolitics*. Cambridge, MA: Cambridge University Press, 2001.

Bart, Michael. "Life in the Vilna Ghetto." http://www.untilourlastbreath.com /Bart4ghettofacts.html. Accessed August 22, 2011.

Beer, Helen. "Karpinovich, Avrom." In *Jewish Writers of the Twentieth Century*, ed. Sorrel Kerbel, 510–13. Taylor and Francis, 2003.

Bikl, Shloyme. "Avrom Karpinovitshes Vilner dertseylungen." In *Shrayber fun mayn dor*, vol. 3. Tel Aviv: Farlag Y. L. Perets, 1970.

Brancovskaja, Fanya. Interview by Helen Mintz, Vilna, Lithuania, August 25, 26, 27, 2010.

Briedis, Laimonas. Interview by Helen Mintz, Vancouver, BC, July 15, 2008, November 30, 2011. Consultation on map, August 25, 2015.

Britannica Reference Centre. "Alexander Dumas, fils." http://library.eb.com/levels /referencecenter/article/31425. Accessed August 11, 2010.

———. s.v. "Michurin, Ivan Vladimirovich." http://library.eb.com/eb/article-905 2487. Accessed August 11, 2010.

Brown, Benjamin. "Danzig, Avraham ben Yeḥi'el Mikhl." In *YIVO Encyclopedia of Jews in Eastern Europe*. New Haven, CT: Yale University Press, 2010.

Bulat, Miroslawa M. Translated by Michael C. Steinlauf. "Vilner Trupe." In *YIVO Encyclopedia of Jews in Eastern Europe*. New Haven, CT: Yale University Press, 2010.

Cahan, Mendy. Interview by Helen Mintz, Montreal, Que., June 29, 2011.

Cammy, Justin. "Tsevorfene bleter: The Emergence of Yung-Vilne." In *Polin: Studies in Polish Jewry*, ed. Antony Polonsky, vol. 14, 170–91. London: Littman Library of Jewish Civilization, 2001.

———. "The Politics of Home, the Culture of Place: *Yung-Vilne, A Journal of Literature and Art (1934–1936)."* In *Judische kultur(en) im neuen europa: Wilna, 1918– 1939*, ed. Marina Dmitrieva and Heidemarie Petersen, 117–33. Wiesbaden: Harrassowitz Verlag, 2004.

Cohen, Israel. *Vilna*. Philadelphia: Jewish Publication Society of America, 1943.

Dawidowicz, Lucy S. *From That Place and Time: A Memoir, 1938–1947*. New York: W. W. Norton, 1989.

———. *From That Place and Time: A Memoir, 1938–1947*. New Brunswick: Rutgers University Press, 2008.

Etkes, Immanuel. "Eliyahu ben Shelomoh Zalman." In *YIVO Encyclopedia of Jews in Eastern Europe*. New Haven, CT: Yale University Press, 2010.

Gillerman, Sharon. "Strongman Siegmund Breitbart and Interpretations of the Jewish Body." In *Emancipation through Muscles, Jews and Sports in Europe*, ed. Michael Reuveni and Gideon Brenner, 62–73. Lincoln: University of Nebraska Press, 2006.

Glasser, Paul. "Weinreich, Max." In *YIVO Encyclopedia of Jews in Eastern Europe*. New Haven, CT: Yale University Press, 2010.

Gliksman, Dr. Volf. "Kacyzne, Alter-Sholem." In Der *leksikon fun der nayer yidisher literatur*, vol. 8 (8 vols.). New York: Marin Press, 1981.

Goldberg, R. "Karpinovitsh, Avrom," In Der *leksikon fun der nayer yidisher literatur*, vol. 8 (8 vols.). New York: Marin Press, 1981.

Golomb, A. "A. Karpinovitshes Baym Vilner durkhoyf." *Di goldene keyt* 60 (1967): 256–60.

Gros-Tsimerman, M., A. Karpinovitsh, and A. Shpiglblat, eds. *Almanakh fun di yidishe shrayber in Yisroel*, 2nd oysgabe. Tel Aviv, Israel: Fareyn fun yidishe shrayber un zhurnalistn in Yisroel, 1967.

Gutwirth, Jacques. Translated by Sophie Layton. *The Rebirth of Hasidism, From 1945 to the Present*. London: Free Association Books, 2005.

Guy, Donna. "Argentina: Jewish White Slavery." *Jewish Women's Archive*. http://jwa.org/encyclopedia/article/argentina-jewish-white-slavery. Accessed March 1, 2012.

Howe, Irving, Ruth R. Wisse, and Khone Shmeruk, eds. *The Penguin Book of Modern Yiddish Verse*. New York: Penguin Books, 1987.

Jewish Telegraphic Agency. "Warsaw Editor Jailed for Article on Hitler." May 14, 1935. http://archive.jta.org/article/1935/05/15/2828928/warsaw-editor-jailed-for-article-on-hitler. Accessed August 16,2011.

Joravsky, David. "Mitchurin, Ivan Vladimirovich." *Complete Dictionary of Scientific Biography*. http//www.encyclopedia.com/doc/IG2-2830904917.html. Accessed December 12, 2012.

Karpinowitz, Abraham [as Avrom Karpinovitsh]. Interview by Boris Sandler. Tel Aviv, Israel, 1995. Unpublished.

———— [as Avrom Karpinovitsh]. Interview by Gennady Estraikh, "Intervyu: Avrom Karpinovitsh." *Di pen*/The Yiddish Pen 7 (February 1995): 33–36. Oxford, England: Oxford Institute for Yiddish Studies.

Karpinowitz-Gelbart, Anna, interview by Helen Mintz. Vancouver, BC, June 7, 2011.

Kassow, Samuel. Vilna: *Jerusalem of Lithuania; A Series of Three Lectures*. National Yiddish Book Center's 1996 Winter Seminar in Yiddish Culture. Ann Arbor, MI. Unpublished, 1996.

Katcherginski, S., and K. Pupko. "Gershteyn, Yakov." In *Lerer yizkor-bukh, di umkegumene lerer fun TSYSHO in Poyln*, ed. Y. Pat, Y. Rotenberg, B. Tabatshinski, and S. Gilinski. New York: Martin Press, 1952–54.

Kharlash, Yitskhok. "Grodzenski, Aaron-Yitzkokh." In *Der leksikon fun der nayer yidisher literatur*, vol. 2 (8 vols.). New York: Martin Press, 1958.

Kopelman Foundation. *Jewish Encyclopedia.com, the unedited full text of the 1906 Jewish Encyclopedia*, "Excommunication." http://www.jewishencyclopedia.com/articles/5933-excommunication. Accessed August 1, 2012.

Kruk, Herman. *The Last Days of the Jerusalem of Lithuania*, ed. Benjamin Harshav. Translated by Barbara Harshav. New York: YIVO Institute for Jewish Research, 2002.

———. "Library and Reading Room in the Vilna Ghetto, Strashun Street 6." In *The Holocaust and the Book: Destruction and Preservation*, ed. Jonathan Rose, 171–76. Translated by Zachary Baker. Amherst, MA: Univ. Mass. Press, 2001.

Kuznitz, Cecile Esther. "YIVO." In *YIVO Encyclopedia of Jews in Eastern Europe*. New Haven, CT: Yale University Press, 2010.

Lempertas, Izraelis. *Musu Vilne/Our Vilne*. Vilnius: Leidini Reme Publication, 2003.

Levin, Dov. "Hirsh Lekert." In *YIVO Encyclopedia of Jews in Eastern Europe*. New Haven, CT: Yale University Press, 2010.

Lipphardt, Anne. "Vilne, Vilne undzer heymshtot . . . ': Imagining Jewish Vilna in New York." In *Jüdische Kultur(en)in Neuen Europa, 1918–1939*, ed. Marina Dmitrieva and Heidemarie Petersen. Wiesbaden, Germany: Harrassowitz, 2004.

Lis, Avraham. "Avrom Karpinovitsh—Vilner dertseylungen." *Tsukunft* 5/6 (May–June 1983): 74–75.

Magocsi, Paul Robert. *A History of Ukraine*. Toronto: University of Toronto Press, 1996.

Melamed, Leo. Email correspondence with Helen Mintz, May 2011.

Mevorah, Baruch, Abraham J. Brawer, and Alexander Shapiro. "Napoleon Bonaparte." *Encyclopedia Judaica*. Detroit: Macmillan Reference, 1972.

Miller, Uri. "'The Family Is Not Rich but They've Got Integrity,' or, A Few Leaves from the Genealogical Tree." www.the-ratner-family.com/Family_story_eng.htm. Accessed September 15, 2011.

Miron, Dan. "Sholem Aleichem." In *YIVO Encyclopedia of Jews in Eastern Europe*. New Haven, CT: Yale University Press, 2010.

Monologn fun yidishe shraybers: Avrom Karpinovitch. DVD. Directed by Boris Sandler. 2012: New York: Produced by Forward Association.

Niborski, Eliezer. Email correspondence with Helen Mintz. May 2013.

Niborski, Yitskhok. Translated by Yankl Salant. "Kacyzne, Alter-Sholem." In *YIVO Encyclopedia of Jews in Eastern Europe*. New Haven, CT: Yale University Press, 2010.

Novershtern, Avrom. "Shir halel, shir kina: Dimuya shel Vilnah be-shirat yidish bein shtei milhamot ha'olam." In *MeVilnah LeYerushalayim: Mehkarim betoldoteihem u'betarbutam shel yehudei mizrah eirope*, ed. David Asaf, Israel Bartal, and Avner Holtsman, 485–511. Jerusalem: Magnes Press, 2002.

———. "Yung-Vilne: The Political Dimension of Literature." In *The Jews of Poland Between Two World Wars*, ed. Yisrael Gutman, Jehuda Reinharz, and Chone Shmeruk, 383–98. Hanover, NH: University Press of New England, 1989.

The Partisans of Vilna. DVD. Directed by Josh Waletsky. 1986. New York: Ciesla, NEH.

Pat, I., ed., "Giligitsh, Yosef." In *Der leksikon fun der nayer yidisher literatur*, vol. 2 (8 vols.). New York: Martin Press, 1958.

Perloff, Hirsh. *Bel-khai un foygl nemen auf yidish, Yiddish Names for Birds and Animals*. London: Whitechapel Presentations, 2002.

Pinsker, Shachar. "Choosing Yiddish in Israel: Yung Yisroel between Home and Exile, the Center and the Margin." In *Choosing Yiddish, New Frontiers of Language and Culture*, ed. L. Rabinovitch, S. Goren, and Hannah S. Pressman, 277–94. Detroit: Wayne State University Press, 2013.

Rojanski, Rachel. "The Beginnings of the Yiddish Press in Israel: Ilustrirter vokhnblat." *Zutot: Perspectives on Jewish Culture* 5, no. 1 (2008): 141–48.

———. "The Final Chapter in the Struggle for Cultural Autonomy." *Journal of Modern Jewish Studies* 6, no. 2 (2007): 185–204.

Roskies, David Hirsh. "Di Shrayber-grupe 'Yung Yisroel.'" *Yugentruf* (September 1973): 7–12.

Rozhanski, Shmuel, ed. *Vilne in der yidisher literatur* (Vilna in Yiddish Literature), Masterworks of Yiddish Literature, vol. 84. Buenos Aires: YIVO in Argentina, 1980.

Salant, Yankl. "Frayland-lige." In *YIVO Encyclopedia of Jews in Eastern Europe*. New Haven, CT: Yale University Press, 2010.

Sandrow, Nahma. *Vagabond Stars: A World History of Yiddish Theatre*. New York: Harper and Row, 1977.

Schachter, Allison. *Diasporic Modernism: Hebrew and Yiddish Literature in the Twentieth Century*. Oxford: Oxford University Press, 2012.

Schram, Peninnah. *Tales of Elijah the Prophet*. New Jersey: Jason Aronson, 1991.

Shapiro, Meir. "Vi M't Geredt in Vilne, A Zamlung fun Oysdrukn." Unpublished, 2010.

Shavit, David. *Hunger for the Printed Word: Books and Libraries in the Jewish Ghettos of Nazi-Occupied Europe*. Jefferson, NC: McFarland, 1997.

Simon, Sherry. *Cities in Translation, Intersections of Language and Memory*. London: Routledge, Taylor and Francis Group, 2012.

Smogorzewski, Kazimierz Maciej. "Jozef Pilsudski." In *Encyclopaedia Britannica*. http://library.eb.com/eb/article-9060041. Accessed October 13, 2011.

Steinlauf, Michael. "*Yung-teater.*" In *YIVO Encyclopedia of Jews in Eastern Europe.* New Haven, CT: Yale University Press, 2010.

Studer, Sandra. *Erinnerungen an das jüdische Vilne: Literarische Bilder von Chaim Grade und Abraham Karpinovitsh.* Koln: Bohlau, 2014.

Turkow, Jonas. *Farloshene shtern,* vol. 1. Buenes Aires: Tsentral-farband fun Poylishe yidn in Argentina, 1953. 2 vols.

Venclova, Tomas. *Vilnius,* 3rd ed. Vilnius: R. Paknio, 2003.

Visit Lithuania. "St. Casimir's Fair Weekend." http://www.visitlithuania.net /index.php/component/content/article/108-other-events/349-st-casimirs-fair -weekend.html. Accessed May 17, 2013.

Volpe, David. "Di sheynkayt fun Vilne." *Di goldene keyt* 109 (1982): 206-9.

Weinreich, Max. "Der yidisher visnshaftlekher institute." In *Vilne: A zamlbukh gevidmet der shtot Vilne,* ed. Yefim Yeshurin. New York: [n.p.], 1935.

Wisse, Ruth R. "Peretz, Yitzkhok Leybush." In *YIVO Encyclopedia of Jews in Eastern Europe.* New Haven, CT: Yale University Press, 2010.

Wolfson, L. "Vilne, Vilne, undzer heymshtot." In *A zamelbukh: Vilne,* ed. Ephim H. Jeshurin. New York: Arbeter Ring, Vilna Branch 367, 1935.

Yad, Vashem. "The Interwar Period—Cultural Life." http://www.yadvashem .org/yv/en/exhibitions/vilna/before/literature.asp. Accessed December 8, 2011.

Yanasovitsh, Yitshok. "Avrom Karpinovitsh." In *Penimer un nemem,* vol. 2, 274–79. Buenos Aires: Kiem, 1977.

YIVO Institute for Jewish Research. "Guide to the Records of the TSYSHO (Tsentrale Yidishe Shul Organizatsye) 1919–1940. 2006, RG 48. "Historical Note." http://digifindingaids.cjh.org/?pID=131232. Accessed August 15, 2011.

Zable, Arnold. *Wanderers and Dreamers, Tales of the David Herman Theatre.* Vicoria, Australia: Hyland House, 1998.

Zalkin, Mordechai. "Vilnius." In *YIVO Encyclopedia of Jews in Eastern Europe.* New Haven, CT: Yale University Press, 2010.

Zilbertsvayg, Zalman. *Der leksikon fun yidishn teyater.* 6 vols. "Malach, Leyb," vol. 2, Warsaw: Elisheve, 1934; "Halperin, Dina," vol. 4, New York: Elisheve, 1963; "Moyshe Karpinovitch," "Shriftzetser, Leyb," "Tsuker, Regina," vol. 5, Mexico City: Elisheve, 1967; "Bronetsky, Sam," vol. 6, Mexico City: Elisheva, 1969.

"Zloty." Internet Encyclopedia of Ukraine. http://www.encyclopediaofukraine .com/display.asp?linkPath=pages/Z/L/Zloty.html. Accessed November 30, 2011.

Bibliography for Maps

Dawidowicz, Lucy S. *From That Place and Time: A Memoir, 1938–1947.* New York: W. W. Norton, 1989.

"Vilnius, Lithuania." 54°41′N, 25°17′E. Google Earth. November 26, 2015. Accessed June 15, 2015.

Lempertas, Izraelis. *Musu Vilne / Our Vilne.* Vilnius: Leidini Reme Publication, 2003.

"Plan fun der shtot Vilne." In *Yerushalayim d'Lite,* Vol. 1 (3 vols.), ed. Lyzer Ran. Jackson Heights, NY: Laureate Press, 1974.

Venclova, Tomas. *Vilnius.* 3rd ed. Vilnius: R. Paknio, 2003.

Vilnius Jewish Culture and Information Centre information pamphlet. Lithuanian State Department of Tourism under the Ministry of Economy.

Zalkin, Mordechai. "Vilnius." *YIVO Encyclopedia of Jews in Eastern Europe.* New Haven, CT: Yale University Press, 2010.

Abraham Karpinowitz (Avrom Karpinovitsh) was born in 1913 in Vilna, Poland. He survived the Holocaust in the Soviet Union and returned briefly to Vilna in 1944. He left Vilna for Palestine in 1947 and after two years in a British internment camp on the island of Cyprus, entered the newly formed state of Israel where he lived until his death in 2004. Karpinowitz wrote seven collections of short stories, two biographies, and a play. He was awarded numerous prizes, including the prestigious Manger Prize (1981).

Helen Mintz is a translator, writer, and performer based in Vancouver, Canada. She was a 2014 Translation Fellow with the Yiddish Book Center. Mintz has written four one-woman shows seeking to reframe contemporary Jewish women's identity. She has performed these shows in Canada, the United States, Germany, and Lithuania.